ELLYN & THE WOULD-BE GIGOLO

ELLYN & THE WOULD-BE GIGOLO

A LAUGH-OUT-LOUD ROMANTIC COMEDY

PRU WARREN

QUI
LEGIT
REGIT
PRESS
She who reads, rules

Cover design by the Killion Group

Published by Qui Legit Regit Press
Alexandria, VA

ISBN: 978-1-7359919-5-5

Discover other titles by Pru Warren at pruwarren.com

72123wch

❀ Created with Vellum

CONTENTS

BLISS & GIGGLES

Sign up for my newsletter, sweetpea! Go to
https://www.pruwarren.com/

My newsletter philosophy? Never take yourself too seriously. Skip the boring stuff. Amuse yourself; maybe others will be amused, too.

There's generally a smoochy gift to thank you for signing up. Maybe a free epilogue, maybe a peek at the next book, maybe something that gave me the giggles. C'mon and check it out; we'll have much delight together!

Thank God my mother didn't live long enough to advise me on how to make my love scenes better...

But since she was the one who first put Georgette Heyer in my hands (and later Kathleen Woodiwiss), I would be remiss in not dedicating a book to The Redoubtable Sally!

CHAPTER ONE—ELLYN

THE GUY AT THE FRONT OF THE LINE HAD ONE HELL OF A shiner coming up around his eye.

He was trying to hide it. He kept his head down so the side of his face was covered with his long blond hair. But I've been fascinated with bruising since I studied stage makeup, and I'm always on the lookout for good bruises.

He turned from the counter, a small cup of coffee in his large hand, and I abandoned my place in line to follow him.

He ducked around the corner of the coffee shop, moving like more than his eye hurt. He found a bench at a table against the wall. Good light from the front window.

"Hey."

He looked up, and a crack of electricity zipped through me. The black eye was so fresh, the skin was still puffing up. This guy must have been hit within the last ten minutes. I shifted on my feet in eagerness.

"Mister, can I photograph your eye?"

"Fuck off, girlie."

He dismissed me from his attentions by concentrating on his coffee but winced at the sip. Too hot.

Undeterred, I pulled out the chair. My camera bag went between my feet, and I unzipped the main compartment.

"Won't take a minute," I said. "Although if you let me, I'd like to take one photo every five minutes for an hour or so. Are you busy right now?"

"Am I busy," he said woodenly.

I reached past the GoPro. *What if I'd had the right tripod and could film the black eye coming up? My kingdom for a tripod; why didn't I rent it with the video camera?* And I prided myself on always being prepared. My trusty Nikon slipped into my hand like an old friend.

"Yeah. Are you busy?" I sat up and faced him, camera in hand. "I want to photograph that black eye coming up. I make movies," I explained. "I study bruises. Like that one."

I gestured to his cheekbone and calculated the light from the front window. The dreary February day was overcast. No need for a diffuser.

"No, you can't photograph me. Fuck off, I said."

I grinned. I love New York.

"I'm not going to publish it or anything. Just going to capture the light coming off that massive shiner. For the good of the film industry. I'm sure you understand."

"You take my picture and I'll rip that camera out of your hands and—" Words failed him, and he splatted his very large hand against the brick wall next to him. I winced at the implied violence to an innocent camera.

"All right," I said, ready to negotiate. "What do you want?"

"Want," he repeated, not understanding.

"How much to photograph your face?"

He grinned, winced, and groaned. *Cheek muscles a tad tender there, guy?*

"Aspirin," he muttered. "It will cost you aspirin."

I was already fishing in the medical pouch. "Advil or Tylenol? I don't have anything with codeine at the moment. Sorry about that."

Now I had his attention.

"You actually have aspirin in that suitcase?"

"I'm a DP. Director of photography. I have everything. Well, I don't have actual aspirin. But acetaminophen, yeah. Does Advil work on you? Here—how many?"

I shook out two pills into the broad palm that was suddenly reaching for me. I thought about it and popped out a third one.

He grunted and made an impatient gesture with that reaching hand. "One more."

"You want four Advil?" I said. "Are you sure? This stuff will get to your liver eventually."

"Four. I'm a big guy."

That was true. I put the final pill into his palm, which was warm and slightly rough—how would a good director visually convey the frisson of heat that brushed my fingers with that faint touch? The bottle was in its pouch and my camera in hand by the time he'd chased the pills with some still-scalding coffee. He winced at the heat but swallowed it anyway. "Thanks," he said.

I'd use my elbows as a tripod and remain consistent in my placement. "Pull your hair back. Look straight ahead."

He grumbled but complied.

The lighting would do. Through the lens, I saw he was handsome. Square jaw that would look good on a fifty-foot screen. Sharp cheekbones to catch the light; if we'd used video, I'd have had to use a matte powder to stop the light from bouncing. Broad forehead. Way too much hair worn long in a ridiculously blond mane.

And a mouse of a bruise coming up below his left eye. The guy who hit him was right-handed, with a pretty big fist. Big end bone of the middle finger against the cheekbone, prominent first knuckle making itself seen next to the eyebrow. Blood had seeped under the skin into the damaged tissue. Black and purple. Angry. It was gorgeous.

Click.

And it was mine.

I checked the shot: perfect.

The timer on my phone would remind me. I set it for five minutes.

"Now you can fuck off," the guy said, letting his hair fall over his face.

"Every five minutes," I said. "For at least an hour. What'll it take?"

"More than Advil."

I looked at the small coffee. "How about something to eat? Something bigger than that to drink? My treat."

He looked up, interested but not persuaded.

"And I'll make you an ice bag."

That did it. He nodded. "Fine."

The camera went around my neck (my usual necklace) and I picked up the camera bag. "Stay here."

"You can leave that here," he said. "It looks heavy."

"Yeah," I laughed. "Right. You're funny."

He was still sitting there when I returned.

"Where's my ice?"

"They're getting it. It's been five minutes. Pull your hair off your face."

Click.

The two images, one after the other, should have been put in a textbook. The black eye had spread, and the edema was increasing—all the lymphatic system's attempts to swell and protect the area making his eye puff up nicely.

"You're a good subject. The camera likes you."

He grunted. "I'm handsome."

And vain. "Nah. Plenty of handsome people look like shit on camera. You were born lucky."

He scoffed. Apparently, he wasn't feeling lucky at the moment. But I was. Best black-eye study ever.

I went back to the coffee shop's waiting area, thinking it would be a shame to ice that bruise. On the other hand, it was hard to imagine a scenario in which a character in a film would not ice a bruise, so I was still going to get a realistic series of photos even if He-Man Jungle Jim insisted on suppressing the swelling. It would be okay.

"I got you soup. I thought maybe your jaw might be tightening up."

I'd also gotten him a venti iced tea and a cup of ice. I pulled a zippered baggie from my stash and poured the ice into it. He reached for my impromptu ice pack.

I pulled it away. "It's been more than five. Hang on."

Used to the routine now, he pulled his hair off his face with a big, affected sigh.

Lighting was still good. Photo acceptable. Bruise beginning to darken. He'd been hit by a *big* hand.

I surrendered the ice and reset my timer. He made an inarticulate noise as he gingerly laid the bag over his eye.

"So what's your story?" I asked.

One large blue eye regarded me. "The fuck?"

His reply had been conversational; the ice was helping. I helped myself to the baguette that came with his soup. "Yeah. Who hit you? How come? What's the backstory here?"

He snorted. "What's the backstory on your hair?"

I had to think to remember today's style. Right—black-and-white stripes. It looked good. He attempted to get the drink straw out of its plastic wrapper with one hand, the other hand being used to plaster a good chill over his eye.

He was going to crush the straw. I took it from him, pulled it out, put it in the iced tea, and handed the cup back. He took a long pull, and the big shoulders came down.

"Someone put the major smackdown on that camera-ready face. I'm just wondering what the story was."

"You bought the right to photograph my bruise. You didn't buy my backstory."

"That's true." I reached out one long arm—it's always useful to be tall—and pulled the cuff of his jacket away from his wrist.

He jerked his hand from me, but I'd already seen the ligature marks. "You were tied, weren't you? When you got hit?"

The side of his face not hidden by the ice bag glared at me.

"I'm not surprised," I added. "Big chest, broad shoulders—you obviously work out. You've got muscle, and you look like a scrapper. You could probably throw down in a fight, and there aren't any marks on your knuckles. Not fresh ones, anyway."

I had a good look at his right hand cradling the ice against his head. A series of crescent scars, silvery and pale, showed where he'd landed blows on at least one mouth—probably more than one—and the teeth had cut him. But those marks were old. He favored his ribs but not his fingers. He hadn't hit anyone in the last few hours, and he sure as hell had been hit himself.

"So someone jumped you, tied you up, and tagged that big blue eye. If you pulled up that sweater, I bet I'd see some nice bruises on your ribs, huh?"

I got the full glare now.

"Yeah. That's what I thought. I wasn't kidding. I study bruises. And your oversized body is telling quite a story." The timer went off. "Ice down. Pull back your hair. Ooh, that's looking beautiful."

The black blood under the skin had spread, and the eyelid was swollen almost closed. I couldn't help but grin.

"You're very odd," he said as he reapplied his ice.

Four perfect shots in a row. The light was holding. "I've been told. I'm Ellyn. What's your name?"

"Why?"

I laughed at his suspicion. "Because I've got you for another eight shots. Why not be civil?"

He thought about it for a while. "Artie," he said grudgingly.

"Guarded much? How many names did you have to go through before settling on that one?"

Surprisingly, the question gave him the flash of a grin. The guy used way too much whitener on his teeth. "A few."

Right. Stage names, pseudonyms, aliases? This guy began to interest me.

I froze, suddenly seeing a possibility.

He didn't notice. He spooned in beef barley soup and eyed the remains of the baguette, still in my hand.

I assessed him coldly. Too tall, no doubt, but definitely handsome enough. Great shoulders, wide chest. Moved well, given that he probably had a few cracked ribs. Age? How old was he? Could have been anywhere from a twenty-five-year-old to a thirty-five-year-old who took good care of his skin.

Aliases. Possibly violent past. Dressed in jeans, a caramel-colored sweater, a nice leather jacket. Way too much hair, but that could be fixed.

It would be risky. But what wasn't?

He'd noticed my silence. "What?"

I shook my head at him, still thinking. A text message pinged onto my phone from Mock.

Hello? Are you coming?
With my cappuccino?

Shit. I'd lost track.

Get down here now. Starbucks

My Starbucks or yours?

Yours. Hurry

You owe me coffee

"Who's that?" Artie asked.

"Friend of mine. Okay, ice down. Pull your hair back."

You can say a lot about Mock, but no one would say he was slow. He appeared in the coffee shop before the sixth photo, a

Thai man weaving gracefully between tables. He spotted us quickly and couldn't look away from my new companion.

"Girl—who is this?"

His interest was obvious. Mock has an eye for beauty. He stole a chair from a nearby table and pulled it over to sit next to me. "New friend, Ellyn?"

"Mock, meet Artie. Artie, this is Mock, the best stylist in Manhattan."

Mock waved dismissively with his hand but beamed. "Oh, go on with you. Hello, Artie. Aren't you *big*!"

Artie's one visible eye rolled between me and Mock.

"Wait until you see what's under that ice pack. We've got . . . thirty-seven seconds to a big reveal."

Mock clapped his hands eagerly. "I love a big reveal! Ellyn, you always find the *best* things! She's got such a good eye," he confided to Artie, who seemed not at all impressed.

"Oh, I'm going to *show* you a good eye," I assured him.

Mock and I both studied the timer ticking on my phone, our mutual anticipation building. I wasn't prepared for Artie's reaction when the timer went off.

With a flourish, he whipped off the ice bag and leaned forward toward Mock, angling his head so his swollen black eye was foremost. "Ta-daaaa!" he sang.

Mock grabbed my arm and gasped in wide-eyed amazement at the darkness spreading across Artie's eye. "Oooh! Look at that!"

Artie settled with a grin. *Streak of the showman in that guy.* The Advil and ice were working; his aches and pains had eased.

"Now that is a black eye," Mock said in admiration. I knew he'd understand. We'd taken stage makeup (a film school classic) at NYU Tisch.

"Wait until you see my series," I boasted. "Hang on. Every five minutes. Artie, pull back your hair, please."

Artie complied. By this point, we had a routine.

"Look at that bone structure," Mock said appreciatively. "Are you in the business? Actor, I mean. Onstage? Heroic star of the silver screen?" Artie shook his head. "Why not? Everyone else in Manhattan is, and you're a looker, no doubt. Camera loves you. Here's the proof. But sweetie, what's with all that hair? That cut is entirely wrong for you."

Artie looked at Mock, confused.

"That's what I thought too," I said. "Now, look at this series, Mock."

I showed him my collection and Mock had nothing but praise. "Look—you can see each knuckle coming up over time. And look at that color. How would you do the puffiness? Prosthetics, maybe?"

We discussed how we could recreate the effect on camera and Artie watched us do it, impassive but alert. But this was no longer the reason I wanted Mock's opinion. Another picture, and then . . .

"We've got a few minutes until the next shot," I said. "How about you and I get your cappuccino, Mock?"

Mock's my close friend. He got my message but responded with nothing more than the lift of one mobile, beautifully shaped eyebrow. "Yes, girl. I need my 'chino. What about you, handsome? Can I get you anything?"

Artie received the decided leer without objection. "Venti Americano. Thanks."

"Venti," Mock said with a wink. "I'm sure."

Artie made a *what else?* gesture with his hands.

"Nothing in it?" Mock asked. "You don't want a splash of soy milk? Something maybe a little Asian?"

Artie laughed, which was impressive. Most butch guys don't know how to handle Mock's come-ons. "Not today. Thanks, though."

I snorted. "Come on, Mock. You can flirt in a minute."

I dragged the stylist to the line at the counter, and he fanned himself with his hand.

"Honey, I can't tell, and I can always tell. Does that guy play for my team or yours? Because—*yum.*"

"Calm down. What do you think about using him for the Aunt Cor situation?"

Mock snapped his attention to me. More than my career depended on this one. "Aunt Cor?" His clever brain had already leapt ahead of his "gay stylist" persona. "What are you thinking? You want to hire him to be a ringer?"

Now he studied Artie like the man was a job, not a bedmate.

"Well, I thought it was worth discussing."

"Do you even know him? How did you find him?"

"Met him right here, half an hour ago," I said promptly. "I know no more about him than you do."

Mock's known me for nine years; we met on the very first day of film school. "You already know more than I do. What have you seen that I haven't?" He waved away my dismissal as we moved up a place in line. "Hurry up. We don't have much time. Tell me."

I considered. "A history of brawling, but not recently. He's got a flair for the dramatic. He's reasonably intelligent and speaks well. He's camera-ready in terms of physical beauty. He's healthy. There are no signs of drug or alcohol abuse visible, although both could be early stages. And he's in trouble. Someone tied him up to beat him within the last hour. So he might be looking for an opportunity too."

Mock nodded. We both stared at Artie, who stared at us.

"Final assessment?" Mock asked.

"Scoundrel," I replied. "Complete scoundrel."

Mock high-fived me. "That's what we're looking for."

We abandoned our place in line and returned to Artie.

"No Americano?" he said mildly.

"Artie," I said, "I have a proposition for you."

He looked at me. "I don't fuck for money." He leered at Mock. "Not anymore, anyway."

Mock fanned himself again and made a cooing noise.

10

"Not a sexual proposition. Would you be willing to come with us? Mock lives upstairs. We could have a discussion in private." I looked to Mock to make sure he was fine with my offering his apartment as our temporary headquarters. He nodded eagerly.

Artie caught his lower lip between strong, white teeth and considered us.

"I've been beaten once already today. I'm afraid I'm not available for violence. What would be in this for me? And I'll tell you right now—it'll take more than a venti Americano."

We didn't have a moment to waste. I cut through his concerns.

"How about a quarter of a million dollars? Would that make it worth your time?"

"Are you kidding?"

"I'm definitely not kidding."

He stood, unfolding from the seat, and I backed up a step. I hadn't realized just how tall he was. Mock made an "eep" sound of alarmed delight.

"Then let's get out of here."

CHAPTER TWO—ARTIE

Two ribs were cracked. I was lucky; Hambone had wanted to be a boxer in earlier days. When Terence the Accountant had given his three thugs one shot each, Hambone had gone for the ribs. Good thing he'd been making excuses instead of training. Otherwise, he could have broken me.

Gorgeous George had planted a fist in my stomach, but he's kind of a wimp, and he's scared of me. I didn't even barf when he hit me. Core muscles to the rescue. Who says ab work isn't worth the effort?

It was Iggy—of course it was Iggy—who'd blackened my eye. We'd come up together, and he really hated that I was better-looking than he was. Terence had refused to let him break my nose. I was worth more to Terence pretty.

But the black eye was bad enough.

I followed Zebra Hair and Gay Asian out of the coffee shop and into the small, dark lobby next door. We crammed into the tiny elevator, three of us plus Zebra's huge box of a bag, hanging off her shoulder like a hot dog vendor at Yankee Stadium. It took up more than its share of room.

The guy came to my armpit, and he leaned into me. The girl's head would have brushed my jaw—she was tall for a woman—

and she leaned away. I was sorry about that. A little body contact with her wouldn't have been the worst part of my day. But she was giving off a nervous energy. Whatever she wanted, I would be able to work a better deal. She had no idea how badly I needed money, and I would keep it that way.

I just had to figure out how to play it.

Gay Asian let us into an apartment the size of a closet. "We've got the place to ourselves. Both of my roommates are at work."

Three people lived in this storage container. Fuck, I hate Manhattan. If you don't have money, you're no better than a cockroach.

I was given a kitchen chair. The little guy sat on the lid of the garbage can and winked as he propped his feet on the rung of my chair, between my legs. Zebra folded herself onto a futon and rested her elbow on the camera bag, which dented into the cushion. She carried it as if it wasn't heavy, but the evidence was there to be seen. She was strong, then.

And pretty. Not that I noticed the oval face, the creamy skin. The eyebrows didn't match the absurd hair; she was probably a brunette—although there was a hint of red in the eyebrows, and the green eyes were a giveaway. Irish background. I wondered idly if she waxed her crotch or if her true hair color was on display in that fascinating triangle. Had she zebra-striped her pubes too?

I have a good poker face; safe to say she didn't know I was checking her out.

"Go ahead, Ellyn," the guy said. Ellyn. Right. I stored away the detail of her name.

"Well, Artie . . ." She paused. "Is your name really Artie?"

"As far as you're concerned, it is," I said impassively.

"You're going to need a passport if this works out. Do you have one? Does it say Artie?"

Travel outside the country. That could work for me. My interest was definitely piqued. "I have a passport. It says Arthur."

I'd given her my legal first name. It had seemed easiest at the time, and now that was paying off.

"Good. Official introductions. I'm Ellyn Wolcott." She held out her hand to shake mine in an ingrained, trained response to meeting someone, no doubt taught by Mumsy from birth. If I hadn't already known she was a privileged white chick, this would have made it clear. I took her slim, cool hand in mine. She was trusting. Vulnerable. With a single tug, I could have pulled her into me.

"And this is Mock Suwan." I let her pull away from me and confronted Mock's fingers, coyly held so I could respectfully kiss his hand. Mock was all bark and no bite. I would have swooped in to startle and delight him if my ribs had allowed it. Instead, I kissed his hand with as much brio as I could muster while remaining rigidly upright, and he giggled.

"What's your last name, Artie?" Ellyn was a very focused person. I assessed her. She liked to be in control, but I decided that was based in competency. She wasn't power-hungry; she just wanted things done efficiently, and she was used to being the most capable person in the room. I could work that to my advantage.

"Don't worry about my last name yet."

She scoffed but got on with it. "But your passport is current? You could leave the country in two weeks?"

"Thirteen days," Mock squeaked.

I'd been to Guatemala on a very productive journey two years earlier. "It's current."

Ellyn nodded, thinking. "Okay. And based on physical evidence"—she nodded at my eye, now beginning to throb again, and the stiffness in my pose from my cracked ribs—"can I assume you're not exactly an upstanding citizen?"

I was adrift. How to play this? Stalling, I demurred. "You think upstanding citizens don't get mugged?"

She shook her head. "You weren't mugged. You were

restrained and beaten with reasonable control. It wasn't passionate. It was . . . thoughtful. Am I right?"

I raised my eyebrows and regretted it when my eye throbbed. "Right enough. Can I have some more ice in this?"

The guy leaped up, coming to his feet almost between my knees. He smiled at me—we were almost eye to eye—and nearly touched my swollen face. "Yes, sweetie. Of course. How silly of me not to think of it."

He bustled around, adding ice to the bag, and Ellyn went on. "I'll lay my cards on the table. I'm looking for a scoundrel. And I can hardly take out an ad on Craigslist, you know?"

Pieces were falling into place. It goes against my grain as a confidence man to deal in truth and reality, but she'd mentioned an impressively large sum, so I would allow her a peek behind the veil.

"A scoundrel," I repeated.

"Yeah. And I think you qualify. Am I wrong?"

"You're taking a hell of a risk, sight unseen."

She held up the camera around her neck. "Not exactly unseen. I've got a pretty good eye. Speaking of which, pull back your hair. Hang on, Mock." She stopped him from handing me the ice. "Let me just finish the series."

It bothered her that the lighting had changed. She turned me, her hand coming unthinkingly to my shoulder with an unspoken demand, to face the small window onto an airshaft. She made Mock turn on the overhead and the standing lamp.

Click.

"Okay. Thanks. You can relax." She checked the photo in the camera screen and nodded to herself. Ellyn looked up and hit me with the eyes again. "I'm going to tell you a story. Yeah, Mock—give him the ice."

I laid the ice where the whole-head throbbing was the worst and sighed in relief. She went on.

"I have this Aunt Cor. Short for Corinne, although she'd like you to think it was short for Cordelia."

"Aunt Cor!" Mock hooted. "She's such a type! Picture *Downton Abbey* crossed with a Brooklyn trucker. Am I right?"

"That's a type?" My head swam, trying to match the two images together.

"Wait until you meet her. Walk-up flat meets penthouse apartment. Earthy and snobby at the same time. She's a pip. I adore her."

Mock's enthusiasm brought my headache back. Maybe Ellyn would spot me a few more Advil. I wouldn't ask, though. First rule: never show an actual need.

"That's Aunt Cor," Ellyn agreed. "And Aunt Cor is running a popularity contest between her four nieces, one of whom is me."

"A popularity contest." So far, I was on untrodden ground. What the hell was she talking about?

"Explain about Uncle Carl," Mock enthused.

"Right, right. Wait."

I was more than willing to wait. The world had been out of control for the last hour or so, and that's a sensation I do my best to avoid. "Any clarity you can provide would be appreciated. I'm not following all this too well. Yet."

Ellyn gathered her thoughts. "Start again. Wipe that clean." She waved her hands to clear away my confusion. It didn't work. She rose to her knees and settled her shoulders. "In the beginning, there was a Wolcott in Nyack. Ever been to Nyack?"

I shook my head.

"It's up the Hudson. Anyway, he had a store. Back then, it was called a dry goods store. And he had a lot more get-up-and-go than most of the Wolcotts of my generation—"

"He was an ancestor of yours, then," I broke in.

"Yeah. He partnered with another guy. They grew to a few stores. Then the sons got involved and things got bigger. Over time, partnerships were formed. Opportunities were exploited. You know—robber baron times."

I nodded to show I was keeping up, even though "robber baron times" meant little to me.

"Over the years, Beckford Department Stores." She looked at me.

"What about them?"

"That's the Wolcott store, multiplied."

"Your family owns the Beckford Department Stores?" I forgot the headache, the cracked ribs, the black eye. Suddenly, Ellyn was a glorious angel. I would marry her.

"Yeah. Some of it, anyway. There's a family trust."

"What's it worth?" We were past worrying if my question was rude.

She shrugged. "Nobody talks about it, but *Forbes* estimates the Wolcott trust to be about $278 million."

I exhaled my lust and greed. She waved me off.

"It's not mine. Don't get excited. We have no shot at that. Artie—Artie, focus. Hear me now: we have no shot at that money. You can't imagine how tied up it all is. But we can get at a little chunk."

"I'm in."

She laughed. She had a great laugh. I adored her. "You don't know what's involved."

"So tell me. But I'm in."

Mock giggled. "I'm in love with this guy."

I winked at him. "If you had $278 million, I'd be in love with you too, sweet thing."

Ellyn fixed me with a stern eye. "Mock and I, we can't decide if you're gay or straight. We need a straight guy, or at least one who can play straight."

"If you need straight, I can be straight."

"Yes," Mock said, "but which are you? Really?"

I knew he was asking for himself.

"I'm bi," I said, "mostly. Especially when it profits me. By inclination, I'm more into her than you, and it's not just because of the money."

Mock made a gesture with his head that encompassed

nodding and shaking at the same time. "I really am in love with this guy."

"Great. You'll do fine, Artie."

Next, she walked me through a discussion that involved big-money words like *trustee* and *family trust* and *law firm*. Not quite the story of my family, but I was more than willing to upgrade. I listened attentively.

Ellyn explained that the oldest male of any generation was the family trustee. He decided how to distribute quarterly profits and was considered the head of the family.

"That was my Uncle Carl. He was the trustee until about a year ago, when he died. He passed the trusteeship on to his wife, Aunt Cor."

Mock hopped up and down on his seat, grinning and loving the tale of vast fortunes. I enjoyed it myself. "But that goes against family tradition. She's not even a Wolcott, except by marriage. The trusteeship should have gone to Uncle Freddy, right, Ellyn? Lots of lawsuits already breaking out because of it."

"Don't break the guy, Mock. Slow down. Let me lay out the family tree. Ready, Artie? You'll need to know this, so pay attention."

I paid attention. She'd had my complete focus ever since she mentioned a quarter of a million dollars. "Go on."

"Carl had three siblings."

This rang familiar; I have three siblings myself.

"First, my Uncle Freddy, number two in birth order. Then my Aunt Muffy."

Mock and I both snorted. Muffy.

Ellyn glared. "All right—Elizabeth. I can't help it that Muffy is her nickname. And then my father, Kip. Christopher. Got it?"

I nodded.

"Carl married my Aunt Nan about a billion years ago, and then he divorced her and married The Tramp. His secretary, Corinne."

"Aunt Cor," I confirmed.

"Right. The family hates her. That's important. Got it?"

"Keep going."

"Okay. Carl never had any kids, but everyone else did. Uncle Freddy and Aunt Cill had Priss—Priscilla. Named for her mother, right? Priscilla, Priscilla? Cill and Priss?"

It seemed an unnecessary detail. *Keep going.*

"Aunt Muffy and Uncle Bob have the twins—Olivia and Farrah. We call Olivia *Liv*."

Mock interjected, "And never were two people less alike. Fraternal twins. *Not* identical."

"Mock loves Farrah, who's a party girl, but he hates Liv because she made fun of his styling. She's a fashion designer."

"She wishes she was a fashion designer," Mock corrected in a huff.

"Can we get on with this?" I asked.

"Sorry. And Kip and my mother had me. So, Uncle Carl has—had—four nieces. Right? Are you keeping up?"

Please. "Priss, Liv, Farrah, and Ellyn. I'm keeping up."

She looked pleased. "Good for you. So, Carl knew the family hated Cor. In his will, he left the family trust to her, which—Mock is right—should have gone to Uncle Freddy, who immediately filed a lawsuit in protest. Lots of lawyers getting rich on that one."

We all nodded, united in a general suspicion of lawyers.

"Carl had bought a company that eventually developed facial recognition software, so he was worth an additional $73 million when he died."

I inhaled. These numbers were catnip. "So, Aunt Cor is in charge of $351 million."

"You're quick. Yeah, more or less. The numbers are vague, but close enough. And, as they say, that starts to add up to real money pretty soon. But now the brothers and sister are insisting that Carl bought the company with family funds and the profits ought to be a part of the family trust, so that's another lawsuit."

"You guys must have great Thanksgivings."

"Yeah. Family gatherings are nothing but peace and pumpkin pie." She'd made an easy joke, but I'm trained to hear the undercurrents, and she was definitely hiding pain. I filed it away. Pain is always useful.

She rallied. "Here's where you come in. Carl knew the family hated Cor and favored Aunt Nan, who was pretty chilly, but— you know. Family."

Mock broke in, loving the details. "Nan is now living in Aspen, furious and icy. She only got a few measly millions in the divorce since Carl insisted all the money was in the family trust. Do you love it? She's like Leona Helmsley, only colder."

Mock clapped his hands, and Ellyn ignored him. "Carl figured it would be rough for Cor after he died and that she would be liable to be sued to death, so he left a special Aunt Cor trust. It's five million dollars."

"After so many big numbers, that seems like chump change," I admitted.

"Right? But it's the number we can get our hands on. The deal with that money is, Cor has one year to decide which niece should get it."

"Ah," I said, understanding. "The niece popularity contest."

"Exactly."

"But she's got all that money. What does she care?"

Ellyn corrected me. "Aunt Cor is in charge of all that money —or maybe not—but she doesn't *have* it. She just lives off the income."

I was calculating investment returns and interest rates. "Which would come to . . . what, about a million every month? Without breaking a sweat?" Shit. Aunt Cor was my kind of woman.

"Something like that."

"So, what's it to her?" I was trying to clear away my financial lust and think like a con man. I answered myself before Ellyn could. "The money is nice," I realized, "but she's used to that now. What she wants is some kind of acceptance from Carl's family. She wants—" *Ah.* The most powerful force behind any con. "She wants love."

Ellyn and Mock looked startled. Dupes are always startled when presented with raw truth. But it was more than enough for me to work with. "Go on," I said. "What's the rest?"

Ellyn gathered her thoughts. "Aunt Cor has decided to leave all the family drama to the lawyers. She's gotten on a cruise ship in the Pacific Islands and is staying on until it hits Sri Lanka. More than two months for her. And she's invited each niece on board for roughly two weeks each. We're going in age order and I'm the youngest, so I'm last. At the end, she'll decide which leg of the trip was the most fun, and that niece will get the money."

"Motherfucker," I breathed, lost in admiration.

"You know it," she agreed. "Crazy, huh?"

"Crazy." It was all about love. It always was—love or greed. Aunt Cor wanted love, and I had plenty of greed. Beautiful Ellyn would be putty in my hands.

"I already know Liv and Farrah have a deal," she said. "The twins have promised each other that if one of them wins, they'll split the total between them. That doubles their chances of getting at least some money."

"Smart. How do you know about the agreement?"

"Priss told me. She's been bribing Luz—that's Cor's maid, who's on the ship with her."

"Let me guess. Priss wants the same arrangement with you."

"You really are quick. That's right. She and I are teaming up. If one of us wins, we each get 2.5 million."

"The numbers keep getting smaller," I commented.

"Because you're used to the big family trust numbers. It's still *2.5 million dollars.*"

She said it with emphasis, and I took a moment to consider. Fuck yeah. That's a lot of green.

"So, you need Aunt Cor to have the best time when you're on board."

She nodded.

"And you'll give me a quarter million if I help make it possible."

Now Mock nodded too. Ellyn went on. "Mock and I need two million to set up our own production company. We'll make our own films."

"No more asshole directors or producers who don't actually pay what they promised."

"Directors who actually listen to their DPs."

"Girl, I'm telling you. Dare to admit your dream. You should *be* the director. Hire someone else to hump the huge suitcase."

"Give up my camera bag? Never. But I would like to direct. I think I could do it. And you would be head of creative. Everything: script, design, locations. Not just wardrobe. You'd be the best ever."

"*We'd* be the best ever." They bumped fists, and she turned back to hit me with the offer.

"I'll give you 10 percent of everything I get if you help us."

"Hang on. What does Aunt Cor having a shipboard romance with a hot stud have to do with her liking you?"

Ellyn grimaced at my self-aggrandizement but didn't disagree. "That's who she is. Luz told Priss that so far, Liv was winning because the weather was better after Liv came onboard. Priss was pissed."

"Priss was stupid to bring that child with her," Mock added. He saw my confusion. "Priss is the only married niece. She brought her husband and her three-year-old with her. And there's nothing as annoying as two weeks locked on a ship with a three-year-old, you know?"

"Especially one named Lovely." Ellyn and Mock were now both giggling. "That's what they call Priscilla the Third: Lovely. Can you fucking believe it?" Ellyn said.

"Even that vampire, Liv, would be a welcome change!" Mock wriggled in delight.

"Farrah's with Cor now, and they're both probably drunk off their asses." Ellyn shook her head. "And that could be good or bad, depending on how big the hangovers are. But I could have a chance to steal here. If you're there to romance Cor and make sure her time with me is the best of the four."

"So, I come onboard as your—what? Friend? Lover?" This con might have nice side benefits. Ellyn was tight-laced, but I thought I'd like to undo those laces.

"Hell no. You're a stranger to me. We do not know each other once we're on the ship. And we'll work together *secretly* to make sure Aunt Cor has a great time."

I saw advantages and disadvantages to her plan, but I could unfold those to my advantage later. I eyed her critically and spoke. "I want 20 percent," I said. My bald statement curbed their amusement immediately. "And half of anything you get over the Popular Niece Fund."

"Anything I get over?" Ellyn said, goggling.

"I'm good," I said. "I'm very, very good. You've lucked into one expert scoundrel. If I talk Aunt Cor out of more than the planned five mil, I get half of everything I add on to your total. Deal?"

They gaped at me. I laughed inside. They'd never considered they could get more, and now that I'd suggested it, they'd forget any concerns about me participating at all. Their own greed—simple, human, inevitable—would eat at them. Instead of me working for them, I'd be a partner in the scheme.

And maybe I'd be an uncle too. An unmarried woman worth $350 million? I could overcome my lone-wolf status for that.

"Done," Ellyn said.

I masked my relief. Mock shrieked and clapped his hands. "We are going to *Pygmalion* the fuck out of this bitch!"

CHAPTER THREE—ELLYN

MOCK'S *PYGMALION* REFERENCE LANDED POORLY. ARTIE'S eyebrows went up.

"*Pygmalion?*" Mock clarified. "We're going to pull an Eliza Doolittle on you, darling." Still no reaction. "Have you never seen *My Fair Lady*, handsome?"

Artie shook his head. Mock whirled to me. "Girl. He's culturally illiterate. We're going to have to make over his brain, as well as his look."

"What's the matter with my look?" Artie sounded offended. No time for that now. I pulled out my spiral notebook; I always brainstorm better on paper.

"Okay. We'll make him a must-watch list. Let's figure out the look first."

Mock's focus was complete. He stopped ogling Artie and began looking at him like a blank canvas. "We'll start with the hair, obviously."

Artie's hand went unconsciously to his shoulder-length blond mane. "What about my hair?"

I needed no further proof that Artie really wasn't in the film industry. Handsome enough to be an actor, but all actors are steeled for rejection. Tell an actor he needs a haircut and he'll look pathetically grateful—at last, someone telling him how to fix himself. Now everything would be okay.

Artie, on the other hand, was working himself up to being actively offended.

"Lamb chop," Mock said, "that style is entirely wrong for you. Not with those cheekbones. We need to go less Cirque du Soleil and more Abercrombie & Fitch."

"Make it Ralph Lauren," I said.

"Oh yes," Mock agreed. "Better. Older, wealthier, much less trendy. Timeless classics that never go out of style. How old are you, darling?"

Artie blinked and opened his mouth, no doubt to add some lies to the mix. I stopped him. "Aunt Cor is in her late sixties. We can't have you coming off as a twenty-five-year-old. How old can you go?"

Artie blinked, thrown off-balance. "I don't know. I've always tried to look younger. Maybe . . . thirty?"

Mock scoffed. "We can get you up to at least thirty-five. We'll have to deal with those teeth, though."

"No, you don't. My teeth are perfect."

"Sweetheart, not even Hollywood is going that white. You look plastic, lover. Don't worry. We'll fix you. That's what we do."

I made notes. "Agnes for the teeth?"

"Of course," Mock said. "She owes me."

"What about the hair? Can you do it?"

Mock stepped back, as far as he could in his shoebox apartment, to look at Artie. "I could. But the potential is so great. We really need Jasmine."

"Ugh. She hates me."

"I'll handle it. Now, angel—how tall are you?"

"Six-foot-five," Artie responded. "But I have lifts. I can be six-six or even six-seven."

"I don't want you taller, beefcake. You're too tall now. From now on, nothing but the thinnest-soled shoes—or barefoot.

You'll be on a cruise ship in tropical waters. Don't wear any shoes at all. So preppy."

Artie looked at me. "Where are we going, by the way?"

I was texting Agnes. "We pick up the ship in Singapore, then through the Andaman Sea, across the Bay of Bengal, a quick stop in India, and finish up in Sri Lanka, where the whole mess comes to an end and we all head home to examine the contents of our bank accounts."

Artie was silent. I looked up. Mock had found a tape measure and had Artie standing, arms spread out like Christ the Redeemer, while Mock measured and measured and measured, sometimes crooning in delight. Artie's silence caught my attention.

"What is it?" I asked him.

"Nothing," Artie replied, but he was thinking about something. It made me suspicious.

"Nothing what?"

Even with the black eye, the smile he hit me with was megawatt. "It's fine."

After five years in the film industry, I am immune to physical beauty. He was hiding something. "How do I know you're a scoundrel?" I said in sudden accusation.

Artie and Mock both turned to me.

"I can't afford to mess this up," I insisted. "What assurances do I have that you can do this?"

He lowered his outstretched arms. "What assurances that I can romance a little old lady?" His tone was incredulous. "You think I couldn't do it?"

"You think he couldn't do it?" Mock was already in love with our scoundrel. "This guy can *get* it."

Artie gave him the megawatts and Mock fluttered.

No way. "I'm going to need some references."

They both looked at me. "References?" Artie confirmed. "What kind of references?"

I worried my lip with my fingers while I thought. "Someone

you've scammed," I said hopelessly, knowing I was asking for the impossible.

Artie began to laugh.

"Okay," he said. "Give me your phone."

"Why?" His easy charm made me suspicious.

"Because mine got taken from me a little more than an hour ago by some rather unsavory people. I'll make a call, and you'll have your references. A really, really good one too."

I unlocked the phone and handed it over to him. He dialed a number from memory.

"Is this the luminous Moonglow Mystic? How are you, my darling? No, I'm in New York. I'd love that. Love it. Evie, I'm longing to chat, but I really need Dash's phone number. Can you give it to me? Thank you, priestess. Okay. Hang on."

He gestured to me, and I handed over my pad and paper. "Go ahead." He jotted down a number, promised a lifetime of love and bliss, and hung up. He handed the phone to me.

"Call that guy."

He was far too pleased with himself. "Who is it?"

"Friend of mine. His name is Dash. Ask him anything you want to know about me."

"How do I know he'll tell me the truth?"

Artie smirked. Mock watched us like we were Wimbledon. "Call him. You'll see."

"Put it on speakerphone!" Mock pleaded.

I dialed. The call went through, and a low, strong voice answered. "Special Agent Ashwood. Who's calling?"

My eyebrows went into my hairline. "Hello?" I said stupidly.

"Hello? Identify yourself, please."

"This is Ellyn." I'd lost my mind. I sounded like an idiot. "Did you say *special agent*?"

"What can I do for you, Ellyn?"

"Wait a minute. Who do you work for?"

"How did you get my number?"

Artie spoke. "Dash—it's Phoebus Apollon. How are you?"

Mock and I exchanged glances. *Phoebus Apollon? Now that was a stage name if ever I heard one.*

I heard an exasperated sigh from the speaker. "Phoebus." The name was drawn out like a curse. "What are you up to now?"

"Nothing bad, I promise. Can you confirm to this young lady that you're with the FBI?"

Mock and I goggled at him.

"I'm with the FBI. What's going on?"

I interjected. "Wait. Why would I believe you?"

Ashwood was silent, and then he spoke. "You shouldn't. And what's it to me?"

"W-well," I sputtered and came to a stop.

Mock spoke. "We need references for this guy Artie. He said you could vouch for him."

Sputtering came through the speakerphone. "Phoebus, I'm supposed to vouch for you?"

"Yeah, man. I'd appreciate it."

"Jesus Christ."

I broke in. "Not that I'd believe you were FBI."

We were all caught in silence until Artie said, "Evie gave me your number. She said you'd help me."

From the speaker came the rustling sound of hands being scrubbed over a face. "I'll bet she didn't. Ellyn, after I hang up, find the main number for FBI headquarters in Washington, DC. When you get to the switchboard, ask to speak with Special Agent Dash Ashwood. I've got a meeting in . . . twenty-two minutes. If you call before then, I'll talk to you."

There was a click and the phone disconnected.

"His name is Dash Ashwood?" Mock marveled.

"Good name, huh?" Artie and Mock exchanged grins. I looked up the number and figured I could probably trust what I found online, even if I didn't trust Artie. It would be an impressive scam if he'd managed to infiltrate Google.

It took a few moments, but the voice that ultimately

answered the call sounded tired. "Special Agent Ashwood. Who's calling?"

"Hi, Agent Ashwood. This is Ellyn again."

"Well, hello, Ellyn. I gather you accept my status as an FBI agent?"

"Yeah."

Mock nodded too.

"So, what can I do for you?"

"Do you know this guy? He says his name is Artie, but you seem to know him by—"

"Yeah, I know him. Big guy. Blond. Grins with a lot of teeth. Looks like he wants to bite people. Arrogant. Thrill-seeker. Surprisingly good in a crisis."

The venom he'd had at the beginning of the description died out by the end, and Artie grinned.

"That's the guy. Can you confirm—" It was hard to say the words. Artie leaned against Mock's fridge, arms crossed. Mock nodded at me in encouragement.

"Confirm what, Ellyn?"

I took a breath. "Is he a scoundrel?"

The agent sighed. "He's a dyed-in-the-wool scoundrel. Don't trust him any farther than you can throw him. The guy was probably born a confidence man; he will scam you out of any money you have. Stay away from him, Ellyn. Stay far, far away."

Artie nodded, smug. Mock clapped silently.

"Will there be anything else?" the agent asked.

"How's Running with Rosie?" Artie broke in.

A chuckle came over the phone. "She's good. She and Enos got married in November, and she's already pregnant."

"Awesome! A little eaglet at last, huh?"

They gabbed together, having a little old home week. Once he ended the call, Artie turned to me. "Is that reference enough?"

Mock and I looked at each other. "Let's get to work," I said.

Our next issue was the budget.

Distributions of largess were common when a Wolcott trustee died. I still had a fair chunk of the $100,000 I'd gotten as a bequest, but this would cut into that total.

"I'll need to pay for his cabin. That'll be $17,000," I figured out loud, and Artie blanched.

"Seventeen thou for a cabin on a cruise ship? How long are we going for?"

"Two weeks."

"More than a thousand a day?"

"It includes airfare. And it's a very nice cruise ship. Could be a lot worse. You'll be staying in one of the dinkier rooms."

"Dinkier?"

Mock was delighted to fill him in. "You'll be in the maid's room. It would have been me, but you'll be so much better at this than I ever would have."

Artie's brows met over his nose. I clarified. "Aunt Cor has both owner's suites for the journey. She gets one and whichever niece gets the other. And both suites include a second room for the maid—or a child, in Priss's case. But if no one rents both the owner's suite and the maid's room, that room can be purchased by someone else, and the connecting doors get locked."

"Don't forget about Rebel," Mock said.

"Rebel is Cor's bestie. She's got the next cabin. All in, Cor has rented five rooms on the ship for two months total, and the smallest is $17,000 for two weeks."

Artie did the math. "I'm going to really love your aunt, I think."

"Good. That will help. I'll have to call her travel agent and bribe her to make sure you get the maid's room as soon as I release it—and I'll have to pay for your cabin without letting my aunt know."

Artie flicked an eyebrow at me. He had no objections to other people spending money.

"And that," I finished, "will leave us with an Eliza Doolittle wardrobe budget of . . . you can spend four thousand, Mock."

"Wait," Artie protested. "I can handle the wardrobe. Give me the $4K."

Mock bubbled over with laughter. "Sweetie! Aren't you darling!" He turned to me. "I can do it. I'll get Spense to let me into the costume department. That will help fill in some gaps."

"Tell him I said thanks. We won't forget it."

Artie sputtered. "I can dress myself, you know."

Mock shook his head. "Resort casual for blue bloods? I don't think so. Old money doesn't wear new clothes. Everything has to be just worn enough—some things from two, even three seasons ago. You wouldn't stand a chance. Do you even know what shoes to buy?"

We all looked at Artie's feet. They were very large.

"I'm good at clothing." Artie was offended again.

"Of course you are, love." Mock patted Artie on the chest, but his hand fell a little low. One might say he patted Artie on his flat stomach. "We'll do this together, honey. Don't you worry about it."

I mapped out the next two weeks. "Can you sail?" I asked Artie.

"No."

"Speak any languages?"

"Some Russian."

"That's not a language anyone speaks. How about cards? Can you play bridge?"

"Poker. I'm excellent at poker."

"Bridge is not poker, and it's much, much harder to cheat."

"I can cheat at any card game."

"No. Dancing—can you dance?"

"Anyone can dance. I can get down."

"Not that kind of dancing. Can you waltz? Rumba? Fox-trot?"

"Fox-trot?"

"Don't look at me; I didn't name it. Can you?"

"No."

"That, at least, we can teach you. What else, Mock?"

"Skeet shooting? Will they shoot skeet off the back deck?"

"Good one. Can you shoot skeet?"

"Actually, that I have done. And I can ride a horse."

"Less useful at sea, but we'll keep it in mind. We're going to need a backstory for him, Mock. What's his line?"

We kicked around ideas. Software designer was nicely ambiguous, but if we ran into another designer, ignorance would be betrayed very quickly. We settled on commercial real estate. Artie said he knew about Wyoming, so that's where we centered his tiny, rural empire.

"Are you from Wyoming?" I asked, suddenly interested.

"Staten Island," he said shortly. Hmm. Less romantic. I turned to Mock to continue our backstory-brainstorming.

"Where'd he prep?"

"Andover?" suggested Mock. "No—Choate. He looks like a Choate boy."

"Hang on." Artie looked annoyed. "Didn't you tell me that Cor was walk-up apartment mixed with penthouse? So, she's ashamed of her background, right?"

I'd never really thought about how Aunt Cor viewed herself, but Artie had a point. "Maybe she thinks the family looks down on her because she didn't come from blue bloods," I realized. "Not because she was a home-wrecking gold digger."

"Which she totally is," Mock added. It was his chief dream to be the hussy who breaks up a marriage and becomes a wealthy trophy wife.

Artie nodded. "Right. So she'd respond best to someone from working-class roots who is a self-made man." He watched as his idea washed over us.

"That is good," Mock admitted.

"Under that theory, I went to public school in Casper, Wyoming. Just a regular guy—that's me." He favored us with a friendly grin, and suddenly I could see it.

"Do we need to get him a cowboy hat?" Mock asked.

I shook my head. "Not on the ship. But a slight Western tilt to the wardrobe? It's not a bad idea."

Mock's eyes were distant. "The Fall 1979 Ralph Lauren collection—cattlemen jackets, chain-stitched boots, pearl-snap shirts with contrasting trim—but taken to a tropical place. And updated, of course. Hmm. An interesting challenge."

He wandered to a laptop and was lost in his own searching. This was where Mock really began to shine. Best to give him room.

"Good idea," I said to Artie.

"I'm not completely helpless," he said.

His easy confidence raised my suspicions, and the FBI agent's words echoed in my brain. *Don't trust him any farther than you can throw him.* Mock and I were putting all our production company eggs in one con man's basket. I revised my expectations. I'd be an idiot if I didn't keep an eye on where this guy went next.

CHAPTER FOUR—ARTIE

Victor always said, "It's better to be lucky than smart."

Today I was lucky as hell. Zebra Girl had saved my ass.

In two hours, I'd gone from looming pain, shattering poverty, and the loss of everything I loved to having a strong line on possibly the scam of a lifetime.

And all I had to do for now, according to the hastily scrawled list in my hand, was to watch *My Fair Lady* and learn the rules of bridge.

Alone, I slumped in the corner of the elevator and immediately stood upright again, wincing. Cracked ribs. Never not an absolute party.

Okay. Ellyn and Mock had given me two tasks, but I had a list of my own to accomplish before movies and bridge rules. And the nicer one—seeing if Bobby still worked at Killerz Gym; he'd tape my ribs for a twenty—had to come second.

I stiffened my spine and flashed a white-toothed grin at my reflection in the elevator door. Perfection. Even the black eye was okay. It gave me a devilishly raffish air. I was Zorro. A musketeer, filled with brio and derring-do. Next stop: I was going back to Terence the Accountant, and I would need all the arrogance I could muster to pull this off.

The elevator dumped me out in the dingy lobby of Mock's apartment building. I managed to put a swagger in my step as I headed around the corner.

Fortunately for my swagger, Terence's offices weren't far. His boys had roughed me up pretty successfully that morning, and the Starbucks across the street, where I met Zebra Girl, had been as far as I'd been able to go before I'd had to sit and recover —in mind, as well as in body.

Maggie, Terence's frumpy receptionist, went wide-eyed when she saw me returning. She glanced over at Gorgeous George, whose phone was forgotten as he looked up, astonished.

"Get Hambone," he said to Maggie.

"No need. I'm not here for trouble. I just need to talk to Terence."

George and Maggie gaped at me. Good. My return had put them off-balance.

"You don't talk to Terence without Hambone. And me," George thought to add. George was a weasel, and weasels are useful. But most people don't assume a weasel is much help in a brawl, and most people are right. George knew his pathetic limitations, and he was no match for me on his own. "Maggie, see if you can get Iggy back here."

I beamed at them from my full height because I knew a smile would confuse them at this point. "Sure. I'll wait for Hambone and Iggy. But tell Terence I'm here, will you?"

"He's with a client," she said nervously. That wasn't so surprising. Terence Dalloway was an unsuspected and successful drug lord because he was also an actual Midtown accountant, with a client list and reviews on Yelp and Google he cared deeply about.

I winked at Maggie, who jumped. The ice had helped with the swelling, but my eye still must have looked a little alarming. "That's fine. I'll wait."

I turned to face George, who hunched his neck into his

shoulders protectively. Caught at it, he attempted bluster. "How are those ribs?"

I threw myself into the chair next to him, forcing myself into a slump without wincing. "A little more painful than my stomach, of course." I gave him a full shark grin, making no effort to mask my contempt for his weak right cross to my belly.

We sat in silence in a reception area designed to be unassuming. A drug kingpin would have a flashy, bimbo-style secretary. Maggie was on the far side of forty and currently sporting a cardigan that matched her blouse. Where drug lords would have fish tanks filled with tiger sharks, Terence had motivational posters of kittens reminding us Friday was coming. I had to admire his camouflage. Even George, assigned to linger in the waiting room like the next appointment, had been dressed in an off-the-rack suit that did nothing for him.

George's eyes darted around the room until Hambone oozed into the reception area. Hambone didn't usually linger in the waiting room and was therefore allowed to dress as he liked. He had Italian mobster pretentions—his people came from Poland, so he wasn't off to a good start—and he wore an unfortunately sleazy silk suit that offended my sensibilities. *Was it so hard to show a little style?*

"Hambone, if you can't afford the good stuff, those knock-off suits are not an acceptable substitute. They're greasy. A nice, worsted wool would look better on you. Good shoes, though."

Hambone, as usual, was easy to distract. He flushed, annoyed. "I thought I broke some of your ribs."

I shifted in the chair to face him, hiding the pain. "Oh yeah? I don't think so. Maybe next time?"

"You're wearing Iggy's black eye for everyone to see," he said petulantly, and I grinned at him.

"Very observant of you."

He was sputtering for an answer when Terence came out of his office, ushering Joe Businessman to the door. "I'll have the reports ready for you next week, Danny. Thanks for coming in. Now," he said, turning to us. "What do we have here?"

"I'm calling Iggy," Maggie said hurriedly.

Terence eyed me and I eyed him. "No matter. We're fine, aren't we, Mr. Petrovitch?"

I couldn't hide it; I hated him knowing my real name, and he knew I hated it. That was why he used it.

"We are fine." I came to my feet and stretched casually, laying my hands flat against the dropped ceiling. Maggie forgot to close her mouth. "I just want to talk."

Terence pursed his lips. "Do I have any more appointments, Maggie?"

"Not until four."

"Okay. Come on back. You guys come too."

George leaped to his feet and I dropped my stretch, one hand landing on his shoulder. He squeaked and darted away, and I laughed.

"I want to talk to you about my options," I said to Terence as we entered his office.

"Hang on." He turned to George. "Is he wearing a wire?"

George shook his head. "I, uh—I don't know."

Terence looked at Hambone, who shrugged. Terence was clearly disappointed.

He gestured to me. "Strip."

If he thought nudity would unnerve me, he was mistaken. I work on my body. I'm good with being naked.

Terence hissed and George laughed when I pulled my sweater over my head. "Can't tell me those ribs don't hurt," the weasel said.

I could see the spreading bruise in the faint reflection of the windows opposite me. "Like I said, George, at least my stomach doesn't bother me."

I slapped the eight-pack and grinned at him again. He ducked his head and shot a look at the boss.

Unlacing my boots was a bitch on my ribs, but I made it

through. I unfolded again and shucked my jeans, casually kicking out of them. Any excuse to avoid moving my rib cage.

I stood before Terence in my skin and stretched my hands to either side. Who drew the *Vitruvian Man*—Michelangelo? Da Vinci? "No wire," I said, stating the obvious.

"Check him," Terence said shortly.

"What, you think some feds hid a microphone up my ass? What would they hear? Digestion?"

"Bend over," he said. "Or leave."

Behind me, George was being forced to do the honors by Hambone. "I need gloves!"

"Spread him apart and look," Terence said, annoyed.

It doesn't take long in prison to get bored by body cavity searches. I bent forward and put my elbows on Terence's desk. Wagging my ass at George, I chided him, "Come on, man. What are you afraid of?"

If he'd had gloves and something to hurt me with, I wouldn't have done it. But he was more fearful of what Hambone—and especially Terence—thought of him, and he grabbed my butt cheeks in two angry hands and yanked them apart.

"Jesus," Hambone said. "Artie, you bleach your asshole?"

"Who doesn't?" I said. "Of course I do."

Having found nothing, George let go and I was allowed to stand. Hambone turned to me, interested. "You do pornos? Because I know a guy."

I smiled. "I no longer fuck for money. Thanks, though."

All three men were taken aback by the statement. I'd gotten to use it twice in one day. Bonus.

I sat in the client chair, wiggling a little so Terence knew my naked ass was on his fabric, and crossed my ankle over my knee. "So. Do you want these two in on our discussion?"

Terence looked like I'd worn him out. He shook his head faintly and gestured George and Hambone out of the room. "Leave the door open," he said. *Didn't want to be in a closed office with a naked man? Interesting.* I noted a potential for latent homosexuality in my mental file on Terence.

"What the hell are you doing back here? I wasn't clear earlier?"

"I need my wallet and my phone."

All accountants like it when things add up, and I wasn't behaving as he'd expected. That put him on edge. He wasn't sure how to handle me.

"Why?"

"Why?" I stretched one arm out along the other chair. "Because they're mine, of course. Also, I have a proposition for you, and I need them."

"*You* have a proposition for *me*."

"That's right."

He consulted his watch. "You came here at ten this morning. I told you what your options were and made sure you had a few reminders of our discussion. Now, four hours later, you're back to give me options? What the hell did you have for lunch?"

I laughed. "Soup, actually. Let me explain."

My foot came off my leg with a thump on the floor and I sat forward suddenly. Terence flinched, and his eyes went to the open door. I showed him all my teeth as I put my elbows on my naked knees.

"I will pay you every penny of the $89,000 Kaz owes you, plus an extra $10,000 for your troubles. In return, you give me my phone, my wallet, and one month to make this happen. Plus, I'd like to suggest a new opportunity for both of us."

I outlined my plan to bolster his business—the non-accounting part of his business—while he sat and listened. It wasn't long before he got up and shut the door so we could continue our discussion in private.

He tipped in his chair, considering. "How?" he said simply.

"That's for me to worry about."

"And what reassurances do I have that you'll be back in a

month with the hundred grand, much less this new opportunity?"

Kaz's $89,000 plus my offer of $10K was $99,000. He'd added his own thousand to the total, but I wasn't going to quibble.

"You know where my brothers live. You know where my sister lives. You know where my mother lives."

"As it happens, I know where your father lives too."

Like Hambone, Terence the Accountant was from my old neighborhood.

"My father, you can have," I said dismissively.

He scratched his chin and then his face. "One month."

"One month and a whole new potential revenue stream for you."

He'd already made up his mind—I would get my time and my chance—but he made me wait, just for the power it gave him. "George!" he barked. Gorgeous George opened the door quickly enough to confirm he'd been doing his best to eavesdrop. "Get Artie's phone and wallet."

We considered each other, both wearing carefully chosen faces, until George scurried in. I held out my hand, but he handed my things to Terence.

"Go on. Get out now," Terence spoke almost kindly to George, who nodded and vanished. "Okay. Here's your phone."

He tossed it to me. Halfway there.

"Your wallet was interesting." Terence looked at it, and I kept my face impassive. "The debit card in the lining was well-hidden, but I found it." He showed me all his teeth this time and savored my discomfort before continuing. "My guy at the bank? He was able to pull the entire $14,000 off the account, so we'll consider this a down payment. You can keep the cash you had."

He'd earned the wince I gave. *Fuck.* That was all that was left from last summer's most profitable scam, a con in Wyoming called "Prophecy Week." Cons in the intervening months hadn't panned out well, and I was living off my savings. To a guy like me, that's death. I live for the thrill. For the hunt. For the chance to fleece sheep. It's what they deserve. I wasn't made to live on a budget or to—ugh—economize.

I caught the wallet when he tossed it. "A down payment," I said with a sneer. "So, you've got $14K and I owe you $86,000."

"No," he said, "you owe me the full amount. A hundred. In one month." This was the problem with dealing with drug lords. All their math errors went in their favor. "Or," he continued, "I'll start with your brother."

"Fucking Kaz."

"You may well say. Now take your clothes and get the hell out of here."

"Can I get dressed first?"

"Not here. Go give Maggie a thrill. I don't need to look at any more of your body. You have one month."

It was easier on my ribs to scoop up my clothes from the floor while I sat. I rose—jeans, sweater, boots, and jacket in an ungainly bundle in my arms, wallet and phone in my hands. "Thanks, Terence." I gave it a cocky attitude.

"Get out."

Maggie flushed scarlet when I did a slow turn for her in the reception area. I dressed slowly and used force of will to make Gorgeous George lace my boots.

"See you in a month," I told them.

"You'd better!" George called, brave behind the receptionist. "We're coming after you if you don't!"

"You're welcome to try," I said.

And then I was on the street, breathing freedom and possibility.

It could happen. I could make this happen.

I was made to separate the stupid stooges—the Wolcotts, accountants, anyone who thought they could beat or use me—from their lovely, empowering money.

CHAPTER FIVE—ELLYN

I wasn't surprised when Bax showed up the next day at our rehearsal hall. I'd told him the plan over dinner, told him about Artie, the enormous beefcake stranger. So when Bax appeared, carrying cupcakes, I knew he was just being protective.

Not that I needed it. I would never point it out to Bax, but I was physically stronger than he was, and I've taken my share of self-defense classes. But Mock did need the cupcakes. In fact, Mock greeted the cupcakes like long-lost friends. I did introductions.

"Artie, this is my boyfriend, Baxter. Bax, this is Artie."

"Cupcakes, I'm Mock. I'm so pleased to meet you."

Mock had no use for Bax. He'd made it very clear that he thought my boyfriend was a spineless convenience for me, no matter how much I protested that I liked having Bax around. But Mock's loyalties could be temporarily purchased with baked goods, so I knew the day's work would go smoothly.

Artie regarded Bax with interest, making no attempt to hide his assessment. He held out a large hand and offered a shiny smile. "Hey. How you doing."

Bax was confronted by a whole lot of man and wasn't sure

what to do about it. He stood straighter and shook the offered hand. Instead of protecting me, Bax was now measuring his own masculinity. He wasn't going to be kind to himself in the comparison. Bax was sweet, not butch, and a valuable part in my life for his thoughtfulness and support, but he worried about guy foolishness, like arm wrestling and the ability to drink beer all afternoon.

I put a hand on my honey's shoulder in affection. "I'm glad you're here. Can you sit in for a few hands of bridge? We want to run through the rules before Eddie gets here."

"Eddie's coming?" Bax brightened. "Are you choreographing a sword fight?"

"Not this time. He's going to teach Artie how to dance. You know—ballroom."

"Oh, cool!" Bax liked all aspects of movement; I'd found him in a hip-hop dance class when I was doing a documentary on the teacher. We'd been together for over a year. He was a good actor and had a job with an off-Broadway company. He was still getting understudy roles and filled in the financial gaps with shifts as a barista, but he was good at his craft, and he'd be getting bigger parts soon. I knew it.

The four of us settled into folding chairs around a table made of a large wooden spool that had once held fiber optic cable. Mock had lucked into the rehearsal space in the community room of a church that would surely be rehabbed as soon as the Episcopalians coughed up the cash. It had been closed for almost two years, and Mock had an in with a caretaker who wanted to be Mock's apprentice stylist.

Artie's eye was now black and purple, but the swelling had receded. From here on, I'd cut back to one photo a day to watch its progress as it faded to greens and yellows and then disappeared. Should be just about the time we got aboard Aunt Cor's ship.

"You play bridge, Bax?" Artie asked. He shuffled cards easily, his hands gracefully arching the deck in a fancy move.

"Some," Bax said with a shrug. Bax was great at bridge. I smiled at him; he looked happy. He'd stopped measuring his manliness against Artie's and anticipated some bold bidding.

For some reason, Artie smiled, too, as he dealt the cards.

"You learned all the rules?" Mock asked. "You know how to bid? What the bids mean?"

"Close enough," Artie said easily. "I looked the rules over."

"Looked them over?" Mock, partnered with Artie, was distressed. Mock liked to win.

"Don't worry about it."

The bidding seemed unorthodox to me, but unlike Mock and Bax, I was hopeless at bridge and couldn't be trusted to know what was normal and what wasn't. The game began, and Mock was the dummy. We played for a bit until a second ace of diamonds appeared on the table.

Even I, as bad as I am at bridge, saw the problem, and Mock and Bax protested immediately. It was clear who the culprit was.

"Artie," I said. "I know you're new at this, but this isn't poker. All the cards are dealt out. You can't just pull out a fifty-third card."

"Sure I can. Watch. I've been holding this one for the last five minutes, and you never noticed."

"It doesn't matter. People count aces. People count all the face cards."

"And here's one to count."

Mock and Bax were both speaking. I hushed them and kept trying.

"Do you see that now there have been five aces in play? You can't do that, Artie."

"I have a blinding smile." He hit me with it; we really needed to do something about those unnaturally white teeth. "They won't notice. They're all biddies, right? Older women are my particular specialty."

Frustration rose in me. "Artie. Even blinded biddies know when there are *two aces in the trump suit*."

"No, it's a really good smile. Here—let me hit you with it again."

"Oh, for Christ's sake." We all threw down our cards. "How about sailing? Did you say you knew how to sail?"

Bax and Mock had found common accord with each other at last and were commiserating over someone attempting to cheat at bridge. Mock decided it was time for another cupcake. The morning deteriorated until Eddie arrived, charming and graceful.

"Dance class!" I said, relieved. "There will be dances onboard. Priss looked at the schedule for the last part, when we have three days at sea across the Bay of Bengal. She said there's a dance competition. The rumba. And I'll tell you now: Aunt Cor really, really likes to rumba."

Artie listened with a raised eyebrow, and Eddie clapped his hands.

"The rumba! Afro-Cuban! It's all about the hips. A great dance. Are we starting there?"

I made him back way up. "Let's think of this as sixth-grade dancing school. I think the box step is the way to start."

"Fine." Eddie was all work. "Put down that bag, Ellyn. You're the girl here."

"I already know how to dance," I protested. "Teach him."

"He needs someone to dance with. Camera bag on the table. You can survive for half an hour without it. Come on—let's go."

Eddie posed me in front of Artie. "This hand on her waist. Hold the other. Ellyn?" I reached up to put my hand on Artie's shoulder. My other hand was lost in the size of his warm grip. Palm to palm, his fingers bent almost all the way across the back of my hand, but his clasp was gentle, and he didn't crush me. His other hand rested respectably on my waist. In the briefest flash, I wondered what it would feel like to have his arm wrapped around me, pulling me into him. *Stupid.* I blinked and eased away fractionally.

"Good," Eddie said. "You look good together. Both of you are far too tall for normal people. Okay—here's what you're going to do."

He walked Artie through the basic box step.

"You went to dancing school in sixth grade?" Artie asked me as we watched our own feet. We were too close; it was an oddly intimate moment. I focused on directing him instead of feeling him.

"Yeah. You didn't? No—forward, side-together back, side-together forward, side-together back . . . that's it. Good."

"In sixth grade, I was"—he nodded his head to the beat Eddie was clapping, but he also thought—"I was helping my brother boost cars."

I missed a step and landed on his foot. Or he missed a step. Either way, I was off-balance, and he had to hold me up for a minute with that strong hand coming around my waist. *Pull it together, Ellyn.* What had he just said?

"You stole cars in sixth grade? Damn. You really are a scoundrel. How old was your brother?"

"Fifteen. Tall enough to reach the pedals. We got a hundred for every car we brought to this chop shop, assuming we could find it. It moved around a lot. That was good money then."

"Wow," Bax said. "That's something."

Eddie clapped to return our focus. "I'm going to put on some music. Try to stay with the beat. And when you're ready, Artie, turn her in little circles. See what I mean?"

He took Baxter in a practiced hold. Bax laughed and off they went, turning easily.

"Got it." Artie's jaw was set. Eddie cued up some Frank Sinatra, and we were back at it.

I helped out by beginning the turn, and Artie caught on quickly.

"That's good," Eddie said. "Now you can stop counting and nodding your head. Right? Good. Just let your feet move. That's right."

He watched us critically. "Artie, you're supposed to be leading

Ellyn. Feminism goes out the window in ballroom dancing, so don't even worry about it. The man leads. You make the decisions."

I rolled my eyes. *Right.* Artie was getting the footwork, but he had a hard time leading.

Unexpectedly, Eddie announced that it was my fault.

"Oh, come on," I said. "I've been doing this for years, and he's just started. This is not my fault."

Mock watched. He stepped forward, his eyes bright. "You know, I'm exactly the height of your Aunt Cor. Artie should practice with me. And I won't try to lead."

He pushed between us and beamed up at Artie. Artie shrugged and let go of me, taking Mock's outstretched hand. "All right. Let's try this."

I backed up, irked—by Mock? Or by Artie letting go? Bax appeared next to me. "May I have this dance?"

Ah. That's the guy I felt comfortable with. "Charmed, I'm sure!"

Bax and I, both experienced, sailed around Artie and Mock, who were turning in careful circles as they danced. I'd forgotten how much I liked formal dancing, and Bax and I had a lovely time. I sang along (I can't resist big band songs) until the dance ended.

Eddie had stopped Artie and Mock, and the three of them were watching us. They clapped at the end. "You see?" Eddie said. "Ellyn was leading the whole time."

"I was not!"

Eddie smirked. "Sure you weren't. Let's do it again. Ellyn, you're with me this time."

With the touch of his hand, things changed. Eddie wouldn't let me lead; he showed me exactly where he wanted me to go, and I began to laugh as we swept in larger and more graceful circles. Eddie was better at this than Bax was. He was better than *I* was. I applauded, too, at the end. *Fun!*

"There. See? Let the man lead. And you be clear in what you

want of her," he said to Artie, who nodded. "All right. We've got the fox-trot. Time to move on. Let's learn to waltz."

Waltzing was even more fun, and Artie and I discovered that we moved well together. The rumba was a challenge, but all agreed it was a sexy and fun dance. And by that time, Artie had forgotten the box step.

"Go home," Eddie advised. "Watch videos. Practice. Do you have someone you can dance with?"

Artie grinned. "I think I can scare up some partners."

It occurred to me how little I knew about this man. Who was he scaring up? Was there a girlfriend? A wife? A harem?

He caught me studying him and grinned.

I shrugged. Not my business.

―――――――――

Jasmine was a hair stylist to the rich and popular. Up-and-coming, perpetually on the hottest lists. Attitude for days. She loved Mock and hated me. She agreed to see us two days later.

Actually, two nights later. She deigned to hold her salon open for an after-hours appointment, and we arrived at midnight. I ushered Artie in, a hand at the small of his back, but he needed no encouragement. This was a temple to vanity, and he was its chief acolyte.

But after considering Artie's black eye with scorn, Jasmine turned to what she clearly regarded as a more worthy opponent: me.

"Who did that to your hair?" She glared.

Behind her, Mock waved his hands. *Don't tell her it was me!*

"I, uh, did it myself. Why? You don't like it?"

"Stripes? Don't be stupid. You look like a convict. An ugly convict. Sit. I'll turn you back into a redhead—which was the only thing about you anyone has ever liked, so of course you changed the color." *Bitch.* "Now. Let's look at this."

Artie started to say something, and Jasmine held up a hand.

"Please. Don't open your mouth. I don't need anything from you but your bone structure. Sit here."

He was summarily dismissed to the chair next to mine, and she and Mock descended into an incomprehensible discussion. She made fun of Mock relentlessly, but he must have said the right things because she kissed his cheek at the end and turned up the music.

"Nobody talk to me. Nobody talk at all. I need to think."

I had occasion to think on Eddie's lesson on leading and following, because the more arrogant and demanding Jasmine got, the meeker I got and the harder I tried to please her—even though I didn't particularly want to. If I could master her autocratic control as a director, no film set would ever defeat me. *Lean back, sit up, lift your head, look down, sit here, hold this.* If Jasmine were dancing a rumba, there would be no doubt who was leading. And at the end, she'd whip out a pair of scissors and slice through her partner's Achilles tendon to prove some unargued point about art and perfection.

Control. Success in this world—for a wannabe director, for a ballroom dancer, for a hairdresser—depended on who had control and who didn't. This was a lesson I didn't think Artie the scoundrel needed to learn. I reminded myself to keep an eye on our ringer.

Mock had his hands clasped beneath his chin like a little girl watching fairies dancing in a magic circle. Artie and I were mannequins whose hair was unforgivably attached. She made it work.

After hours of smelly potions and bizarre treatments, I was a plain old redhead again. The only difference I could see from the way I was born were some pretty honey highlights, but that seemed like too little payoff for hours of fuss, when she could have just washed the dye out of my hair and called it a day.

Artie, on the other hand—damn.

His hair was short but shaggy. Straight, yet with body. Wind-blown, tousled, and still neat. His cheekbones could cut, and I'd never noticed what a great neck he had. Strong. Long. Like something you could cling to. Jasmine was an artist.

Artie looked like the freshest and most beautiful version of old money.

"Too young!" Mock announced. "I told you. He has to look thirty-five!"

"That man can't look thirty-five. Not without crimes against art. This will have to do. His hair, at least, is irresistible. Even with the remains of that shiner on his eye."

"Maybe too clean-shaven?" Mock asked thoughtfully.

"Depends. If he's after younger women—or men—then with a few days of scruff, he'd have to beat them off with a stick. Like this? Ideal for older women."

Mock and I exchanged significant nods. Artie would be shaving twice a day, then.

He was having a hard time getting used to his new look. He kept turning his head and running his fingers along his neck. That movement alone was proof he'd had long hair for a while.

But he also smiled into the mirror. He preened. He posed. He liked what he saw. As previously suspected, our boy was vain.

Of course, that wasn't surprising. No need to deny it. He was damned good-looking.

I grabbed Mock's elbow and turned him away from the others. "Oh my God," I said.

"What?"

"This might work."

"You're just getting that now?"

Panic and excitement fizzed my nerve endings. "Christ. We've got so much to do!"

CHAPTER SIX—ARTIE

ANYONE WITH ANY EXPERIENCE COULD HAVE PICKED ELLYN out of a crowd. She was hopeless at the con.

I'm sure she thought she was cool as milk. The problem was that as we moved slowly up the gangway to the ship, she looked everywhere but at me.

That's a dead giveaway.

There were six or eight people between us and everyone else eagerly explored the sights—from the ship's berth in the hugely crowded Singapore harbor to the ship itself, frequently counting portholes or windows to point out to their traveling companions where they thought their cabins were.

And they looked at their fellow passengers.

Of course they did. All humans are snoops. We want to see who's going to be with us on our vacation, who might be next to us at the bar, who might share a table in the restaurant, who could sprawl out in the next deck chair.

And lots of them were looking at me.

Of course.

I was taller than everyone else, I was younger, I was far better-looking. I had a smile that could melt judges, social workers, soft touches at the Staten Island Ferry Terminal. If she'd known what she was doing, Ellyn would have checked me out. The fact that she didn't was glaring and obvious.

Still, Joe and Jane Citizen, inching up the gangway and onto the ship, weren't paying attention. Of course they weren't. People were sheep. Suckers, one and all. That's what made my job so easy.

I'd already met and assessed most of the new arrivals. The cruise line had provided transportation from the airport in a posh van, along with sightseeing and lunch, and I'd found an excuse to chat with all of them—not because I was looking for a scam, but because by now, it's instinct. I never knew when an interesting opportunity would present itself.

The adorable man and woman in front of me were on their honeymoon. Quentin and Paula. Cheap shoes. Glaze of excitement. They told me her family had pooled together to give them the cruise as a wedding gift, and although they would've rather had some mortgage payments in the bank, they were still excited. They had the smallest cabin at the bottom of the ship and no money. I smiled warmly at them and dismissed them as being fully uninteresting.

The couple behind me, however, was a different story. Hannah (*Call me Hannie; everyone does!*) and Chris Kettlesworth. Older. She had skin like an old wallet from decades of tennis with the club pro. He had their travel documents in a leather fanny pack he wore without irony. *Financial planning*, he'd said with a CEO's grin as he shook my hand. I didn't even have to peek at their documents to know they were on a higher deck and in a bigger cabin than Quentin and Paula.

I leaned casually on the gangway's railing as we chatted to avoid looming over them. These people had disposable income, and I wasn't specifically on the hunt—but if something came up, who was I to turn away? It's a fool who doesn't pay attention when possible profit is commenting on the heat behind you.

Ellyn made it into the ship before me and was greeted by a purser who would direct her to her cabin. Quentin and Paula,

Hannie and Chris, and I—we edged forward, grinning at the excitement of a new journey. I would need stronger sunscreen. Mock had forbidden me the straw porkpie hat I'd wanted (it had a madras band and would have been perfect), so I was bareheaded in the sun.

The baggy shorts, though—those were comfortable, and in a faded red that looked old-school and wealthy. A white polo (*God, no insignia*, Mock had insisted. *You are not going to be a walking billboard for Vineyard Vines, as much as they would like that.*) and boat shoes with no socks. He'd vetoed the needlepoint belt with my name in naval flags as being too 1970s.

If not now, when? I was still annoyed by that. Details are important.

So, except for the sun cooking my head and frying the back of my neck—pale skin once covered for decades by my hair—I was comfortable in the heat and humidity.

Once on the ship, the air dropped to arctic temperatures, which was a reprieve from the steamy heat . . . for just a moment. Then the chilled air made all the women shiver in their gauzy sundresses and colorful summer clothes.

We'd entered into a bottleneck. It soon became apparent why the line had inched up the gangway so slowly. A cluster of guests waited for porters to return to show them to their cabins, so I got an unexpected look at my prey.

Aunt Cor Wolcott had come to the reception area to meet her niece.

Ellyn had her back to the gangway and held herself so rigidly I longed to goose her just to see her jump. We'd planned for me to accidentally meet Aunt Cor at the bar later, and Ellyn wasn't rolling too well with the derailment of her plans. I'd explained that plans were only outlines of what might happen and we'd need to be ready to improvise, but Ellyn knew what she wanted and didn't like considering she might not get it.

So here we were, mere feet from each other, and she wasn't happy about it.

Cor was, as advertised, the exact same size as Mock. They were both about a foot shorter than me, and both built on very round lines. Unlike Mock, Cor held her curves in place with some powerful undergarments. It must have been tough breathing in all that Spanx.

She had a round face, a carrying voice, and white hair piled in a 'do that must have needed to be reset every morning.

And she was a talker.

"Sweetheart, I hope you brought a sweater. The ship is positively arctic. I've spoken to our steward about it, and he just smiles and doesn't do anything at all. Rebel and I are permanently blue. We'll have to spend all our time on deck. Did you bring sunblock? That pale skin of yours—it's like Wooly's. You'll burn if you're not careful!"

Ellyn and the porter next to them were both trying to nudge Cor out of the crowded reception area, but she scanned the incoming passengers and wouldn't be moved. I merited an interested smile and made sure to break off eye contact quickly. *Don't want to alert the quarry to my pursuit.*

"And Ellyn, you have your little camera? That's wonderful. Oh, that camera bag—must you carry it everywhere? Well, never mind. There's so much to see. You'll love to take pictures of all of it, I'm sure. The food buffets are just gorgeous, and on this leg, there's a dance troupe from Bali for entertainment. So colorful! Oh, and a dance contest next week! I hope you and I can find partners. I know how you love to rumba!"

Sometimes the gods smile on me. It would be sacrilegious to ignore the opportunity.

I pushed gently past Hannie, who was chatting about their recent trip to the Galapagos, and leaned forward, eyes and expression innocent.

"Excuse me," I broke in, "I couldn't help but overhear. Did you mention a dance contest . . . and a rumba?"

Ellyn might have swallowed her tongue, she looked so

alarmed, but Cor didn't notice. She had eyes only for me. No wonder.

"I did. How do you do?"

She stuck out a hand covered in rings and bracelets—and even the fastest assessment confirmed a bewildering mixture of trash and very real, very large gemstones.

I took it gently and bowed over her hand. "How do you do? I'm Arthur Petrovitch. Staten Island, New York."

"Not really! I'm from Jamaica!" Cor was delighted. Ellyn, expecting her Wyoming real estate story, watched with her mouth hanging open.

"Oh, a Queens girl—you're from the *good* side of the tracks!" I said with a twinkle, and Cor and I shared a delighted laugh.

"Oh, Mr. Petrovitch, how nice to meet someone from home!"

"I was thinking the same thing. Please call me Arthur."

"Arthur! All right—I will! Well, I'm Cor, then. Cor Walcott. And this is my niece, Ellyn."

She presented Ellyn as an afterthought, and she deflated slightly when she turned to the far younger, far slimmer woman. And indeed, Ellyn was luscious, her Irish-lassie red hair pulled away from a face Botticelli could have used as the model for an angel.

I made a point of giving her a patently obvious smile and a cursory "how-de-do" before turning back to the older woman.

"Cor, what were you saying about a rumba?" I held my hands up, one in the air and one on my tight abs, and did a hip shimmy that had both ladies and the porter cooing in appreciation. "Because I do *so* love to dance."

"Oh, my," Cor breathed. Inside, I grinned. The hook was set. "Well, you must tell your wife there's a dance contest in a few days."

I put on a sad-clown face. "Alas, no wife, Cor. Just me."

"No girlfriend?" she said hopefully. She peered past me to see if I had a traveling companion somewhere.

I shook my head. "Unmarried. Footloose and fancy-free. I've

finished my latest novel, and I'm treating myself to a little solo vacation before getting back to it. I was lucky to get a last-minute deal on a cabin."

Behind her, Ellyn had regained enough presence of mind to telegraph her annoyance to me. Her foot, in a canvas sneaker, stomped in irritation against the ship's deck.

"A novelist!" Cor gushed. "Have I read anything you've written?"

"I write under a pen name—Ambrose Pensiter. Is it familiar? No? Well, that's not surprising. Don't think anything of it. I've only written three, and only one was reviewed by *The New York Times*, so it's not surprising that you haven't heard of me."

Ellyn blinked. A second porter, bearing my key, had joined the group and was trying to get us to move out of the crowded reception area and to our various cabins.

I reached out to turn the ladies, using the force of my will to get our little troupe moving. To an observer, I was politely ushering them down the long hallway. But once Cor was facing away, my thumb slid under the hem of Ellyn's silky shirt and brushed lightly against the small of her back—a daring intimacy in the midst of meeting her aunt. The excitement generated by that secret connection fed my need for adrenaline. Ellyn jumped at my touch and shot me a glare little-masked by the false smile plastered on her face.

Her reaction added to my pleasure. I dropped my hand and turned solicitously to the older woman. "Do you rumba, Mrs. Cor?"

"Oh, just Cor, please, Arthur. And yes, I do. I quite love it!"

We'd moved out of the crowd far enough that I had room to come to a halt. "Not really? Well—would your husband mind if I asked you to partner with me for the dance contest, Cor?"

She made a little moue. "My husband died not quite a year ago. But he hated dancing. I'd love to partner with you!" Her face brightened.

"It would mean practicing," I said with a warning tone.

"Every day. Cor, I believe you can't just fake your way in a really good rumba."

Ellyn shook her head in disbelief, and Cor nodded as vigorously. "Oh, I quite agree! Arthur, you're so right!"

"Wonderful!" I straightened and turned to the porters. "Well, let's get settled in and maybe we could meet in an hour or so to discuss it. In the restaurant bar, maybe?"

Ellyn's lips were pursed in irritation, but Cor was thrilled. "Perfect!"

We'd reached the elevator. "Well, I'm in 517," I said, knowing exactly where her rooms were.

"517?" she said blankly. She turned to Ellyn, a sudden question occurring to her. "I thought you were bringing that plump gay boy—the Thai fellow who wanted to return to the motherland or some such thing."

Ellyn inhaled and lowered her shoulders, clearly making a play for patience. "Mock. I told you he couldn't make it."

"But cabin 517—that's the extra room—"

"I released it. Remember? The travel agent got your money refunded for the last leg of your trip?"

We were riding up in the lift. Cor worked it out. "So you released cabin 517," she said to Ellyn, and turned to me. "And you got it."

"What great good fortune for me. My decision was last-minute, and I was thrilled to get a place on the *Empress of the Indian Ocean*."

"Oh, well, it's a lovely ship," Cor agreed, looking at me with stars in her eyes. She would be putty in my hands.

The elevator dinged, and I held out a hand to usher the women out before me. Ellyn scooted away from my arm. "Here we are. Well—what did we decide? In the bar in an hour?"

"Let's make it the poolside bar, Arthur. Up on deck seven. It's freezing everywhere inside, and that bar has a pretty woven awning. Breezy and not too hot. Won't that be nice?"

The ship's store would have a heavy-duty sunblock, and I'd charge it to Ellyn's cabin. "Just perfect. Until then!"

I left them both gaping outside my door. I tipped the porter with Ellyn's money, closed myself in, and indulged in a brief war dance and victory grin.

Cor was a sweetheart, like her niece. Suckers, the pair of them.

All my problems were solved. Time to put my plan into action.

CHAPTER SEVEN—ELLYN

MOCK REALLY WAS—AS HE HIMSELF PUT IT—THE FINEST stylist in all the land. Artie was a masterwork: preppy, handsome, perfectly dressed. Aunt Cor couldn't take her eyes off him. Score.

Of course, I couldn't take my eyes off him, either—only I was glaring.

The flight to Singapore had been direct; I didn't have to worry about him wandering off the plane. But twice I'd had to peek through the curtain to the economy section to reassure myself he was really there.

I eyed him uncertainly. He really was too large to be wedged into a steerage seat. On the other hand, I didn't have Aunt Cor's budget and couldn't afford to upgrade him. And if you buy a last-minute ticket, you end up in the middle seat. Sorry, not sorry.

But I hadn't had a great flight myself.

That alone was surprising. Aunt Cor's travel agent had taken Cor literally when he'd been told to ensure everything was first-class for her nieces. Singapore Airlines had gone beyond anything as pedestrian as "first class." I'd been assigned a suite—an opulent little room with a sliding front door and a separate bed. The walls only came up to shoulder height, so people passing along the aisle to the toilets could peer in at you, but that was the only possible annoyance. It was by far the easiest way for a person to endure almost nineteen hours in the air.

And yet I couldn't sleep. I couldn't focus on a movie. I couldn't read. I was edgy and twitchy. There was restless energy under my skin.

I lay in the dim gloom during the endless night and tried to settle my conscience. It was clear by then that I'd hired a con man. I was pulling a con on my own aunt. Things were complicated, but there was no sense in pretending that was anything but a nasty thing to do to someone.

On the other hand, my family was notoriously tight about money. I didn't mind. I'd made my own way and was proud of it, and the occasional largess (like the legacy from Uncle Carl) meant I was better off than most of the people I knew. I had friends who had written excellent scripts that went unchosen. I could see how they would become strong movies. But no one would loan us the money for Mock and me to start our own production house. And we'd make it work too. We'd turn a profit quickly, and I could see if I really had it in me to be a good director.

No, a *great* director.

Not that any banks had listened.

So, my future was tied to what Artie had aptly titled the Popular Niece Fund. This was my future. And Mock's future.

And I'd put it in the hands of a con man.

I had a horrible night, drifting in that miserable in-between state that happens on planes when I'm too awake to get any sleep and too asleep to actually wake up. Nerves, I suppose. I was worried about the plan. About trusting to a scoundrel to pull this off. About exposing Aunt Cor to a wounded heart, and maybe worse.

And given that I had such a miserable night, it annoyed me to see—both times that I'd peeked—that Artie was sound asleep in his seat, tipped almost into the lap of the irked passenger behind him, his wide shoulders encroaching onto the lady on one side and the turbaned businessman on the other. No worries for that guy. He slept peacefully. Hmph.

Once we'd arrived, the tropical sun had seemed too bright. I was skimmed in travel grit. I was grumpy and had a headache. And I had to keep an eye on Artie without looking like I was keeping an eye on him.

We both made it through customs, through the baggage claim, and onto the van that took us to the ship via a "deluxe driving tour of cosmopolitan Singapore" and a lunch of local and exceedingly spicy delicacies at an outdoor restaurant. The whole time, I ignored him. But I could hear him chatting in a friendly manner with our fellow travelers. I decided I hated him. He'd somehow slept the night before in his two square inches of space while I'd been treated like a pasha yet had grains of sand in my eyes that wouldn't come out without ten solid hours of sleep.

And when I'd finally gotten onboard the ship, Aunt Cor was such a bundle of energy I had to force myself to smile pleasantly and return her hug. She'd met me at the ship's check-in and happily took up much-needed space in the overcrowded area.

"Ellyn, I'm so glad you're here! You know Farrah left this morning, and she was just no fun. She was either hungover or drunk. No fun at all! I mean, I know it's a vacation for you girls, but I think she might have been a little more friendly, don't you?"

This was a blatant hit. Aunt Cor was very well-aware her nieces were competing for her affections—and for her five million—and she was making sure I was in full suck-up mode.

Well, I could do that.

I shifted my camera bag to the other shoulder (the porter had tried to take it, but back off there, buddy) and held my arms out wide. "Well, I'm here now. Let's have us a great time! What do we have planned?"

She went into a long rant about all the wonderful things we could do together while I tried to clear my head and make sense of her list. And then, just when my nerves were already stretched thin . . .

The large head of Artie the Scoundrel intruded into my cone of awareness.

And he made shit up on the spot. Staten Island? A novelist? Practicing for a rumba competition? I wanted to strangle him where he stood. But I couldn't, and he knew it.

He gave the full grin to Aunt Cor, who loved it. His teeth had been dialed back so they were no longer blindingly white; now he looked like a strong, healthy man with a strong, healthy interest in a woman more than twice his age. And she bought it.

If only I'd gotten any sleep at all, I was sure I could have kept up with them. But my head was woolly. I might have broken into unspecified twitching if this stress kept up any longer. And that was before he started painting the skin of my back in little ribbons of heat. With Cor walking along right in front of him. Idiot.

Artie disappeared into his cabin. He and Aunt Cor had delightedly planned to meet at the poolside bar, and I was determined to be a part of that meeting, if only to keep track of the wild fabrications.

The porter unlocked my cabin and handed me the key. Aunt Cor came in with me to show me things I couldn't have possibly discovered by myself, like where the bathroom was and how to open the sliding doors to the balcony. She helped me unpack and made lots of theoretically helpful comments about what I'd brought. The room was much bigger than I'd expected, with a sitting area and an ocean liner of a king-sized bed that called to me.

But there was no way a nap was in the plans. I needed to prove to Aunt Cor I was more fun than my cousin Farrah, at least. And it was only a matter of time before she teed up some complaints about Priss and Liv, too, so I'd be sure to toe the line for my two weeks with her.

So, when invited, I went across the hall with her. Her suite was identical to mine except an insane shopping fairy had wandered through and thrown piles of crap into all the corners. There were tropical woven baskets, two—no, three—entire rolls of batik fabric, a paper-mache flamingo as tall as me on a two-foot-long spike for the garden, the matching three-foot-tall paper-mache frog, furled poolside umbrellas in rattan, large woven hats, shoeboxes with tissue paper and bright sandals spilling out of them, and two small palm trees in pots on the balcony. Cor lived for the shopping experience.

"You're not going to get those trees past customs, are you?" I asked.

"The natanguras? I have someone at the State Department working on it. Wooly bought a few senators in his day; I decided it was time to cash in. Aren't they wonderful?"

This was the life of Cor. She'd use Carl Wolcott's money and connections to bring two exotic plants in past any quarantine so her gardeners could plant them in entirely the wrong climate and try to keep them alive. And when they died, she'd never notice.

"When was the last time you spoke to the State Department?" I pulled out my pad to make a note.

"Oh, I left it to the lawyers."

"And what have they said?"

She thought about it. "I'm not sure. I don't think I heard back from them."

"Want me to call them?"

"Darling—it's such a relief to have you here. Thank you!"

Was I clear-headed enough to do this now? Would I remember to do it if I postponed until I was more awake? What time was it in the US? What time was it here? What time was it in my brain?

Cor paid enough for her lawyers to be woken up; I made the call and chatted with an underling who put me through to a partner. I handed my phone to Cor and took it back when she only confused the issue. He and I worked things out and he promised to follow up.

I said my hellos to Luz, her ever-present maid. Luz was a gaunt, pale woman with black hair and the expression of a mournful vampire. Aunt Cor wouldn't travel without her, as Luz had spent years as a hairdresser in Queens and could repair Cor's up-do, as well as care for her clothes, rooms, and life.

Aunt Cor pulled out the ship's calendar of events, and we had to discuss in detail the shore excursions and onboard opportunities. I sat in the armchair and realized gravity had suddenly gotten a lot stronger. All my muscles and bones were melting into the seat, and I had to blink to snap out of it. With her usual scary attentiveness, Luz brought me a tall, icy soda.

"With caffeine," she whispered.

I smiled my thanks and drank deeply. It helped to chase away some of the fogginess.

Rebel finally made her entrance. Rebel, born Rebecca, had been Cor's best friend since they were in secretarial school together. She was a sturdy woman with a smoker's raspy voice and an abiding commitment to supportive footwear. Where Cor was cuddly and mothering in a manipulative sort of way (features that must have appealed to my Uncle Carl in contrast with his first wife, my chilly Aunt Nan), Rebel was loud and brash and thought Cor hung the moon. Not entirely surprising, as Cor was now worth more than several small nations, but at least Rebel was a premarriage friend and thus not fully chiseling off Cor. They were devoted to each other.

Rebel had been in the ship's salon, having her practical, strong fingers painted a surprising shade of crimson. She greeted me with feigned interest. I was the fourth niece to intrude on her extended vacation with her wildly wealthy best friend, and she'd long since lost any willingness to pretend she was glad to spend time with us.

Still, Rebel and I had generally gotten along on family vacations in Nantucket or at dinners at Cor and Carl's massive apartment in Manhattan, and I assumed that if Rebel were the deciding vote, I would have gotten the millions. But my cousins were cleverer than that, and I needed to play every angle I had.

Speaking of which . . .

I leaned near Aunt Cor and kissed the air. "I want to get settled. I can come with you to meet that stranger at the bar, right?"

Rebel zoned in on that like a heat-seeking missile and, after promising they wouldn't go on deck without me, I left the two of them to their increasingly excited speculations about the tall blond man Cor had met.

I let myself into my cabin and took a moment to stand in the sudden silence.

I didn't dare sit; both bed and sofa might absorb me and not let me go for eight or ten hours. I needed to stay alert and keep up with the plan.

Which Artie had gleefully destroyed with the exuberance of a poo-slinging chimpanzee in the zoo.

Fury rose in me. Was he even in his cabin still? He'd better fucking be where I told him to be.

I crossed the acres of carpeting and banged on the connecting door before consciously thinking about it.

When he yanked the door open, my fury evaporated, and I fell back into my suite.

"Have you seen the size of this room?" He was even angrier than I was and loomed over me.

"What is the matter with you?"

"*Look* at it!" he hissed. "Go and look. It won't take long. While I look at *this* fucking palace."

I peered into his cabin and put my hand over my mouth to smother my sudden laugh.

It was clearly designed for a maid—for Luz. It made Mock's apartment look luxurious. Most significant was a single bed wedged in between bulkheads. It had an entertaining coffin-like aspect that made me giggle.

Artie followed me in. With both of us in the room, there was no space for oxygen. We'd have to take turns inhaling.

"That bed isn't even six feet long. Do you know how long *I* am? Do you?"

"You've told me. You're six-foot-five. I get it; it's not a great room. But it's what we've got."

"No, it's not. You've got a bed I could sleep in. You sleep in here. Give me that room."

"Fuck off. That's my room."

"Don't be greedy—"

"Artie. You work for me. Get over it."

"Get over it? You want me to look good, then I'm going to need to sleep. Fucking Mock could barely sleep in that bed."

"Sleep on the floor. I don't care." I pushed past him and returned to my room, where oxygen was rich and plentiful. He followed me, and I wheeled on him. "And what the hell is up with you being a novelist from Queens?"

"Staten Island." He threw himself on my sofa—my broad and soft and supportive sofa that I wanted to lie on very badly. He stretched his arms along the back with a sense of ownership that made my nose flare in contempt. His mood shifted, and he grinned at me. "I heard it in her voice as soon as she spoke. She's a city girl. She loves me."

"She would have loved the real estate guy from Wyoming. What are you going to do when she looks up your so-called pen name?"

"Ambrose Pensiter. He's a guy. I've read his books. He's good."

"Jesus. You couldn't leave it alone, could you? Just follow the plan?"

"My way's better. Admit it."

"What about all of Mock's western touches in your wardrobe? How are you going to explain them?"

"Oh, I weeded them out before we left. Don't worry about it."

That made me furious. I was too tired to adapt, to roll with the changes. "You *weeded them out*? You mean you knew you weren't going to follow the plan before we left New York? And you didn't tell me?"

"I did tell you. I told you I could figure out my backstory and I could handle my wardrobe. It's not my fault you didn't listen."

He was in a full sprawl, leering at me, and I was hot with anger. "And Jesus Christ, stop feeling me up! You've only just met her. You can't have your hands all over me, damn it."

"It was just one touch. Not my fault you don't tuck in your shirt. Don't overreact, Red."

Don't overreact. Nothing could be more likely to make me overreact than accusing me of overreacting. I paced to calm myself. Nothing was broken. This could all be mixed into the plan. It would be okay. It had to be okay. My future depended on it. We just had to keep dancing, that's all.

I wheeled on him. "Dancing—fuck me. What the hell are you going to do about the fucking rumba? You've had one lesson with Eddie and now you're ready to enter a competition? You're going to screw this up for me."

He stood and moved to my bathroom. "Don't worry about it. I told you I'd practice, and I did. Jesus, this is bigger than my entire cabin." He closed the door in my face; he'd chosen to pee in *my* bathroom. I growled and clenched my fist.

I was texting Mock, venting my ire and commiserating with him over our now-less-than-certain production company, when Artie reappeared. "You have a bathtub, as well as a walk-in shower. A bathtub. My bathroom is so small, the toilet paper has a cover so the shower doesn't get it wet."

That made me feel better. "Get out of here. You can't be in here. Cor's coming to pick me up to meet you on deck. Go. Leave me alone."

"Fine. I'm taking your sunblock, though. You've got really good SPF. Smart for a redhead. You've got to take care of all that white, white skin."

"I can't protect my white, white skin if you take my sunblock. Give me that!"

Damn it, he was through the door, and it locked behind him. With my sunblock. That he'd boldly filched from my kit while exploring my bathroom. The scoundrel.

We'd been onboard for less than an hour and already he'd pushed my Little Engine That Could right off the rails. No famous film director would have let this happen. Where had I gone wrong?

Didn't matter. I could get it back. I needed all my wits about me for what was coming next, and I was balanced between uncontrollable fury and the overwhelming desire to take a nap. The next few hours were going to test my mettle.

CHAPTER EIGHT—ARTIE

ELLYN MAY HAVE THOUGHT OF HERSELF AS A WORKING GIRL, but nobody who lives paycheck to paycheck could have afforded that sunblock. It went on like silk, smooth as the small of her back. I was moisturizing while protecting myself. And it smelled good.

I was definitely keeping this.

I had time before meeting the new object of my affections on the top deck. I abandoned grumpy, overtired Ellyn and began my surveillance of the ship's staff. I needed a steward, a porter, a bartender, a cook's assistant—or anyone who could help me out when we made it to Phuket.

Like everywhere else on the globe, the staff wasn't paid well on this luxurious cruise ship, and they were all open to the gift of a US twenty-dollar bill in exchange for some future friendship. I'd made a lot of progress by the time Cor and Ellyn found me sipping a mai tai under the rattan awning of the poolside bar.

Cor waved at me from ten feet away like someone stranded on a desert island. "There you are, Arthur! How lovely to see you!"

I kissed her cheek in greeting, and she flushed with pleasure. "Don't you look lovely, Cor!"

"Oh, you sweet talker! Now, you remember my niece, Ellyn." Ellyn looked drawn and tense and wore an obviously false grin. *Not an asset*, I thought. "And this is my dear friend, Rebel, and my maid, Luz."

I nodded to both of them, projecting the feeling that any friend of Cor's was a friend of mine—but that Cor was my true focus.

"I was just talking to Basilio here." I gestured to the bartender, capable but still smiling as sheeplike guests began to pack in, all on deck and eagerly awaiting the moment the ship pulled away from the dock to embark on our grand adventure. "He suggests we see if the yoga studio on deck six is available for practice."

"Oh, I haven't been to the yoga studio yet," Cor said brightly, as if she planned on whipping out a Dying Warrior pose at any moment.

"It should be empty right now. And I suggest we all take mai tais with us, because what could possibly make a rumba more fun than that?"

We chuckled together in delight, and Rebel pushed up with us to order hers. "I want a piña colada!" she cried in the deepest, roughest voice I've ever heard on a woman.

It certainly got Basilio's attention, and soon we were all trooping together down a stairway near the stern, holding highly alcoholic beverages and already giggling. A tone had definitely been established.

My twenty to Basilio was already paying off; my second mai tai was as virgin as the first, but Cor was never going to know I wasn't a tad tipsy as our dance practice wore on.

The yoga studio was small, but vast windows gave a sun-filled view of the harbor beyond the ship. The floor was smooth bamboo, ideal for dancing.

I found the sound system and plugged in my phone. Considering my audience, I scrolled through my prechosen music and pulled up a Dean Martin playlist.

When I turned, Cor was wearing a gauzy scarf tied around her waist over her camp shorts. Her practical shoes had been exchanged for bright red sandals with high heels and an ankle strap that bit cruelly into the generous flesh of her foot. Ouch.

"Don't you look lovely!" I enthused. "Now, how did you pull that off while my back was turned?"

She tittered coquettishly and gestured to the gloomy maid, who held a large tote bag in one hand and a club soda in the other. "Oh, I had Luz bring a few things. It makes it so much easier to rumba when I have a skirt flowing around me."

She held her arms out and dipped her ample hips, shuffling her feet in the beginnings of the basic step. I was reassured and grinned as I took her hand.

"This is going to be fun!"

"Oh, so much fun!"

Ellyn and Rebel had found seats on a low bench that ran around the room. As tired as she was, Ellyn ought to have been half-asleep already. Instead, she leaned forward, her elbows on her knees and a thumbnail between her teeth. She had no faith in me at all.

I was happy to prove her poor opinion wrong.

"Let me show you how I think we should begin," I said.

I made sure to angle us so I could watch Ellyn as I began, just to enjoy the look on her face.

I would have suffered the torments of the damned before admitting I'd been practicing the dance with my mother in her tiny kitchen over the past two weeks. Hildy Petrovitch hadn't had the easiest life (my dad was not the prince she deserved), but in her younger days, she used to go out dancing, and she was thrilled to spend more time with me.

And when my sister, Wendy, caught us in the act, she wanted in, too, so between the two of them, I knew how to rumba. Plus, they'd been fascinated by the details of my mission. They were long since accustomed to my profession and loved to hear about the marks I conned, for all that Wendy was now married to a mostly honest cop. We'd watched and dissected dozens of videos and chosen the choreography I could do . . . and that we thought Cor might be able to do.

Both my mother and my sister were tall for women, and as soon as Cor and I began, it was clear I'd have to modify things. We could hardly stretch out at fingertip length and make a nice line. On the other hand, we could do turns where she passed cleanly under my arm as I spun her.

I could make it work.

And it was soon clear that although Cor loved to rumba, she was no better at it than I was. Once I realized that, I got into a groove of rhythm, encouragement, and hips. It was fun, and Cor was flushed and happy.

We sent Luz for more drinks, after which our hip action got slinkier. Rebel and Ellyn began to applaud some of our more successful moves, and when Cor got tired, Rebel insisted on a turn. She was even more wooden than her friend, but Cor beamed in satisfaction.

"Fulfill a little fantasy of mine, won't you, ladies?" I held out a hand to each of them, and they purred with scandalous delight. "Let me dance with two women at once. May I have this dance?"

They blushed like girls, and we weren't skilled at all, but they had a wonderful time spinning away from me and being pulled in to lay their hands against my chest. They laughed to each other in delight, and I grinned. So easy.

Cor and Rebel had both worked up a slight sweat, and Ellyn pulled out a small towel from her camera case to blot away their shine. I was coming to understand that the camera bag was almost magic. Ellyn carried one of everything in it.

I retrieved my phone and offered a general congratulations for an excellent practice. "We should keep practicing," I said, "if you can spare the time. I really think we could be pretty good, Cor. Don't you?"

Her eyes were shining. "I think we're going to win hands down! Let's practice every day. Don't you think, Ellyn?"

Her niece, suddenly drawn into the conversation, was startled but tried to keep up. "That's a great idea," she said lamely. "Um, why not?"

"Why not, indeed!" Cor chortled. "Arthur, won't you join us for dinner?"

"Really? That's so kind of you! I'm alone, as you know, and assumed I'd be assigned a random table."

"Nonsense. You're with us now! We've got a table for four people at seven. Luz, you'll eat in your room."

I was in, and Luz was dismissed. It was hard to tell if she was pleased or disappointed by this change of plans; Luz didn't have much expression. I could tell a twenty in her hand would have made her an ally, but Ellyn had already told me Luz was the bought-and-paid-for agent of Ellyn's cousin, Priss, so I didn't muddy the waters. Especially as Ellyn was keeping me her secret weapon, even from Priss.

"Well, we must go and change for dinner. Shall we see you in the restaurant bar at six for cocktails?"

The timing surprised me, but I didn't let it show. Dinner at seven, drinking at six? More cocktails and an extra hour in which to drink them. I'd need to stop by and make friends with that bartender beforehand. I needed to make sure I wasn't keeping up with the Wolcott party when it came to alcohol. Drunkenness is to be encouraged in the suckers but discouraged in the skilled confidence man. Sobriety would be a rare but valuable asset with this group.

"Perfect. But let me escort you to your cabin—which is practically my cabin!"

We fawned over each other as we tottered to the rooms. To her credit, Cor kept up in the high heels without once betraying a wince. "And do you play bridge, Arthur? Would you join us in the card room after dinner?"

Ellyn's glare burned between my shoulder blades. If she could have slipped in a knife and still kept me alive to work on her behalf, she would have done it. But she needn't have worried.

Even if I'd been a master bridge player, I would have declined. It was important to avoid the Too Good To Be True scenario that lets a mark start getting suspicious.

"Hopeless at it, I'm afraid. I'm so sorry."

"Well, never mind. We've got lots of time. It's a vacation! One day we'll teach you!"

"I'd be most honored. Thank you, Cor."

We parted as dear old friends. I had a great blue blazer for the evening—plain as mud and without ornamentation, despite Mock's intention of sewing on the patch of some athletic club—and I looked great in it. Young CEO all the way. I was eager to show myself to the world in it.

"We'll see you at six, Arthur!"

"Until then, my dear!"

I closed the door on Ellyn's hostility and refused to answer when she tapped on our connecting door. *Stew on it, Red. I'm managing this just fine, and you'll have to deal with it.*

CHAPTER NINE—ELLYN

THERE COMES A MOMENT WHEN THE BODY IS SO FATIGUED that the brain floats around, disconnected, like an out-of-body experience. Cor kept trying to get me to drink, and I kept refusing.

"Well! One niece can't stay sober, and one niece won't even share a toast! You haven't touched your first glass of wine. How will you ever catch up?" She was huffy about it, her attempt to manipulate me coming up against my determination to avoid falling asleep in my mango salad. The restaurant was elegant, the people around me poised and handsome, the carpeting under my sandals thick. All of it blurred together into a paste of input that my brain wasn't handling very well.

"I won't make it to the main course if I start drinking now, Aunt Cor. Nineteen hours on a plane. I'm jet-lagged and exhausted."

"You're a lightweight, that's what you are. Am I right, Arthur?"

Damn him. He kept up with her, drink for drink, and the only effect was a slight looseness in his speech—that and the relaxed state of his epically huge shoulders, which looked particularly impressive in a blue blazer that fit him like a glove.

And it should have. Mock had stayed up for two nights hand-tailoring it to fit. There were very few suits big enough for those shoulders that drop in far enough to show off the slim waist without couture alterations. Luckily, like all great stylists, Mock was fast with a needle and thread. As a result, Artie looked like a fashion ad. I decided I hated him.

He was seated between Cor and Rebel and kept them both tittering with sly references to dancing with two women at the same time. Plus, he drew both of them in via tales of Staten Island. Give credit where credit was due—never before in the history of seduction had that line of conversation been useful. My mind stumbled over "seduction" and "Staten Island," and I resolved anew to remain silent if at all possible.

"I used to go dancing on the pier," Cor said, gesturing grandly with her planter's punch.

"I heard about that," Artie cheered. "That must have been something to see. All the women in their beautiful dresses and the music from the orchestra . . . gorgeous. You know that pier was pulled down for the new power plant?"

"I know." She and Rebel exchanged frowns. "Such a pity! Wouldn't it be fun to go dancing on water, Arthur? Can you imagine it?"

"Imagine it? I thought you and I were dancing on the ocean itself this afternoon!"

I rolled my eyes—safely, as it turns out, as no one looked at me. I wondered if I could pillow my head on the beautifully displayed dish of chili crabs the waiter set in front of me.

"I wondered, Arthur dear—do you cha-cha?"

"Do I cha-cha?" He reared back in mock outrage. "Of course I cha-cha! Don't tell me you do too?"

"I do!"

"Well, should we practice tomorrow, or stick with the rumba?"

"Oh, I don't know. It would be fun to have the rumba perfect for the dance competition."

"That's true. Well, we've got an entire vacation, don't we? Let's rumba for the next few days, win the competition, and then get going on that cha-cha!"

"Cha-cha!" she cooed.

"I can cha-cha," Rebel said, longing for some attention.

She got some, too—but never more than Cor got. Even in my sleepy daze, I had to admire how skillfully he played them both. He teased that he had always wanted to try two women at once, but there was no doubt where his focus and admiration lay.

I would have admired it more if I'd been able to keep my brain between my two ears instead of occasionally floating off into the ether.

At last, Cor took pity and released me. "My niece is asleep on her feet. And that's fine, dear. Rebel and I are off to play bridge. Are you sure you won't join us, Arthur?"

"I thought I'd take a walk on the deck and admire the moonlight."

"Silly man. It's the dark of the moon."

"Is it?" He fixed her with a dopy, slightly drunk smile. "I thought the evening was particularly radiant. How can there be no moon?"

She fluttered and tittered. He stood and held her chair, and we escorted Cor and Rebel to the door.

"Until tomorrow, you enchanting creature," he said with bold arrogance.

"Until tomorrow, Arthur! Good night!"

And then it was just him and me in the broad hallway.

He turned to me, and all pretense of tipsiness dropped away. "Let's get you back to your cabin before you fall asleep standing in a corner."

I goggled at him as he got me walking. "Aren't you—why aren't you—" I couldn't formulate the thought.

"Paid the bartender before you guys got here. None of my drinks had alcohol in them."

So fucking smart. "But the wine. I saw you drink—"

"I'm a big guy. I can handle a couple of glasses of wine with dinner. And I switched to daiquiris pretty quickly, you'll notice."

I guess he had. Uselessly, I tried to think of the many rounds of drinks. The waitress had always been careful to serve him last. I thought it had been simple "ladies first" etiquette, but apparently there had been more going on than I'd realized.

Hmm. Clever.

We came to a halt, and I realized I stood in front of my cabin door. I looked at it stupidly, and he took my bag out of my hand, fished out my key, unlocked the door, and handed bag and key to me.

"For God's sake, get some sleep. You look like the walking dead."

"How can you be so charming to her" —I gestured at Cor's cabin, empty behind us—"and so rude to me?"

I knew the answer. I knew all 350 million of the answers. But he surprised me with the gracefulness of his reply.

"You're not the dancer your aunt is. Good night."

"Night."

Once inside, I stumbled around, stripping off clothes, washing my face (*oh, so good*), finding the oversized T-shirt I slept in, and stupidly puzzling over how to turn off the lights in the cabin.

The room was icy cold, and I was sitting woodenly on the large bed, caught in sleepy anticipation of pulling up the covers and surrendering to nothingness, when the connecting door between our rooms opened.

Artie walked right in, in a T-shirt and boxer briefs.

I'd seen him in just the briefs during his fittings with Mock, but the sight was still impressive. The bruises over his ribs had faded as nicely as the one on his eye, and he looked large and golden and sturdy.

"Did I give you a key?" I asked stupidly.

"Picked it," he said shortly and pulled down the covers on the other side of the bed.

"What are you doing?" I was confused.

"I'm going to lie here for a while."

"No. Get out. This is my room."

"Right. I'm getting out. In a bit."

"Artie."

"Hit that light and lie down. It's freezing in here."

"This whole ship is freezing. You can't sleep here."

"Sure I can. Watch."

"No—Artie—"

"I don't fit in that bed. If you don't want to share this bed with me, go sleep in the other room."

"No. Wait."

"I'm just going to lie here for a minute. Lie down. I can't pull up the covers with you sitting on them."

"No!" Somehow, I was lying down. Somehow, he was tugging up the covers. "You're leaving soon?"

"Absolutely." He stretched out and groaned in satisfaction.

"When?"

"Few hours."

"How many hours?"

"Does it matter? Let's say eight."

"You can't share a bed with me."

"Why not?"

"I have a boyfriend."

"So?"

"So—so—" I couldn't formulate an answer. The covers were heavy, and I began to warm up. "So get out."

"I'm not going to fuck you, Ellyn. I'm just going to sleep."

I wrinkled my forehead. Dimly, I thought there was an insult in that but couldn't decipher what it was. "Jeez," I said helplessly.

"Yeah. Come over here."

"What?"

"Come here." He held up one impossibly long arm, waiting for me to come over to his side of the bed.

"No! Get out!"

"No, just come here. I'm still cold."

"I'm not sleeping with you." And yet somehow, I was. Had I moved, or had he? How was I curled against him, my head on his chest, my breasts against his rib cage, his arm around me?

"Good. Put your leg over mine."

"Why?"

"Because it feels good. Do it. There. Isn't that better?"

He was warm. Blissfully warm. From the crown of my head all the way to the top of the foot, I snuggled against him, heat flowing from him into my chilled body. But it wouldn't do just to give in, so I made a big deal about arranging pillows and pulling my hair out from under me.

"Jeesh," he complained. "You're fussy as hell. Are you settled yet?"

"Shut up."

"You shut up."

"I don't like sleeping with someone. I sleep alone."

"Oh yeah? Me too. I hate sleeping when someone is beside me. What about Baxter?"

"What about him?"

"You don't sleep with him?"

I was too tired to dissemble. "I send him home. I sleep better when I sleep alone."

"I get it," he said. "He fucks you and then he has to go."

"Actually, I fuck him and then he has to go."

"I bet." I could hear the grin in his voice.

I raised my head to glare at him. "What's that supposed to mean?"

He pushed my head onto his chest. "It means shut up and go to sleep. That's what it means."

"You shouldn't be here," I grumbled. I was an addict, pressing closer for his warmth and his faint, delicious male smell.

"I know."

"If Cor finds you here . . ."

"She won't."

"How do you know?"

"Because you locked the door. Go to sleep."

"How do you know I locked the door?"

He sighed. "You're a city girl. You live alone. There's no way you didn't lock that door."

He was right, of course. I'd thrown the bolt almost without thinking about it.

"If she knocks, though—"

"If she knocks"—his deep voice rumbled in my ear—"you say 'come in' like you're asleep and confused. By the time you realize your mistake and stumble over something on your way to the door and fumble with the locks and pull it open with your gorgeous hair all tousled and in your eyes, I'll already be on the other side of the connecting door, and no one will be the wiser. Now shut up and go to sleep."

"I sleep alone," I tried one more time.

"I know. Me too."

And then I was asleep. Like a trusting, foolish idiot.

CHAPTER TEN—ARTIE

THE AIR CONDITIONING WAS CRANKED TO "ARCTIC." THAT WAS the only explanation for how easy it was to sleep with Ellyn—that, and the fact that she was so dead to the world, I could move her to suit myself. Roll her over and spoon her when I wanted to shift positions, or persuade her to spoon me when I wanted to sleep on my other side.

She was warm and pliant, and somehow, I never got to the usual point where my skin began to twitch and a clinging woman started to cut off my air.

I slept really well, in fact, and woke with morning wood.

She didn't know, of course. I eased out of bed and took care of it in her luxurious bathroom shower. I found my workout clothes and went in search of the gym.

It was a tiny room tucked away on the top deck. Great views, but not much bigger than my cabin. Most vacationers probably didn't put too high a priority on fitness. There were three women in there, and seven by the time I left. I assumed—since all of the women were watching me go through my routine in the mirrors (while their lackluster stints on the exercises bikes took place at zero resistance)—that they were enjoying the view. I did look good running on the elliptical for a few miles, and my regular routine was impressive: planks, push-ups, and some of the more advanced balance poses from the yoga discipline.

I liked being watched while I worked out. It helped me focus on form. And I could read admiration in the faces of the watchers, and that gave me a zip of extra energy.

They actually applauded when I finished, joined by the guy who restocked the towels. I bowed and assured them I'd be back tomorrow at six thirty.

Then I went in search of some fruit and a chat with the nearest bartender I could find.

You wouldn't think I'd be able to find one at 7:15 in the morning—a bartender, I mean, the fruit was easy to come by—but Basilio was setting up in the poolside bar. They opened for breakfast cocktails at 8:00 a.m.

Of course they did. Sheep love alcohol, and nothing clears away a hangover faster than a Bloody Mary or a mimosa.

I pulled out one of the tall chairs and leaned my elbows on the bar. The air was fresh and cool, and the sun hadn't hit that painful glare yet. It was a nice morning.

Basilio made me a yogurt shake while we chatted, and he provided me with invaluable information, for which, of course, I tipped him again, and heavily. The places that cater to the richest people tend to be the tightest with their staff, and that's just stupid. Wealthy patrons never think their valet or their maître d' or, in this case, their bartender might decide to plump up the rent money by sharing a little info with an interested listener.

All of which made my job easier.

Then I went to the cabin to take a shower and wake Ellyn.

"Hey," I said, landing heavily on the bed next to her.

She was buried under the covers, little but red hair visible in the nest she'd made. "Huh."

"Wake up." I dragged a pillow out from under her and propped it behind me, crossing my ankles.

"Fuck off. What are you doing in my room? What time is it?"

"Almost eight. Time for breakfast."

"What? I've been asleep for . . . uh?"

"About eleven hours. Eleven and a half, actually."

"Oh my God, I have got to pee so bad."

She bolted out of the bed. I admired the sight of her pert ass, exposed by the baggy sleep shirt. She tugged it down and shut the bathroom door. "Ugh! Who steamed up my shower?"

Assuming she didn't actually need clarification, I called after her. "I'm told I'm not the only shark in these waters."

"Just wait a damn moment."

The closed door didn't do much to muffle the sound. She peed for an impressively long time; the woman had excellent bladder capacity. The faucet ran, and she appeared in the doorway, brushing her teeth. "What did you say?"

"I said I'm not the only shark in these waters."

"What are you talking about? Hang on." I waited until she reappeared. "What, now?"

I patted the bed and she sat gingerly, bending one long leg under her and fisting the hem of the nightshirt to hold it firmly down between her legs. This made me grin.

"Your aunt has picked up several would-be suitors already. Looks like I'm going to have competition for becoming your uncle."

She blinked, confused. "My—what?"

"Sweetheart. You didn't think I'd ignore the fact that your aunt is now a widow? You think I'd skip over the part where I could marry the whole fortune?"

"Well, yes. When you had a shot at a quarter of a million dollars. That's not good enough for you?"

She was getting angry, and I enjoyed the view. She gave a flounce of annoyance, which bobbled her breasts. Nice.

"The quarter mil is good. I still want it. But why shouldn't I go for the brass ring? I could work the cons until I'm ninety, but this would be a lot easier. Anyway, you *want* me as your new uncle. I could throw a lot of investments your way. You and

Mock would never have to take out a bank loan. Ever." Her anger was derailed by that. "You could buy all your own movie cameras."

"Nobody buys movie cameras. The tech changes too quickly. You rent."

"You could rent your own cameras. You could buy your own camera rental business."

She frowned, processing the new information, and got up to pace. "You'd be my Uncle Artie."

"Uncle Arthur," I corrected. "And you, my little niece. Good plan, huh?"

She turned, her shoulders set. "Let's stick with this plan first, okay? Can we just make sure she has a great time with me and worry about your wedding later?"

I crossed my hands behind my head. I could afford to be magnanimous. "Sure. Plus, I need your help, anyway."

She fished clothes from the bureau. "Why? What for?"

"Because," I said patiently, "I'm not the only shark here. Aunt Cor has already drawn a few real gigolos to her side."

She wheeled. "The fuck she has. What are you talking about?"

"I got it from the bartender at the poolside bar."

"Vasily?"

"Good memory. Basilio—the Filipino version of the name. He said he would have told me about these guys last night if he'd known I was after Cor."

"He knows you're after Cor?" Her voice held panic. Amateur.

"Relax. These guys always know what's going on. He's going to be a huge information source. There are three guys."

I moved to the edge of the bed and focused her attention. She sat on the sofa and listened.

"There's a fake British colonel who takes the cheapest cabin at the very bottom of the boat. He sails this route twice a year, looking for a wealthy protectress. He calls himself Saint James

Fennimore—known to his intimates as Sinjie. He wears an ascot. An actual ascot."

I couldn't wait to meet this guy. The balls to pull off an ascot.

"An ascot?" Ellyn tried to keep up.

"The necktie. Like Fred from *Scooby-Doo*."

"Fred from . . .?"

"Then there's a young guy. Basilio says he's common and stupid but very, very pretty, like a dashing highwayman. He's been oiling up to the older women on the cruise and he's somehow found out what Cor is worth, so she's his top target."

"What's his name? Stud McHotstuff?"

"Nice one. No, it's Brock. Brock Halliday. He's not likely to be your next uncle, but he could get in the way, and we should watch for him."

"Yeah. Okay." She fiddled with her camera, and it seemed to be calming her. "Did you say three guys?"

"Yeah. The third guy might actually be competition. The other two have been here since your aunt came onboard, but the third boarded just one stop before ours." I stood and opened the sliding door to the balcony, letting in a wash of jungle-hot, humid air and the not-terribly-nice odors of a port town; we were already docked for the day outside of Kuala Lumpur. Ellyn wrinkled her nose.

"The third guy?"

"Marcus Vanderfleet. Not a gigolo. He's traveling with buddies. They did a sex tour in Indonesia"—Ellyn winced—"and now they're cruising the Andaman Sea and the Bay of Bengal. He's some kind of businessman. Owns a manufacturing company making something; I don't know what. He thinks all the people in this part of the world who aren't in the sex industry are in the making-things-much-cheaper-than-the-US business, and he's angry about too many rights for workers in America."

"Pig. I was the director of photography for a friend's senior project—a documentary on the demands of fast fashion. Manufacturing in Asia is cheaper for horrible, horrible reasons, and part of that is because buyers like Marcus don't object to the abuse of garment workers."

I held up my hands. *Not going to get into a human rights discussion with an annoyed redhead.* "Anyway, Basilio says it's occurred to Marcus Vanderfleet that a large infusion of cash might go a long way to solving his business problems, and Cor would be the answer. So, he's making a play for her too."

"Well, I don't like him. He's not allowed to be my uncle."

"Right. That's my job."

"I'd back you over a man who does sex tours of Indonesia and doesn't care about his workers, Uncle Arthur."

"Now you're talking."

"So what's next?"

"Well, we have one big disadvantage and three advantages."

"Hit me with them."

"The disadvantage is Sinjie and Marcus both play bridge. A lot."

"Oh, shit."

"Yeah. That's apparently where they're making their most progress."

"You need to learn to play."

"Absolutely not. I'm not going to meet them on their field of battle. I'm going to draw them onto mine."

"You sound like a general formulating battle strategy."

"This is nothing less. That brings us to our three advantages —what we have that they don't."

"Yeah?"

"First, me. I'm deadly attractive, smarter than they are, and extremely charming."

"Modest too."

"That's beside the point. The second advantage is you. You're family. An insider. And you're pulling for me."

"You're damned right I am."

"That's good. Finally, Sinjie Fennimore doesn't tip as well as I do, thanks to your money, and Brock doesn't tip at all, so the staff will be working for me."

"Okay. How'd you get my money to tip with?"

"Oh yeah. Right. Well, Mock gave me some of the clothing allowance. I needed sundries."

"Sundries?"

"Sundries." I tried to look righteous.

"Like sunblock?" she suggested archly, and I smiled.

"Sure. Sunblock. Also bribes for the staff, which I knew you'd never think to do."

"Well, that's true. How much of my money did he give you?"

"Two hundred."

"If I texted Mock right now, how much would he tell me he gave you?"

"It's the middle of the night at home. Let's not bother Mock."

"He's probably at a club where he and his boyfriend are picking up guys together."

"Nice!"

She pulled out her phone, and I sighed.

"A thousand."

"You talked my business partner out of a thousand dollars, and he didn't think to tell me?"

"I charmed him. I'm very charming."

"Uh-huh," she said suspiciously. "What did you do to persuade him?"

"Nothing."

"What?" She waved her phone at me again.

"Oh, all right. I let him give me a massage."

"He gave you a massage, and you got money out of it?"

"I have a very nice back."

"Is that all he got to?"

"Actually, yes. As I've said to others lately, I no longer fuck for money."

She regarded me with renewed suspicion. "Are you liable to give my aunt a social disease?"

"I'll have you know I'm a fanatic about health and cleanliness, I am regularly tested, and I am clean." She offended my dignity, and I let her know it by my tone and impressively upright posture. She wasn't at all impressed. "It was quite a good massage," I admitted. "He walked on my spine."

"And paid you a thousand dollars. Of *my* money. Your body isn't that good."

"Oh yes, it is."

Our argument might have gone on if the cabin phone hadn't rung.

Ellyn glared at me and answered.

Aunt Cor wanted to meet for breakfast on the sundeck. I signaled to Ellyn that we needed fifteen minutes and fled.

CHAPTER ELEVEN—ELLYN

Uncle Arthur.

He wanted to be my fucking uncle.

The nerve of that guy! I fizzed with frustration and made little sounds of disgust whenever Cor and Rebel weren't looking at me—and that was a problem, because it was my job to make sure Cor had a wonderful time.

With me *or* with Uncle Arthur.

Ugh.

Cor and Rebel were both in shorts and colorful, tropical camp shirts, sturdy walking shoes on their sturdy feet. I'd pulled on a sundress and sandals, and Cor stared at me when I knocked on her door to pick them up for breakfast.

"That's what you're wearing?"

"To breakfast? Is this wrong?"

"Well, sweetie, we're going shopping—in Kuala Lumpur, some of the best shopping on the planet! Will you be able to walk in those shoes? And maybe you shouldn't bring the whole camera bag?"

"Aw, hell, Corrie," Rebel said, pushing her friend out the door and pulling it closed behind her. "We'll buy the girl some better shoes. Let's go to breakfast. I'm hungry."

She nudged us down the hallway, and before long we emerged in the bright sun on deck.

"Oh! Look!" Aunt Cor spotted him immediately and waved. "It's Arthur! Good morning, Arthur!"

He was seated in a corner of the deck, his back to us and an empty plate in front of him. When had he found time to order and be served—much less finish—breakfast? We'd been plotting and arguing mere moments before.

He looked up, surprised, and closed a book on his finger. He wore a pair of tortoiseshell glasses I hadn't seen before and looked for a moment like the most handsome man anyone had ever seen. I shook myself and snapped out of it.

"Cor!" he exclaimed in real (or fake real) surprise. "How nice to see you again! I had no idea you were an early riser too!"

We were closing in on nine in the morning. Hardly the crack of dawn.

"You must join us for breakfast."

"Oh, I wouldn't want to disturb you, and I'm just finishing. Doing some light reading."

We all stared at the book, and I realized he'd forced us to look at it, like a magician forces a card on an unwilling dupe. The book was hardback, thick and well-worn. "Whatever are you reading, Arthur dear?" Cor asked.

He shrugged. "It's not very good vacation reading, I'm afraid. It's a history of Burma—or Myanmar, as it's known now. I'm fascinated by the place, you know."

"Are you? How interesting." Cor clearly wasn't interested, but we all liked the way Artie looked while discussing it: like a hot professor. In a porn movie. Any minute now, a young, large-breasted co-ed would come to beg for a better grade.

"Well, I hope you enjoy your breakfast," he said with a genial smile. "Are you going into Kuala Lumpur today?" At Cor and Rebel's eager nods, he added, "Perhaps we'll be on the same bus! I'm looking forward to seeing the Petronas Towers."

"Oh, no." Cor was being seated at a table by a solicitous

waiter. She stopped and turned to Artie. "No, don't take that tour. Come with us. We've hired a local guide, and we're going to all the most authentic shopping spots."

"Shopping? I don't want to intrude."

"Nonsense! He's got a lovely van, and it seats six. We've just got room for you."

"We do?" Rebel asked, confused.

"Of course we do," Cor said stoutly. "Luz can stay on the ship. I'm sure Arthur would like to see the real Kuala Lumpur and not those silly towers."

He looked charmingly abashed. "Do you think so?"

"I do think so. We'll see you on the dock at nine thirty exactly. I insist!"

He put his hand on his broad chest and gave a little bow, surprisingly graceful for being seated. "It would be my honor. And perhaps I might be allowed to buy you ladies lunch? I don't have a huge budget for my trip, but there could hardly be a better way to spend my vacation dollars."

"You're sweet. Of course you can. And maybe we'll buy you a little something in return. I'd like to see you in one of those Nehru jackets!"

"Oh my!" He blushed—he actually managed to blush. And he was blushing through my sunblock, which I was wishing I had.

"So—nine thirty on the dock?"

"I wouldn't miss it for the world. Good morning, ladies."

He made his exit, and Rebel turned to the far more important task of choosing what she wanted for breakfast.

"Why can't Luz come?" I asked.

"Hmm, dear?"

"You said the van seats six. You, me, Rebel, Arthur, and the guide makes five. Why can't Luz come?"

"Sinjie, of course. Oh, that's right—you went to bed so early, you haven't met Sinjie yet. I partnered with him last night at bridge. Oh, we had the best hand. Really, it was something memorable, and Sinjie is so bright about cards. It's a pleasure to partner with him. I was almost void in diamonds, and Rebel was the dummy . . ."

She went into a tedious history of every trick, which Rebel argued with and complained about. I smiled and nodded and exclaimed in all the right places and kept Aunt Cor happy, but inside I thought we would get a chance to check out the ascot-wearing Saint James, whose name was abbreviated as Sinjie. I hated him already.

I was not going to endure an Uncle Sinjie at Thanksgiving dinner.

I could, however, endure the altered perspective of life so close to the equator. Even at this hour, the sunlight was already midday-harsh and the shadows were intense, so I took some dramatic portraits of Cor and Rebel while they ate. They both protested but sat straighter, stretching their necks to avoid double chins and looking at me from lowered faces so I'd take the most flattering photos.

Then we exclaimed over the photos and discussed my flaws as a photographer, and I did a detail study of the lattice we were sitting under that captured the azure of the clear sky. The air was hot and humid, and the port smells were beginning to bake in the sun. But the persistent breeze at least made life bearable as long as we were in the shade.

Standing on the docks was a different issue. I was regretting my loss of sunblock but grateful for the cool sundress and open sandals when Arthur appeared. "I'm not late, am I?" he asked.

He was in a white button-down shirt, worn by age to an appealing suppleness. The rolled sleeves showed off strong wrists and forearms, and his navy shorts were appropriately baggy and fell almost to his well-shaped knees. He wore a woven pair of espadrilles on his feet that made me want to kiss Mock right on the mouth; his footwear was "casual yacht club" all the way.

"Not at all, dear. We're waiting for the driver. And Sinjie."

"Oh?" Artie gave an inquiring smile.

"My bridge partner," she simpered. "I do hope you boys won't be jealous of each other."

"I don't see how we can avoid it, Cor!" he said with a charming wink. She fluttered in delight. He compounded his annoyance factor by turning to me. "Ellyn, isn't it? I worry about you in this sun. Would you like some of my sunblock?"

And he handed me my own tube. He was so annoying.

I fought the urge to dent his handsome shin with my open-toed sandal. Instead, I smiled sweetly. "How nice of you. Thank you. I seem to have forgotten mine."

I applied a liberal coat and made a point of tucking it into my camera bag. "I'll just hold on to it for you, shall I?"

He was forced to nod and smile.

"That's good," Cor said. "You're so pale, Ellyn. All her family is, Arthur. You should have seen my Wooly."

"Wooly?"

"My husband, Carl Wolcott. The man would get a sunburn at midnight. Like a ghost—he was so pale. The whole family, redheads. Not that most of her cousins have remained red! I don't know why; it's the most glorious color. Ellyn, you know your cousin Priss has gone back to her natural color."

She went off on a diatribe about dyed hair. Priss had gone blond when she was ten, although she'd apparently given up living as a blond since then. Liv had dyed hers that flat black goths favor. And Farrah the party girl changed her hair color weekly; the last time I'd seen her, it was purple on top and faded to flamingo pink.

"Can you believe it?" Arthur said in companionable amazement. "Do you know, I saw a woman in New York City recently who dyed her hair to look like a zebra."

"No!"

"Ridiculous. I almost laughed out loud when I saw her!"

I smiled sweetly at them both and added a second mental divot in his other shin. He had no way of knowing whether Cor had seen me with my striped hair or not. Risky.

Of course, I thought grumpily. *Cor's been on this ship for six weeks.* Maybe his sin hadn't been too terrible. Still—annoying.

An older man made his way toward us. He waved and called out, "Madam Cor, there you are!"

"Oh, Sinjie! We were waiting for you!"

She introduced us and I shook his hand. I had to give it to him: Sinjie was a good-looking older man, with a white, neatly trimmed beard and twinkling eyes. He was dressed entirely in white and wore some modern descendent of a pith helmet—a woven creation with a deep brim. No ascot. I was disappointed, but the hat took some courage to wear, so I had to award him points for that.

Cor did the introductions. Colonel Saint James Fennimore had such a plummy, upper-crust British accent I had a hard time believing it was real, but he held to it.

He gestured to a short Malaysian man at his elbow.

"My dear," he said, "this is the guide I told you about. This is Khalish. He knows Kuala Lumpur even better than I do."

"Oh, then we're so happy to have you with us, Khalish! I'm Mrs. Wolcott, and these are my guests."

Cor spoke slowly and loudly, which seemed to confuse Khalish.

"A lot of people in Malaysia speak English, Aunt Cor," I tried, but she was largely indifferent.

"Now, I will pay you half now, and half when we get back." She pulled out a wallet from her purse and a ripple of interest went through the group. "That's the way the steward said to do it," she confided to us as she counted out bills into his extended hand.

Khalish was very attentive, as was Sinjie. I assumed some of that cash would be making its way into the colonel's pocket. Old Sinjie would get a kickback for putting wealthy Aunt Cor into Khalish's hands and van.

Artie, on the other hand, stepped up protectively. "Cor, I insist you put that wallet in your front pocket. Do not put it back in your purse—and don't put your hand on that pocket. You'll just be advertising where your money is."

He took her elbow, neatly nudging Sinjie out of his place of honor, and continued to educate Cor about dips and pickpockets as they followed Khalish to the van. "I did quite intensive research for one of my books, and I can't advise you too strongly on this."

"Really?"

He seated her behind the driver and took the spot next to her, leaving Rebel and me to climb into the back seat. Sinjie was relegated to riding shotgun.

"You know Kuala Lumpur so well, Sinbad." Artie smiled and planted a large hand on the older man's shoulder from his position behind him. "You'll help Khalish get us where we're going, right?"

"It's Sinjie, actually. Short for Saint James."

"What an unusual name! How did you come by it?"

Artie continued to engage his opponent in genial conversation, forcing the older man to crane around painfully to answer. Rebel smirked beside me.

The drive into the city was eye-opening. Malaysia was like no place I'd ever traveled before, and I begged for several stops so I could photograph the landscape. The docks around Port Klang were industrial and ugly, with shipping gantries that stood like leviathans above the water. The roadway into the city was crowded with houses and shops, interspersed with thick jungle; the contrast was startling and remarkable. We went too quickly.

Once in the city, Khalish took us to an enormous, freezing-cold shopping mall, gleaming with chrome and glass. He'd proudly brought us to Louis Vuitton and Chanel and Armani.

Aunt Cor pouted in the center of this marble palace.

"I can get all of this in New York," she said. "Is this really the real Kuala Lumpur?"

"Yes, miss," Khalish answered nervously.

"No," Rebel said, "I read it in the guidebook. We need to go to the Indian market."

"That's not the right place for you ladies. It's not always terribly safe," Khalish tried, but he was overruled.

"We want to see the real Kuala Lumpur! Take us there!"

Khalish looked to Sinjie, his actual employer, who offered no guidance. Then he scanned Artie, standing head and shoulders above anyone around him. "Well, perhaps with this gentleman— I mean, these gentlemen"—he quickly included Sinjie—"it will be all right. I'll bring the van around."

Soon we were off again. Khalish spent the entire time on the phone, calling people and speaking rapidly in Malay. I followed along on my GPS and noticed we were going in circles while he talked to his contacts, but whatever. Everyone deserves to make a living, and if Khalish was going to sell patrons to various shops, more power to him.

Eventually, we found ourselves in the middle of a shopping district so crowded the van could only inch along.

Khalish found the garage he wanted (having passed at least five that he wouldn't drive into) and turned to us.

"Perhaps the gentleman could take that money," he suggested nervously, "so you don't have to worry about it."

"Certainly not." Cor was offended at the thought.

"You will leave your purses here? The young lady would like me to lock her camera bag in the van?"

None of us liked that idea. I appreciated Khalish's attempt to make sure he was the only one who robbed us, but my camera bag didn't leave my sight. I put the strap across my body and secured it.

"Miss, a clever thief will cut through the strap and take that bag right off of you."

"No, he won't." The bag looked normal, but it was canvas over steel mesh, and the strap had a steel cable running through it. I'd locked it to my body with a carabiner through my belt. It was going nowhere. Khalish shook his head in resignation.

"Good luck," he said to Artie.

"Well, I've barely got any money at all." Artie smiled. "I'll be glad to act as bodyguard!"

"As will I," Sinjie said hurriedly. Cor and Rebel were delighted.

"Let's go!"

The street was a kaleidoscope of color and sound. The textures were dizzying, and the people were alternately fascinated by and indifferent to us. Cor and Rebel were in heaven, exploring tiny stores that reeked of incense and stopping for small savory or sweet pastries at the endless array of cafés. Soon, Khalish carried purchases and Artie had large tote bags over both shoulders that held colorful saris in impressively large sizes, scarves, huge quantities of necklaces and rings, and a headpiece a Las Vegas showgirl would have blushed to wear.

And eventually, he also carried a Nehru jacket in midnight-blue silk, richly embroidered on the shoulders and arms, in which Artie looked like the heroic British aristocrat at the casbah. The shop owner did a fitting before lunch, and it was ready by the time we finished eating. Artie tried it on and everyone in the place—even the hetero men—sighed with pleasure at the sight.

Artie held to his word about buying the group lunch (with my cash), pleading the poverty of a humble novelist but insisting on picking up the tab. Cor was thrilled, and Sinjie tried to mask his annoyance with a benevolent smile.

Somehow, as usual, they all decided to follow where I went. I don't know what it was about me, but even with Khalish right there, Cor and Rebel (and soon Sinjie and Artie, too) were asking me where to go next. As if I knew.

But on we went, sometimes pushing past Khalish to explore a shop and sometimes heeding his recommendations.

And I filled an entire memory stick with photographs. Everywhere I looked, there was a new scene to consider. Beautiful teen girls in cropped T-shirts next to mothers in headscarves.

Opulent displays of fruits I couldn't name. A riot of materials hanging to catch what little breeze could push its way down the packed street. Small children sitting under a table and playing with a kitten. The shine of a lantern in an oil-slicked puddle.

I was dazzled and drunk on the light.

Artie played the role of hero. He was as good as his word; he kept the dips and pickpockets away from my aunt and away from our group. When a monsoon broke out, he was the one who tucked Cor and Rebel under an awning and leapt across the road to buy cheap, colorful umbrellas, and he was the one who waited patiently, holding an umbrella over me while I caught the rush of color reflected in water sluicing down a rainspout.

He flipped his shaggy-short hair off his forehead with a laugh, sprinkling raindrops around him in a crown, and we all exhaled our appreciation.

Sinjie, attempting to carry even a few of Cor's purchases, was utterly routed. In this first battle of his campaign, Artie was the undeniable winner. But one battle does not win the war, and a new general was about to enter the field.

CHAPTER TWELVE—ARTIE

Sinjie wasn't what my old mentor, Victor, would have called "a worthy opponent."

He and Khalish were getting kickbacks from every shop we entered. The shopkeepers passed cash along as soon as Cor and Rebel focused on their shopping. Every purchase earned "the Colonel" a little more folding money.

At Khalish's not-so-subtle direction, he nudged us from one street-side bakery to another, and we walked past two identical cafés to get to a third, where the owner folded colorful Malaysian ringgits into Sinjie's palm with the welcoming handshake.

As the host of that meal, I should have gotten the kickback, but I played ignorant and smiled all the while.

I was counting, though.

I could have lifted Cor's wallet four separate times myself, but the short-term profit would have blown my long game. And my hands weren't quite as small as they'd been when I'd been a skillful pickpocket back in Times Square.

So, I watched and waited and smiled and protected. I played the oblivious hero. I tracked Ellyn through the crowd by her flaming-red head and glared at a few street toughs who were eyeing her massive camera bag. She was an idiot to have brought it, but she wasn't happy unless she had it with her. My sexy future niece. I could indulge her.

The inky-blue Nehru jacket was the absolute bomb. I looked fantastic in it. One look in the tiny shop mirror, and I knew. My new short haircut had revolutionized my look; I had to hand it to Mock. The long "sun god" hair had served me well, but this cut lifted me to a new level of handsome.

I guided Cor into insisting she get me a pair of white trousers to go with it, fitted down the leg to show off my muscles. The shopkeeper and I had a long discussion on the proper shoes to wear with it—leather sandals? That would be traditional, but black patent leather would be sharp too. Cor suggested white shoes, but he and I disabused her of that fashion travesty.

We ended up with the classic sandals. I'd need a pedicure; I'd get it at the spa on the ship and charge it to my cabin. Ellyn could pay. I eyed myself in the shop mirror, set in the middle of the space so customers had to leave the dressing area and be cajoled and berated by the owner. I tried a smile. My teeth could have been whiter, but Ellyn had insisted on making them dingy. She had no appreciation for perfection.

Cor was thrilled with her purchases—both the outfit she got for me and all the haul she'd pulled for herself and Rebel. Ellyn wanted very little. She bought a few paisley shawls but spent most of her time either photographing the world around her or looking ahead to where we'd go next.

Ellyn needed and expected no help with her bags. Cor, on the other hand, dimpled at me when I kept carrying her acquisitions for her. She decided, with my help, to get some large tote bags to make my burdens easier. We had a blast. Spending her money was so much fun, I knew this was my future wife.

And Sinjie wouldn't be an obstacle.

That evening at dinner, however, I did come across a stumbling block.

The expected Marcus Vanderfleet joined our table for dinner.

Great name, I thought with envy. *Vanderfleet*. He did not sound like his father had worked for the Manhattan and Bronx Surface Transit Operating Authority. More like he'd grown up on manicured lawns with butlers to fetch another brand-new baseball when little Marcus hit another one into the Long Island Sound.

Never mind. I knew from Basilio that Marcus was interested in Cor's money more than in Cor herself. He wasn't broke, but he was closing in on an ugly reality. All was not so rosy for this one-percenter, and he was no better than me.

Plus, he was a sheep, and I was a wolf.

I watched his confusion with amusement; Marcus was not used to pretty young ladies offering him a firm handshake when they met, but Ellyn was true to her upbringing and greeted him with an outstretched hand. Marcus laughed indulgently as they shook, as if he was doing her a little favor.

Naturally, we hated each other on sight. There's an instinct men have for each other. Primitive man survived on recognizing a competitor in their hunting ground, and Marcus and I had our hackles up from the first moment.

To start with, he wouldn't ever consider himself a scammer. He wasn't conning Cor, in his opinion. His interest was pure and honorable: He was out to save his factories. He was an actual businessman with a backstory that would check out under the closest scrutiny. That alone gave him an unfair advantage.

And second, he recognized my intention to win Cor's affections. My camouflage of innocence wouldn't stand up to scrutiny.

It took longer than expected to actually meet Marcus because he missed the obligatory hour-long cocktail session. Cor and Rebel giggled through endless gin fizz drinks, suggested by Sinjie "because the gin would protect them from tropical malaria."

"Oh, well—if it's medicinal," Rebel chortled and ordered another one.

I affected interested surprise. "I thought the Brits drank gin and tonics in the tropics because tonic water has quinine in it. Is that wrong?"

He blustered and revised and finally had to admit I was right, which I knew, but that gin fizzes tasted better. I showed him all my teeth in a grin. *I see you, fella.* He turned away, submissive to the better man. *That's right.*

But when we sat down to dinner, up bustled a big, barrel-chested man oozing confidence—clearly, the arrival of "the Vanderfleet." He pulled out the chair opposite Cor.

"Sorry I'm late, Corinne. We just got off the links. Now, who do we have here?"

He absorbed all the energy at the table. I sat back to give him his moment and to assess. He was introduced to Ellyn and didn't leer at her in her ice-blue slip dress. Points to him; she looked hot. Instead, he asked her about her camera, which she wore instead of a necklace.

He turned to me. "Petrovitch? You're the guy who's going to rumba with our Corinne?"

"That's right."

"Good for you." He dismissed me by picking up his menu. "I never could stand dancing. Too fussy for me. Or shopping. You buy out the town again, Corinne?"

She dimpled and launched into an exhaustive list of her acquisitions. He paid her very little attention, and I watched her closely. Why didn't she mind?

Then I realized why. His treatment was what she was used to. She must have talked to her husband with the same parrot-like chatter, and he probably ignored her as blatantly.

She liked it.

This was normal to her.

The realization made me wonder if I needed to shift my strategy. On the other hand, she already had one businessman ignoring her. What would make me stand out in comparison? Was I supposed to ignore her more?

And after I'd spent the last twenty-four hours sweeping her

across the room in bold dance moves and holding her bags as she shopped?

No, I couldn't change now.

My gaze fell on Ellyn. She'd become mesmerized by a reflection through a water glass that cast a rainbow on the linen tablecloth. She messed around with her camera but didn't take a shot. She looked up and found me watching her.

She jumped a little and smiled faintly.

She would have to be my ace in the hole.

And it would work out well for her, too, because in addition to marrying her aunt, I'd be able to point that five million at her. She could even keep my share. I was going for the grand prize.

Marcus attempted to grill me during dinner about my agent and my publisher; I deflected by insisting I left my world as an author behind and only wanted to focus on the next book, which would start in Myanmar.

"You mean Burma?" he said suspiciously. "That's a closed society. Human rights abusers." He looked at Cor and flashed her some incisors. "You know how I care about human rights, Corinne."

Right. As long as the rights didn't interfere with labor costs.

"Well, that's going to be part of my hero's transformation." I went into my prepared diatribe about a Burmese man coming to the United States; eyes glazed over. He waited for me to take a breath and turned to Ellyn.

"So. You're competing with your cousins for Corrie's five mil, huh?"

Forks and knives clattered to the table, and all eyes flew to him.

He feigned surprise. "What? We're not supposed to talk about this?"

"I told you that in strictest confidence, Marcus! Really!"

"I'm sorry, Corrie." He reached a long arm across the table and patted her hand. "I'm a simple guy. You know that. I didn't mean to let the cat out of the bag."

"Oh my. Well, now that we all know, I suppose it's better."

I raised my hand meekly. "Am I not supposed to know?" It was important I played this right: interested as any person would be, but not interested enough to imply I had a stake in the outcome.

Aunt Cor looked at me, and that was the moment Marcus chose to pull his hand away—which made her look back to him. Nice play. He kept her attention.

"You see, Arthur," she said, now looking at her dinner, "my dear late husband Wooly—that is, Carl Wolcott—left me a little bequest."

"Little!" Marcus scoffed. "Five million!"

He spoke the sum in a loud voice, not caring who overheard. He spoke like a man used to discussing large figures. He spoke, I realized, like good old Wooly probably spoke.

"He wanted me to pick which of my four nieces would inherit that sum. So, I've invited each niece to join me on one leg of this ocean voyage, and Ellyn here is the youngest, so she's the last niece to travel with me."

I let awkwardness creep into my voice to show that, unlike Marcus, I was uncomfortable talking about anything as crass as money. "It's hard to imagine anyone could be a more charming traveling companion than lovely Eileen here."

"Ellyn," my future niece growled.

"Of course. I'm so sorry—Ellyn. What a nice way for you to decide! So, you've been onboard for a while, then?"

Cor gave me an extended travelogue, with Rebel adding details. She'd started in Fiji ("far more crowded and smellier than you'd think") and sailed through the Coral Sea with Priss and her husband "and the darling baby." Rebel didn't seem to think the baby was quite as darling as Cor did.

"We went to Bougainville. That's in the Solomon Islands, Arthur."

"Ah?"

"That's where I got my natangura palms. You saw them, Ellyn —on my balcony."

"Like I said, Corinne," Marcus commented, "you're not going to be able to get them through customs."

"Yes, I am. I told you, Wooly knew people at the State Department. Ellyn called about it for me. Oh, Arthur, it's so fascinating. These palms, they're . . . oh, what's the word? Rebel, what was the word?"

"I don't remember."

"Well, there's a word. It means this is a plant that can only flower once before it dies! Isn't that romantic?"

Um. Okay. Sure.

Next, fashion designer Liv had arrived with her boyfriend, Xavier. They'd been with Cor and Rebel through the Arafura and Banda Seas. "That's Papua New Guinea and south to northern Australia. Much more crafty shopping—beads and batiks. Remember, Rebel? I got that stunning feather headdress?"

Rebel remembered. "You look like Big Bird in that."

"Nonsense! Liv said it was stunning, and she would know. She's got the very best taste, Arthur. Never wears anything but black, even in this heat!"

The ship's restaurant was arctic in temperature.

"That headdress is quite amazing," Cor went on dreamily. "I got it in Kairuku-Hiri—in this tiny port town. All birds of paradise feathers, Arthur. No—the headdress, not the port! It's all the most breathtaking yellows. I feel like a goddess in it."

"I'm sure you're quite radiant."

"Well, *I* really think I am." She clearly kicked Rebel under the table. Marcus attacked his steak as if it had insulted him.

Then Liv had gotten off the ship and Farrah had gotten on with her friend Lucy in Dili. "Capital of Timor-Leste. Did you know that's its own country, all on its own? So curious."

"Indeed." But she didn't need my confirmation. She kept plowing on.

"And Farrah and Lou—they lived in the ship's bars and the

nightclub! When we were in port, they drank on the docks. Really—drunk half the time and hungover the rest. They couldn't have enjoyed the Java Sea much, and that is a pity. We went to Bali, you know."

"I bought a mask," Rebel said with contentment.

"And I bought a beautiful flamingo for my garden. Why, it's quite as tall as you are, Arthur!"

"Are flamingos native to Bali?"

My question, innocently asked just to show I was keeping up, stumped her. She looked at me blankly. Rebel spoke.

"There was a frog too."

"Oh yes!" Cor said happily. "A frog! Made by the same local craftsman! I'm going to put both of them in my garden."

"It's all about shopping with this one," Marcus said in a fond but patronizing tone. I decided Marcus might have to stumble across a painful accident with a long recovery period. In bed. Behind locked doors, if possible.

"And now it's Ellyn's turn for the Andaman Sea and the Bay of Bengal. Oh, there are so many new treasures to find. We're going to have a wonderful time, aren't we, Ellyn?"

She held out an imperious hand to Ellyn, who took it with good grace. "We are. And we'll see the coral waters of Phuket in Thailand and go to an island range I've never heard of called the Andaman and Nicobar Islands . . ."

"And each place has different crafts and cultures, and Ellyn has a photographer's eye, and we're going to do some wonderful shopping!"

"Absolutely right!"

The topic seemed to have come to a close, and I was trying to decide if a person who didn't know any better would bring up the five million again when Marcus did it for me.

"So that Priss wants the money for a country club lifestyle, and gloomy Liv wants a fashion career. Farrah wants to party all night." Marcus did a grotesque imitation of dancing, elbows held up and hands in fists as he gyrated in his chair. "What do you want the money for, huh, Ellyn?"

This time, I saw Cor wince.

Ah. Got it.

She liked being ignored by a powerful man, but overt discussions of money and motive were too close to admitting people might be interested in Cor more for what she could give them than for who she was.

That was my in.

Ellyn explained about the production company she and Mock wanted to start and her hopes for becoming a director.

"You want to make movies?" Marcus asked. "Why? You think there's money in the entertainment industry for a little independent like you? Why don't you get in with one of the big boys? Go to work for Disney—or the porn industry. You could do well there!"

He chortled, and everyone winced. Leaving aside the question of whether he was advocating that Ellyn film or star in pornos, he'd brought up a subject considered distasteful by the three women at the table.

I immediately betrayed my gender and threw him under the bus simply by looking at my empty dessert plate and folding my napkin. "Well," I said, and let the thought tail off, deepening his social faux pas.

We were saved from a silence I quite enjoyed when Sinjie strolled over—and damned if the man wasn't wearing an actual, honest-to-God ascot. I'd never seen one before in the flesh, so to speak. I almost leapt to my feet and shook his hand. He pulled it off, too, by refusing to acknowledge his tie was ridiculous. Points to Sinjie.

"Fennimore," Marcus said, and I heard the loathing in his voice. So it wasn't just me. Marcus didn't get along with men, apparently.

"Vanderfleet." Sinjie showed Marcus his teeth and turned to Cor. "My dear, I believe I'm partnering with you tonight."

"No." Marcus's voice was flat. "You got her last night. Tonight, Cor and I are partners."

Cor was flattered by the attention but also made uneasy by the obvious undercurrent of tension. "Now, boys," she began, but I broke in.

"I hoped we could have a short rehearsal this evening, Cor. A little rumba before you play bridge?"

I held up one hand and cradled air before me with the other, smiling at her with a wink. She flushed a pleased pink. "What a lovely idea!" She turned to Sinjie. "I'll join you all in an hour or so. And I think you'll find that this evening, Rebel and I are partnered against the two of you."

She'd gotten in the perfect exit line, and I stood immediately to help her from her seat. Cor was turning out to be a tough little fleeceable sheep, and I was coming to admire her. She left the field of battle the clear winner.

On the arm of the undefeated champion. *Gauntlet tossed, boys. May the best future uncle win.* And I had a red-haired ace up my sleeve.

CHAPTER THIRTEEN—ELLYN

ARTIE SWEPT COR OUT OF THE RESTAURANT LIKE HE'D WON the Palme d'Or. All very well and good for them, but it left me and Rebel with the now-seething Marcus and the smug Sinjie.

Marcus turned from glaring at the door and glared at me instead. "I don't suppose you play bridge, do you."

His was definitely not a question. I could have been the bridge grand champion; he didn't want me.

"Rebel, shall we join them?" I said hurriedly. She and I stood, made "goodbye" noises, and fled.

"I'm freezing," I said. "Could we walk on deck for a few minutes?"

Rebel nodded and pushed out the doors. "You'll be sweating in minutes," she predicted. "This is jungle air out here, unless you're actually at sea." She fished a cigarette out of her bag and lit up.

The ship had left port and was moving slowly north. We were heading to Thailand, but the journey was to take two days, and we were crawling along between the shorelines of Malaysia and the westernmost arm of Indonesia.

The air was clammy, but the baked garbage scent of the port

was gone, and the warmth was a relief. I'd need to remember to bring a sweater everywhere on this ship. Or an arctic parka.

"Where do you stand on all these men, Rebel?" I asked as we walked slowly along the rail.

"All these wannabes?" she asked.

"Yeah. They all know she's got money, right?"

"Of course. They're not idiots. Anyone can see the way she spends. At least this new guy is a babe."

I nodded. There was no sense pretending Artie hadn't been made by a benevolent god to fulfill the dreams of women everywhere. "So, he's one of three who are after her?"

"Four. You haven't met the kid yet."

"There's a kid?"

"Well, not a kid. About your age. Skinny, dark, and handsome. Named Brock. But Cor's not into cradle-robbing, so he's not such a big deal."

"Should I be worried?"

She stopped and leaned on the rail. I stood upwind, and she exhaled her smoke so it wouldn't blow into my face. "You worried about her? Or the money?"

I huffed a little laugh. Rebel was a good friend to my aunt. "I'm not worried about the money. My parents have told me often enough: it's tied up in the family trust. No lawyer can bust it out. I doubt those three—those four—are going to be able to. I'm worried about her."

She nodded and flipped her butt into the ocean. "So far, she's just having fun."

"Anybody have the inside track?"

A shrug. "Sinjie's a gigolo, I think, but Cor doesn't care. Marcus is a bully and Cor likes that. And this new guy—Arthur the Handsome. I don't know. Seems like a good guy, but she's got access to a lot of money. Even good guys can go bad for that much."

I nodded thoughtfully. "Anything I should do?"

Rebel nudged me with her shoulder. "Just be her friend. She'd be glad of it. Your family's not too wild about her."

"I know it. Uncle Freddy went wacko when Carl's will was read. He's supposed to be in charge now, you know."

"I know. Cor knows too. But he doesn't get it until Cor dies, and boring old Carl made that airtight."

Boring old Carl. I'd never thought of Carl as boring. He was the man who decided how much money his brothers and sister got each quarter; in my family, he was revered. It was the pope, Dolly Parton, and Carl up there in the pantheon of goodness and morality. But Rebel knew him differently from me.

She stood from the rail. "Let's go. I don't want to leave them alone for too long."

"No kidding. He might knock her up, and then where would we be?"

She and I laughed, and she eyed me as we walked to door. "I would have thought you'd be on the lookout for someone like him. Or he'd be looking at you. You're both beanstalks; you'd look good together."

"Rebel!" I protested. "I have a boyfriend."

She scoffed as I held the door for her. "If you can call him that."

"What? What's the matter with Bax? I thought you liked him."

"He lets you walk all over him."

"I do not!"

"Let's take the elevator. My feet hurt." The stink of cigarette smoke hung around her and the elevator wouldn't make that any more enjoyable, but I'd found a new kinship with Rebel. The elevator it would be.

"Anyway," I said, "I don't have enough money to attract a guy like that."

"Unless you win the two and a half million."

I turned to her, surprised she knew. "Five million," I corrected hopefully.

"Right. I forgot. I don't know that you and Priss have a deal to split the total, because Liv and Farrah have a deal."

"Jeez, Rebel." The elevator let us out on the right floor, and we stepped into the hallway. "How do you know? Does Cor know?"

"Of course. I don't keep secrets from her. And I know because Luz doesn't keep secrets either. So Priss thinks she's got the inside track, but Cor's not an idiot."

I shook my head to clear it. On the one hand, the plot to increase our chances to get some money had been uncovered. On the other hand, by telling me so, wasn't Rebel equipping me with information my cousins didn't have?

Or at least, I didn't think they had it . . .

I was confused. I needed to talk this out with Mock.

No—I needed a scoundrel to interpret. I needed to talk this out with Artie.

He and Cor were concentrating so hard, they barely looked up when Rebel and I slipped into the yoga studio. They were counting together to get the steps right, and Cor had a glow of perspiration on her forehead.

This had turned out to be important to her. She was really working at it.

I found I was smiling at her determination, and my smile confused me all the more. I needed to remember my goal: I needed the millions for my production company. Cor's happiness was a path to that end, and that was all. Didn't need to be any more complicated than that.

They were working on a pass where they both spun out to the lengths of their outstretched arms and then she spun into him, keeping on the rhythm and clasping hands to begin the next form. It was pretty, and Rebel and I applauded when they got it right.

Cor laughed, and she and Artie came to join us.

"That was wonderful," I cried.

"It really was!" Rebel and I were both delighted with what we'd seen—and with the smile on Cor's face.

Luz appeared out of nowhere (had Cor called her? Or did she use her secret maid mysticism to know she was needed?) and gave them bottles of water. I handed Cor the towel from my camera bag so she could blot her face.

"We're working on it," Cor said modestly. Artie beamed at her. "Arthur, I think you should wear your new Nehru jacket for the competition."

He smiled. "An Indian look for a Cuban dance? No, I've got a great white dinner jacket. It's very sharp. Let's save my new look for when we debut our cha-cha. What are you going to wear?"

"I have a lilac gown that would be ideal with a white dinner jacket!"

"Perfect." They regarded each other with great approval. Rebel nudged me, and I suppressed my grin. As long as Cor was happy, we could all accomplish our goals.

They practiced until a large presence resolved in the door. Marcus had come looking for his bridge game—or rather, his investment capital.

"Oh, hello, Marcus dear. I'll be just a moment."

Cor discretely blotted her face and handed the towel to me and the water to Luz, who faded away. She invited me sweetly. "Won't you join us, Ellyn?"

"I'll come peek in the room to see it, but then I think I'll try a little lunar photography on deck."

"Well, if you must. Arthur, can I tempt you? We could teach you bridge?"

Marcus harrumphed his discontent at the idea.

"I think you could tempt me to just about anything, Cor," Artie said, "but I've got a fascinating book in my cabin. I think I'll turn in for the evening. Thank you for the dance."

He bowed over her hand but didn't kiss it. I suppose he thought the kiss would be too overt, and I assumed he was right, as her eyes crinkled from the pleased smile she gave him.

"Ah*em*," Marcus said from the door.

"Yes. Coming. Rebel, are we ready?"

I saw them seated in the card room. It was near the night-club, but the pounding pulse of techno was muffled by the deep carpets. Faces were rapt in concentration, and the pall of cigarette smoke was astonishing. I wouldn't have lasted a single game, but Rebel pulled out her cigarettes with gusto and settled in for a long night of trumps and bids and whatever else made bridge so addictive for some.

Aunt Cor tried to pay attention to me when I said good night, but Sinjie dealt out the cards with a practiced flick, and Cor was clearly eager to focus her energies there. As long as she was happy, I was good with it.

I did walk the deck for a while (I was cold once again) but then made it to my cabin. I stood for a moment outside my door, looking across the hall to Cor's suite and thinking about Luz. Was she useful? Un-useful? Asset or liability?

My suite was still dark and unpopulated. I was relieved I hadn't been visited by someone who would invade my bed and steam up my shower.

I resisted wondering if he could steam up my bed. Or invade my shower. *Banish the thought. Immediately.*

A hoodie over my dress wasn't stylish, but it was warmer. And it toned down my look, which was good. It wasn't as if I was all dolled up and wondering if he'd show up again to join me in bed.

I sat on the sofa and enjoyed the silence.

For seven minutes.

Then I couldn't stand the strain any longer and banged on the connecting door.

"What?" A grumpy voice snapped from the other side.

"C'mere," I demanded. "I have information."

His sigh was audible through the door, and then it was yanked open. He was huge. I'd forget how big he was until suddenly confronted with a vast chest and a head that towered over mine.

"Yeah?"

"Well, don't bark at me. Come in. I'll tell you what I learned. I want your opinion on some things."

He sprawled across the sofa, shirt sleeves rolled up and feet bare below the dark dinner-and-dancing slacks. "So?"

I told him about Rebel—about her question. *When it came to worrying about all the guys looming around her, was I more interested in Cor's happiness or the money?*

"What did you say?"

"I said the truth. None of you guys have a shot at the actual money. It's all tied up."

"But she's in charge until she dies."

"Yeah."

"That's all I need. So, what did you tell Rebel?"

"I guess I said I cared about Cor."

"And she liked that."

"Yeah. Plus, she said she knew about my deal with Priss. Get this: because Luz told her about it."

Artie nodded, showing no evidence of surprise. "And does Cor know too?"

"Yes! Rebel said she didn't keep secrets from her bestie, and Luz wouldn't either."

"Luz is smart. Don't bite the very wealthy hand that feeds you."

"That doesn't surprise you?"

"What, that Luz knows who signs her paycheck? Of course not. She'll make a few bucks off of Priss, and probably Liv and Farrah too. And she'll keep Cor informed. It's sensible."

"So—what do we do?"

"Do? Nothing. You're a sucker, but you're lucky. You've played it exactly right. You're coming out of this smelling like a rose. You haven't tried to bribe Luz, have you?"

I shook my head.

"Good. Don't. Cor will like that one of her nieces isn't trying to get an unfair advantage."

Of course, I *was* trying to get an unfair advantage, and that advantage was pushing blondness at me at that very moment. I refused to pick up my camera and photograph him in that expensive, subtle cabin lighting.

He went on, "And you've expressed concern to Rebel about me and the other guys, which—good job, by the way. She won't suspect we're in this together."

"Right." Just how slimy was I? I didn't like thinking I was in cahoots with a scoundrel, acting against Cor's best interests.

Artie watched me. "You really are a sucker. Cut that out."

I looked up, surprised. "Cut what out?"

"Don't feel guilty."

"I don't!"

He ignored my protests. "You're not doing anything to hurt her. She's going to pick a niece to give the money to. Why shouldn't it be you? You're a nice person, right?"

I raised an eyebrow, thinking about bringing Artie in as a ringer.

He shook his head and insisted, "You are. Get over it. She's fine, you're fine, and I've got a shot at being your uncle. What's bad here?"

"You make it sound so easy."

"It *is* easy. I've got a book. Anything else?"

"Are you really reading?"

"Yeah. Anything else?"

"No. You're not sleeping here tonight."

"Don't flatter yourself, princess. Good night."

He was gone before I could come up with a retort.

I was still thinking about what I was attempting to do to Cor, and my forehead was getting tired from being wrinkled. I shook off my mood. I had a billion photos to download and review. The Indian market in Kuala Lumpur was a photographer's dream. Time to get busy.

When I opened the door to the balcony, the room got warmer, but it also fogged everything, including my lenses. I put on socks and closed the door again. When I was done with my photos, I got ready for bed and turned out the lights.

I flounced into my enormous, empty bed, still thinking hard and still out of sorts. It took a while to finally get to sleep.

Then the connecting door clicked open, and his weight settled onto the bed. I tried not to smile. Pretending I was still asleep, I rolled over and into his arms.

And then I could sleep. God knows I needed the rest to face what the next day would bring.

CHAPTER FOURTEEN—ARTIE

ELLYN'S BED WAS LONG.

Not long enough that my feet wouldn't hang over the edge if I sent them straight down. Mattresses haven't been long enough for that since I was thirteen and hit my first truly painful growth spurt. But the bed was long enough—and wide. I could slew sideways and be fully supported. Within seconds, the day's assorted tensions were bleeding slowly out of my muscles. They got heavy, and relaxation started to settle in.

Ellyn pretended she was asleep when I slid in next to her, and I let it go. She turned into me easily and settled without a fuss. The lack of argument was soothing.

I tried to keep track of the things I needed to remember—including learning how to cha-cha. Having learned the rumba, how bad could the cha-cha be? Still, it would be stupid to let that idea slip. A few videos in my cabin, and if I needed to practice, I could force Ellyn to partner with me. She was condescending and arrogant, but dancing with a chair isn't the same as dancing with a woman. I know. I've tried.

Besides, Ellyn and I moved well together. Not that it mattered.

I needed a place to hide my shipment once I had it. The

mention at dinner of lawyers and the State Department and diplomatic intervention—that had potential. That could be a game changer.

There had to be some way to nudge Marcus Vanderfleet out of my path. Sinjie was no real threat; he was a beta in an alpha world and he knew it. Cor would want to go shopping with him, but she'd never trust him in her life. Too wimpy. Too . . . British.

Vanderfleet, on the other hand, was an arrogant asshole alpha who didn't listen when she spoke. Sadly, that turned out to be what she'd been trained to expect from a serious relationship. How could I best use that knowledge—not just to get him out of my way, but also to cement my future love affair and marriage to Cor?

How would Victor advise me, if he were still alive?

I pictured him as I always did: in bed, sheets artistically draped to hide what he'd felt was an old man's belly. He would have a cigarette in one hand and stroke my hair with the other.

"Darling boy," he'd say, "stop thinking about the man. Keep your eye on the woman. Unless you want to keep your eye on a man—in which case, look at me."

Victor had always made me smile. To his sorrow, I never fell in love with him, but he was one of the few people I actually revered as a teacher and a counselor. If he wanted to enjoy my body, I had no objections. Homosexuality was nothing to me; like all sexual relationships, it was a means to an end. In Victor's case, it was the (very small) price for a brilliant apprenticeship in scamming people. I'd done a great deal more for far less protection in juvenile detention.

"This Marcus Vanderfleet is a type." The ghost of Victor was still advising me, and I listened attentively. "He's a bully and a blusterer. There are two ways to take out a bully. What are they?"

Years later and a world away, I smiled into the darkness of Ellyn's posh suite, remembering Victor's rules.

"You can stand up to a bully," he said, "but you'd be an idiot to do it. This is not the playground at PS 48. Don't hoot like a silverback gorilla. Don't make threats. Don't challenge him. Bumping chests will just make things worse—unless you want to bump chests with me? No? Probably for the best."

Alcoholism and COPD had given him far less vigor than he let on, but Victor was brilliant with words, and I wouldn't interrupt him if I could help it. Even in a drowsing dream.

"What's the second way, Arthur darling? I know you know it. If you don't want to confront a bully, you . . .?"

I chuckled. "Humiliate him," I said out loud, "where his lady love can see."

Ellyn stirred against me, the press of her breasts against my ribs lifting a warmth through me. Wreathed in his smoke, Victor smiled.

That's right.

And that was the answer to this question, at least. I should remain subservient to Marcus Vanderfleet and watch for my opportunity. It would come. It always did.

Victor would have approved.

And in the meantime, Aunt Cor's face lit up every time she saw me, and her niece had a perfect, heart-shaped ass that made it a pleasure to walk behind her. I had new clothes that showed off my shoulders and a brilliant new haircut. Plus, I could anticipate several opportunities coming up where removing my shirt in public, like swimming or sunbathing, would demonstrate the precise definition of my abdominal muscles.

That ought to humiliate old Marcus, I thought.

No, no. I didn't want him secretly shamed by his beer gut; I wanted to crush him into a powder and invite Cor to leave her footprints in the remainder.

Good. That was a better idea.

In addition to learning the cha-cha, it wouldn't be a bad idea to increase my ab work tomorrow in the gym. I'd find Basilio and use him as my starting point for the inevitable chain of twenty-dollar bills that would lead to the second cook's assistant, or whoever could get me into Myanmar when we docked in Phuket.

And I would continue to keep my hands off the pushy, opinionated Ellyn so as to remain focused on Cor. The hands-off part was theoretical, of course, as I was currently sliding my fingers through her hair for the pleasure of the sensation and relishing the warmth of her palm curled around my neck. Her deep, even breathing let me know she'd actually fallen asleep.

That was a smart thing to do. I set my mental alarm clock for 5:45—there was a lot to accomplish tomorrow—and then I went to sleep too. Let the ghost of Victor stand guard against all the things that would almost certainly go wrong.

CHAPTER FIFTEEN—ELLYN

THE SHIP'S WHISTLE WOKE ME; WE MUST HAVE BEEN COMING into the harbor at Langkawi.

I woke slowly. The bed was empty but hopelessly disordered. Artie had once again decided my bed was the better place for sleep. All of my pillows were in the wrong place, and the covers at the foot of the bed had been untucked. It was annoying. I slept neatly. And I slept alone.

The ship's engines came to a halt—we'd made it to the dock. I knew I should roll over and at least peer through the sliding doors to see what the island looked like. Although not as famous as our next stop (Thailand's famous Phuket Island), Langkawi was supposed to be very beautiful.

But I was too comfortable. And then the shower shut off.

It was like the ship's engines, a sound or vibration so omnipresent I didn't really understand I'd been hearing it until it stopped.

Artie had left my bed, but he hadn't left my suite. This was really getting to be too much. I would have to put my foot down.

As soon as he came out.

I didn't realize I'd fallen asleep again until his muttered curse woke me.

"Oh, shit," he said indistinctly.

That snapped me fully conscious. "What?"

He appeared in the doorway in a crisp button-down and another pair of baggy, preppy shorts. Just looking at him made me feel slothlike.

"Do you have a redheaded cousin?" he asked nervously.

"All of us are redheads. Why?" I rose on my elbows, and his eyes dropped to my chest. Apparently, my bosom wasn't tempting enough because he looked back at my eyes as I spoke again. "Is that my toothbrush?" He looked at his own large fist blankly, surprised to see what he held. "You were brushing your teeth with my toothbrush?"

Disgusting. Anger woke me up. We were going to have this out right now.

He stopped me. He threw the toothbrush back into the bathroom and stood in front of me, one hand raised like the world's largest traffic cop.

"We've got bigger problems than that. Do you have a red-haired cousin with a dark-haired husband and a small child who is screaming its head off? Yes or no?"

With growing suspicion, I realized I *had* been hearing a crying toddler. "Why?" I got out of bed to head to the window, but he wrapped one meaty hand around my arm and stopped me.

"For fuck's sake, don't go to the window now."

"Why not?"

"Because she just spotted me in your bathroom, brushing my teeth."

"What?" I couldn't wrap my head around it. "Priss just looked at you? What is Priss doing in Langkawi, anyway?"

"Apparently, she's boarding the ship. And if she had this cabin for two weeks, it's a safe bet she knows which windows you've got, and in whose bathroom she just spotted a large man brushing his teeth."

"What the hell were you doing in my bathroom anyway, you creep?"

"Calm down."

"You can't be in my room at all! I thought we only had to worry about people coming in the door. Who the hell knew someone would be looking in from outside? We're on a damned ship! What are we going to do?"

I paced—away from the windows—and he stood with his head down, lost in thought. "Okay. Here's what we're going to do."

He stepped forward and stopped me by putting his large hands on my shoulders.

"First, you're going to calm way, way down. And second, I'm going to give you a fast lesson in believable lying. Ready? Ellyn—focus. I need your attention now."

"Right. Wait, what? I'm a great liar. What are you talking about?"

He shook his head. "You're not. You're a sucker. One of the sheep. But I'm going to turn you into a wolf. For this morning, at least." He ignored my outraged protests. "When your cousin bursts in here in about ten minutes, you're going to be asleep."

"Shit—the bed!" I began remaking it.

"Stop that. She'll never notice."

"This is a woman who has shared a room with me every summer and holiday since the dawn of time. She knows I don't sleep with my feet uncovered. I am a very tidy sleeper. She says I sleep like a princess."

He began making the bed with me in quick and efficient movements that I appreciated, even in my panic. "Really? I hate having my feet covered."

"No kidding." My scorn was apparently evident. The sheet and blanket were completely untucked from the foot of the mattress.

"All right. She's going to wake you from a deep sleep, insisting she saw a man in your bathroom. Now, listen, Ellyn—are you listening?"

"Yeah?"

"You've got to laugh. Laugh at her. Ask her if he looked like Bix."

"Do you mean Bax?"

"Whatever. When she insists, you go to the bathroom door and yank it open to look around—like you're beginning to believe her, and you want to make sure there's no one in there."

"The bathroom! Did you steam it up again?"

"Shit. Yeah." He peered cautiously through the bathroom window. Priss and her family must have already boarded. It wasn't the kind of place where a lot of people got on board, so she'd be through reception in no time. If she let the porter take them to their cabin first, we'd have a few more minutes.

Artie scooped up wet towels from the floor and began wiping all the surfaces. "Ask her to describe the man she saw. You're interested, a little alarmed, and you *do not* contradict her. Got it?"

"I don't?"

"No. You want to know what she saw. Get her to describe me. When she does, you laugh and say she got it wrong by one window. There's a handsome blond guy in the room next to you."

He pointed at the connecting door.

"That won't work," I said. "This room has a balcony, and that one doesn't."

"Don't I know it," he muttered.

I continued, "She'll know she was looking at this suite's bathroom window."

"She won't if you sell it right. Remember how worn out you were when we arrived? The overnight flight from New York? The bus tour of exotic Singapore? Were you in your right mind when you got here?"

I remembered that light-headedness. He saw my understanding and kept going.

"Neither is she. Plus, she's in Langkawi. With a toddler. How did she get here? What's she doing here? Is there any way in hell she's rested and intelligent? No. She'll believe you. Seriously."

"I can do it." There was a chance this would work and our efforts not wasted. "I know how I'll distract her, too—I'll tell her I'm worried the guy in the next cabin is making eyes at Aunt Cor."

"That's brilliant. Nice enhancement. We'll make a wolf out of you yet."

I glared at him.

He went on. "Of course you're worried about it. The only way you wouldn't be worried is if you and I were in this together. In fact, you're worried about me and Sinjie and Marcus fucking Vanderfleet. She'll forget all about spotting me. Good. Okay. Now, get into that bed. No, on your side."

"I think I know how I sleep."

"I think you know how you go to sleep, but you don't know what you look like when you wake up. On your side, curl up, hold that pillow like it's me."

"Oh, fuck off!"

"I'm getting out of here. As soon as they're all in here, I'm heading on deck so there will be no answer when she knocks on the door. Play stupid, play curious, find out what the hell she's doing here. Can you do it?"

"Get out of here."

"Stay calm. You can handle this."

"Get. Out. Of. Here."

The door clicked closed behind him and I lay in bed, wound tight with tension and cursing him for putting me through this.

He was right, though. Not ten minutes later, someone started banging on my door.

I remembered how he'd said to play it, and I let the first one go. She knocked again, and I called out sleepily, "Come in."

The handle moved uselessly, and Priss called out to me. "Ellyn? Who's in there with you?"

"Priss?" I called. Making sure to stumble audibly over a sofa cushion left on the floor, I pulled the door open, making sure my hair was a mess over my eyes.

On the other side, my cousin Priss had her fists on her hips. Behind her, a bleary-eyed Trip held Lovely, who was howling.

And behind them, Luz peered from Cor's door, cracked open on the upheaval. Luz saw me, nodded, and closed the door again.

"What the—Priss?" I let my confusion take over. I looked around to confirm we were on the cruise ship and not on a summer vacation in Nantucket. "What are you doing here?"

She pushed in past me, looking around the suite. "Are you shacking up with some guy?"

"What? Hey, Trip."

Trip nodded at me with a smile I recognized as utterly fake. He held a howling child with indifference. I knew Lovely had been screaming in his ear for so long, he'd tuned her out in self-defense.

"A guy. A big blond guy." She pushed into the bathroom and looked around, confused.

We'd skipped over about six of Artie's steps, but I was well-rested. I could roll with it. "Uh—is there someone in there?"

"No." She came out and looked suspiciously at the bed, made up as neatly as ever.

"What are you doing here?" I pointed Trip to the sofa and plopped on a chair. "We're in Malaysia. Aren't we?"

Trip sat gratefully and his arms unbent slowly, rust practically flaking off the elbow joints. Lovely wriggled off his lap and onto the floor. She ran to her mother and wrapped her arms around Priss's knees, bringing Priss to a halt.

Priss inched over until she could collapse on the bed. She picked up her daughter, but Lovely didn't want to be held. She craned over backward and I thought she'd go tumbling, but Priss just lowered her gently and let the toddler lie on the bed, still howling.

Trip fished a pacifier out of his pocket and tossed it to Priss, who fielded it neatly. She popped it into her daughter's mouth, which closed on it in surprise. Priss rubbed Lovely's stomach, and Lovely visibly relaxed. Within moments, she'd fallen asleep.

All three of us heaved a sigh of relief.

"It's been a very long night," Trip said.

"Can you tell me what is going on?" I said.

"Big blond guy. Bathroom. Right there."

"Did you see him?" I turned to Trip, who needed only a pacifier and someone to rub his stomach to put him to sleep too. He shook his head.

"I can't even see." He grinned, his fatigue etched deep on his blandly handsome face.

I looked at Priss and let awareness dawn in my look. "Oh—really big? Like, big chest? Short blond hair?"

She nodded. I pointed to the connecting door.

"You just miscounted windows. You must be exhausted."

"I beg your pardon—I think I know which windows were ours for two weeks. I *am* tired, that's true, but I'm not that tired. He was to the right of the balcony, not the left."

"Yeah, but he wasn't here, and he *is* next door. He's this novelist guy. Arthur Somebody. He's after Cor, I think."

"What?" Her surprise cut through her jet lag, and she was distracted from arguing about which window he'd been in. *My idea, con man.* "What do you mean, he's after Cor?"

"He's sure paying a lot of attention to her. They're rumba-ing together. You know, there's a whole fleet of guys after her."

"Rumba?" Priss had the *are you speaking a language I speak?* look common to all who have gotten off an intercontinental flight.

"Long story. What are you guys doing here?"

Priss blinked at me and pasted on a patently fake smile. "We've come to help!"

"Help?"

"With Cor! So you and I can win!"

"I don't understand. What do you mean?"

"I've been talking to Luz. She said Cor was distracted and talking about what a good fashion designer Liv is. I can't have the twins splitting this pot, Ellyn. You and I have got to win."

"So you flew your family in from Connecticut to get back on this ship?"

She smiled in triumph. "We'll be with you all the way to Sri Lanka."

I tried to wrap my head around how this would help. "Sri Lanka?" I repeated, trying to make sense of it.

"I'm going to help you."

"But—this is my turn with Cor."

"Oh, I won't get in the way of that. Besides, if you win, we win. If I win, we win. Doesn't matter who Cor likes best, right?"

Her mildly crazed eyes could just have been jet lag, but I'd now been around a con artist for long enough to question the motives even of people I'd trusted—like my cousin. Were her intentions really so pure? I'd withhold final judgment.

Trip roused himself from his stupor. "Priss, let's settle this later. Can we go to our cabin now?"

Priss kicked off her shoes. "Oh, we'll stay here. Ellyn will swap with us."

"Excuse me—I'll do what?"

She turned, untucking her tidy travel blouse from her neat travel slacks. "Well, there are three of us. We should have this room, and you can stay on deck two. It's only fair. Besides, Lovely is already asleep."

Her logic gave her a predatory grin.

"She can nap here, but then you guys have to go to your cabin."

"Don't be unreasonable, Ellyn."

"Unreasonable?" I stood, the better to handle the emotions rippling through me. "This cabin is across the hall from Cor. This is my time with her."

Not to mention this cabin had a connecting door to my partner in crime. Well, my partner. Not crime, exactly . . .

"But this is where we stayed when we were on board before." This seemed to be definitive to Priss. It was not to me.

"It's where I'm staying now. Priss—you've got to stay in your own cabin."

"It's a double. On deck two. We can't be expected to stay there, and not with Lovely. Why, she had that room all to herself before! She's used to having her own space." She pointed with an imperious finger at the connecting door.

"Well, we don't have that room anymore." I put a hand on her shoulder and nudged her to the door. "Take your husband. Go to your cabin. Get some sleep. I'll watch Lovely, and we'll talk later."

Priss glared at me. "This is not going as I had intended."

I shrugged. She glared at Trip.

"Bring the baby."

She stormed out, and he nodded and stood. Tiredly, he scooped up his daughter (who never even came close to waking), smiled at me, and followed her out.

Damn. I needed to find Artie.

CHAPTER SIXTEEN—ARTIE

THE ARRIVAL OF THE COUSIN WAS AN INTERESTING TURN OF events. Before I'd ducked out of my cabin, I'd overheard Priss tell Ellyn about discussions with Luz, the morose maid. Ellyn thought nothing of it because she was basically an honest person. Also known as a sucker.

To me, that was the most interesting moment of the conversation.

What had Luz said? And to whom had Luz said it? Who else was liable to show up as surprise voyagers on our opulent little cruise ship?

If Ellyn was to be believed, two of the cousins (the un-twin-like twins) had formed a pact to split the five million if either of them won it. So Priss and Ellyn had entered into a matching agreement in self-defense.

But whose idea had this been? The twins? Or was it the suggestion of a master puppeteer?

Was Luz quietly yanking strings and keeping herself in extra pocket money by selling information to three of the four cousins?

And if so, why wouldn't she offer to sell it to Ellyn too?

Of course, I knew why. It was because Ellyn was a natural

mark. She believed the best in people. She was the kind of person who would walk up to a stranger in a Starbucks and pay to photograph their black eye and never wonder if that black eye belonged to a good or bad person.

Ellyn really didn't know what a scoundrel was.

If I weren't already planning on taking advantage of that, she would have aroused long-dormant protective urges in me. I ruthlessly pushed those sentiments away. As Victor liked to say— *don't get to liking your marks. They are not your friends. They are your meal ticket.*

Right.

I went on deck to score some breakfast. Already I had a reputation brewing with women who got up early enough to covertly observe my routine in the gym. This morning's extra ab work had been received with a murmur of approval. And most of the staff knew I'd pay for information, so I had a good reputation going there too.

Breakfast was very productive, and I made my contact for tomorrow's Burmese side trip. I texted Terence the Accountant to finalize the details.

By the time Cor appeared with her entourage, my mood was excellent. And we had a full house this morning, as Sinjie pulled up a chair to have a cup of coffee with us, and later Marcus dragged over an entire table and then an umbrella to ensure he wasn't sitting in the sun.

And at last, the third of Cor's purported hopeful lovers appeared: a slim boy named Brock who had made an art out of leaning.

"Hello," he murmured through a fall of black hair, leaning and looming at Ellyn.

She took one look at him and laughed out loud, for which I decided I would soon kiss her. "Honey, I have no money at all." She shook his hand, though. As usual.

"Pity." He leered at her, holding the grip for a moment too

long. Then he grabbed a chair and sat behind Cor, resting his hands on her shoulders and massaging.

Cor, surprised, jerked around. "Oh, Brock dear, there you are. Where have you been?"

"Busy," he said with a flick of mobile eyebrows. He attempted to imbue his words with great meaning, but now both Ellyn and I were laughing, and he didn't like that. He glared at me.

I did nothing more than flex my pectoral muscles at him, and he winced. We established a pecking order in that minute.

Marcus, however, was immune.

"I suppose you're going shopping again today," he said with a patronizing and paternal air.

"Oh no," Cor said. "There's practically nothing to buy on the island."

"Really." Marcus favored her with a smile. "So, I can have you today?"

Cor shivered in alarmed excitement. "I beg your pardon. What on earth did you have in mind?" She gave him a coy smile.

"Langkawi Sky Bridge. It's this pedestrian walkway high in the air. Said to have great views. And you can take a tram, so you don't get all sweaty hiking to the top."

"That sounds . . ."

"What about kayaking?" I asked. They turned to me. "See the world from water level. Unless you don't want the exercise?" I blinked innocently at Marcus.

Oh, now he'd gotten the message.

He swelled his barrel chest at me and grinned. "Not at all. I like to take some exercise every day. I'm good with kayaking—if that's what Corinne wants to do."

Cor and Rebel were exchanging uncertain glances. "I'm not very strong," she said unnecessarily.

"Don't give it another thought," Marcus said grandly. "I'll put you with me, and I'll be your power. Artie here can take you, Rebel."

They all swiveled to look at Ellyn. "What?" she asked. Then, confronted with their expectations, she pulled out the daily activity sheet and her phone and soon she had the whole thing arranged. She didn't seek leadership, and yet leadership was often thrust upon her. Sucker. *The price of competency, Red.*

I simply smiled. It was a ship-based expedition, and I already owned the staff.

"Wait," Cor said. "Luz said Priss is back on board! We'll need another kayak for Priss and Trip."

"Doubtful," Ellyn said. "My bet is that we won't see them until tonight. They were exhausted when they came onboard."

"You children. You tire out so easily! All right—just the seven of us, then."

"Bathing suits and shirts, then? Shall we say in an hour?" I smiled at them all. "Don't forget your sunblock!"

Marcus turned away, discounting my words. *Fine with me. You're playing right into my plans. With best wishes from Victor.*

We'd all separated to prepare, and I waited a bit before knocking on the connecting door. Ellyn pulled it open with an expression of distrust. I held up her sunscreen.

"Where the hell did you get that? I thought I had that hidden."

"Do my back for me."

"What? No. Get out of here. And give me that."

I let her take the sunblock from my hand and followed her in. "Come on, help me out. I'm going to cook Marcus."

"You're what, now?"

I took off my shirt and sat on the bed, facing away from her. "He's a golf player. I guarantee he wears one of those stupid hats, and he's got a bald patch like the melting polar ice cap. He's ignored it under the 'if I can't see it, it doesn't exist' theory, and it will fry in the sun."

She sat behind me, and her hands began smoothing the lotion over my shoulders. I resisted the urge to purr and flex and kept talking instead. "I'm going to humiliate him."

"How?"

"The guy who does the kayaks. I've already paid him. Anyway, I'll get Cor in with me and give him Rebel. Then I'll push him with a pace that will wear him out, and he won't put on any sunblock. We'll stay out all morning. By lunch, he'll be wiped out and cooked, but he won't realize how bad his sunburn is until around dinnertime. He's going to have a fever and chills. And a few days later, he's going to start to peel. He'll look like a leper. Get below the waistband, will you?"

She didn't fall for it. "I think you can do that part yourself."

"Okay, give me that. I'll do you."

"I beg your pardon." But she turned and pulled the red braid out of the way. She wore a racing tank under a sarong tied at the hips and looked like a modern-day Aphrodite.

I put the lotion on my hands and made sure to get under the straps of her suit. "He's my biggest competition, and I can get rid of him for days with one morning on the water. Quit wiggling."

"You don't have to put sunblock there." She tried to squirm away, but I pulled her closer again and raised her arm over her head with one hand while running the lotion around her armpit, headed toward one creamy, luscious breast.

"You get a sunburn here, and you'll be the one with the fever. Come on—I'm not trying to feel you up. Sit still."

I made her let me put sunblock under the other arm too. Then I handed it to her.

"After you do the rest of you, take this to your aunt and make sure she's covered." Ellyn didn't like taking directions, but this was important. "Get the part in her hair, the tops of her feet, and her *armpits*," I said with significance. "Get her ears. Her, I need healthy and happy. Got it?"

"Stop telling me what to do. And I think your plan could be improved."

"Excuse me?"

She was thinking. Then she caught me with a direct gaze from green eyes. "Yeah. You're wrong to put Cor in with you.

Get the guy to insist that Cor go with Sinjie or Brock. The kayaks need to be balanced, so you go with Marcus."

As she spoke, I saw it. Especially with my shirt off, I didn't need to separate from Marcus. I needed to get as close to him as I could, so the contrast between us was as obvious as possible. "Nice," I admitted. "Do I want the front or the back?"

"Doesn't matter. As long as you guys are a little in front of Cor, she'll have a great view of both of you at the same time. And you're going to look . . . better." She flexed her hands like she was still putting sunblock on me, and I grinned.

"You're a devil. That's exactly how it's going to play out." *Smart girl.* "Now go finish putting on the sunblock. And make sure your aunt's protected."

She pushed me through our connecting door. "I know how to put on sunblock. Redhead, remember? We're going to need more."

"Good thing you had a second tube in your camera bag. Boy, it's like Aladdin's cave in there. I didn't get through half the pockets."

"Get out!"

We met an hour later at the dock. Already my plan was working. Marcus and Sinjie both had pale, old-man legs, while I've done work to get an even tan. And heaven knows I earned these calves in the gym.

Rebel and Cor were both in tent-like cover-ups and giggling like girls. They both smelled good—like Ellyn's sunblock, and that bode well.

Brock had shown up. He ogled Ellyn even as he maneuvered to stand next to Cor, and I watched Ellyn's utter disinterest with satisfaction. *Back off, bucko. My niece's creamy breasts are not for the likes of you.*

Brock had opted to "forget" his shirt and he flexed his pecs at me.

I laughed and pulled off my shirt. I flared my lats at him,

emphasizing my big shoulders and narrow waist. *Pull-downs. Side planks. Oblique twists. Crunches. Read 'em and weep, kid.*

Brock blinked, and Marcus took advantage. He had Cor firmly by the elbow as we approached the kayaks, and I let him do it. *Go ahead, boss man. See what happens.*

What happened was that Basilio's cousin, Datu, decided the weight in the boats needed to be more evenly balanced. He put Marcus in a kayak with me. *That's right.*

I tossed my shirt to the deck and looked a challenge at Marcus. He couldn't keep his shirt on after that. As suspected, there was no evidence of sunblock on his chest, shoulders, or back. He had muscles—but they were coated by a generous layer of fat. This would be too easy.

Marcus insisted on sitting behind me, "where the power comes from."

I acquiesced. "Certainly."

The dark horse, Brock, got the honor of sitting behind Cor, who entered her kayak with a nervous titter. And Sinjie found himself forced to be gracious about squiring Rebel.

Ellyn was given a one-man kayak. She was delighted; she'd rented a waterproof camera from the ship store, and she was thrilled she needn't appeal to anyone else or lead the others to go where she wanted to take her photos.

The water was still and crystalline over a perfectly visible sandy bottom, where fish darted and sea grasses waved in the gentle currents. We followed a tree-lined shore, lush in greenery and accented with stately palm trees. Any movie shot here would have to be a romance. Maybe I could understand now why people were always trying to spend their winters in the islands. It beat the hell out of slush and an overcrowded subway car.

As Ellyn had advised, I set a steady pace that kept us just ahead of Cor so she could see Marcus's naked back and mine. Let her contrast and compare the two of us from an impartial place of judgment. I worked on my traps, rhomboids, and serratus muscles all the time. My back looked good.

If I had any compassion at all, I would have taken mercy on the guy. But he stood between me and a quarter-million payoff . . . and possibly the marriage to the auntie of my dreams.

Sorry, Marcus. Should have shaved your back. And used even a bit of sunscreen. *Can't say I didn't warn you, boss man.*

Ellyn stayed with the group for as long as it took to get past the boat harbor. Then she followed her own path, drawn by images I couldn't see or possible viewpoints no one else expected. The quiet click of her camera echoed over the water, often followed by a soft "yeah" of satisfaction. As long as she remained in sight, we didn't have to worry about her.

The morning was brilliant, the breeze cooled any sweat, the sound traveled easily over the water so we could talk from boat to boat. And I didn't have to see the bald patch on Marcus's head to know it was cooking. Unless he'd been very careful with some high-quality sunblock, the rest of him was too.

How satisfying.

Thank you for the ghostly reminder, Victor. His wisdom had outlived him. *Don't out-bully a bully. Humiliate him instead.* It was so simple.

Cor wanted to see what was around the point of rocks before us, and what Cor wanted, this group would move heaven and earth (not to mention tropical blue seas) to get. Off we set—not rushing, but certainly pulling with more determination than previously.

The rhythm of the paddling settled into my bones. Occasionally Marcus would "accidentally" catch his oar in the wavelets and splash me, but it was more cooling than annoying, and when I didn't rise to the bait, he gave up.

"Isn't this lovely!" Cor was having a good time, and Brock attempted to whisper sweet nothings to her and failed, since we could all hear everything he said. His sallies were mostly considered entertaining jokes and inspired laughter rather than sighs.

Things were working out nicely. When Cor's kayak pulled

away from mine, I started to croon a teasing love song to her, singing an old Irving Berlin classic.

"What'll I do . . . when you . . . are far . . . away? And I . . . am blue? What'll I do?"

It was better than singing in the shower; the water created an ideal acoustical space, and I sounded great. I kept going—but with the next line, something changed.

Someone was singing a harmony.

I looked around. It was Ellyn, paddling a little away and lost in her own thoughts, singing as easily as if she were all alone.

And she could sing.

I stayed with the melody and she flipped about, sometimes creating a high harmony, sometimes lacing her voice with mine, sometimes taking the low line.

"What'll I do . . . when I . . . am wondering who . . . is kissing you? What'll I do?"

It gave me goose bumps, it was so beautiful.

I thought she was unmoved until she glanced at me with a shy smile. We went through the entire song. When I forgot a verse, she remembered, and when she forgot, I remembered. We made it all the way through the hauntingly lovely song, and I forgot completely about Cor and the obstacles and the painful solar radiation now soaking into Marcus.

There was only her voice and mine, joining together and creating something wonderful.

The hair on my head stood up, and I'd forgotten to paddle entirely by the end. Ellyn was smiling, and her nipples were pebbled. We were both digging it.

The others applauded. "Wonderful!" Cor cried. "That was so fine! Sing something else now!"

"Yes, by all means," Sinjie said, not meaning it.

"Damn," Brock said. "That was hot."

"It was like dancing!" Rebel's comment was innocent, but it jerked me to awareness. There was someone I was supposed to be forming an unseen, powerful connection with, and it wasn't the gorgeous redhead. It was her aunt.

"What if we all sang something?" I suggested.

"Like what?" Marcus growled.

When in doubt, look to the classics. "Tea . . . for two," I sang, "and two . . . for tea . . ." Even Brock knew it.

"It's me, for you—and you, for me. Can't you see how happy we would be?" Within a few notes, everyone was singing, everyone was laughing, everyone was having a wonderful time.

But the hairs at the back of my neck were still standing up.

The skin on my forearms was still showing goose bumps.

And I felt a silvery connection to Ellyn, unbroken no matter what we sang or said or did.

Uh-oh. Trouble.

CHAPTER SEVENTEEN—ELLYN

ARTIE WAS ARROGANT.

He was one of the vainest men I'd ever met.

He was a liar and a thief and a cheat. He was everything I hated.

And I couldn't get him out of my heartbeat.

If he'd never opened his mouth, I would have been fine. If he'd never sung a note, I could have existed for the rest of my life happily ignoring a con man in favor of sweet, uncomplicated Bax.

But he had to start singing. And Irving Berlin, at that.

It was a song just begging for harmony, and I was singing before I even thought about it. And now I had a web of notes stretching invisibly between me and that scam artist, and I didn't know what to do about it.

Suddenly, his spine rippled with muscles. Suddenly, his smile dazzled. Suddenly, his deep voice calling across the water was a magnet.

I began to get quite fussy about the whole thing. *Damn him.*

We finished our kayaking trip where we started, and the staff, in the shadows of the enormous cruise ship, advised us to enjoy a lovely swim from the beach a few steps away.

The water was cool after our paddling. The colors were stunning, the chance to float in blueness surrounded by blueness was hypnotic, and I stayed well away from the largest, most beautiful member of our party. And he stayed away from me.

I focused my attention on the way light entered the camera underwater. I've read studies on how to photograph or film coral reefs, and this was the first time I'd had a chance to play with it. I had pretty good lungs and I could stay underwater for a while, but I yearned for a snorkel before long.

Nevertheless, I got some great pictures of fish, and a wonderful one of Rebel and Cor giggling that I took with the camera half-submerged, so their bodies floated gracefully below their laughing faces. That was a keeper.

And I got one shot of a very long, strong pair of legs stretched out across the water, defined by mouth-watering muscles.

No. Delete that one.

I returned to photographing fish with fixed determination.

Soon, Cor announced she was hungry. It was time to get ready for lunch, she said, and we all needed to shower in our cabins and meet on deck.

Obedient to our queen, we did as we were told.

Cor and Rebel were giggling all the way to our cabins, and Artie followed us with a benevolent smile on his arrogant face. We all chortled happily and let ourselves into our rooms, and there was silence at last.

I leaned against my closed door and looked blankly at the suite, already perfectly made up by the silent stewards who came and went without a sound. The chilled air was icy on my wet skin.

But I could still hear the song. Not with my outer ear, no—the sound was still resonating inside me.

I stood at the connecting door.

And then I opened my side.

And he opened his side.

"I'm sorry," he said.

"I know."

"This is a real mess."

I nodded. "A real mess."

"What'll we do?"

It was an unconscious echo of the song's lyric. I shrugged. And we stared at each other.

Someone moved. Me? Him? We met in the doorway, and his hand all but burned my skin as it slid to my waist.

I reached up and slid my hand along his cheek, his jaw, over muscles clenched with wanting.

I leaned in.

He leaned in.

"Such a mistake," I whispered.

"A really, really bad idea."

His breath was on my skin, and his scent was in my nose, and I arched up that tiny bit farther . . .

And his lips were on mine. So lightly. Barely moving.

It was like being hit with electricity.

I gasped lightly and he pulled me closer, my chilled breasts brushing against his sun-soaked body. He inhaled—did I smell as good to him as he did to me?—and leaned down.

In one moment, it was skin against skin, and in the next, it was a kiss. We'd taken a step somehow, passed through an invisible border. We'd hit a transition. I held him to me, and he folded me into him, and this time when I gasped, his tongue slid against mine, strong and soft and electric.

A burst of adrenaline went straight to my crotch.

I slanted my head to pull him closer, and he bent me over his arm. I clung to him, dizzy with excitement. His cock, suddenly hard, pressed against me, and I moved my hips for the reward of his moan. That low, rumbling noise excited me as Bax never had.

That was the thought that brought me to awareness: sweet Bax, who didn't deserve this. I pulled back, panting.

"Holy shit, Ellyn," he muttered.

"Damn." I was still stroking his cheek, and I made myself stop. I held my hands up, braced against the air so I didn't brush against him. He surrendered his grip on me, and I stepped away.

It was too intense. My desire morphed through confusion and straight into anger. That seemed the safest reaction. "You had to sing, didn't you?"

He'd ridden the same wave of emotions and came back at me with the same anger. "Well, how the hell did I know? Nobody said you had to add the harmony."

I still shivered from his touch, and he was still hard, but we were determined to ignore that. I had a boyfriend. I wasn't a disloyal person. And I couldn't be all over Artie if I expected him to romance my aunt.

Which he had to do if he wanted his payday.

Oddly, that thought stung, although it shouldn't have. Artie had never pretended otherwise about his motivations. He was here for money and nothing more. I increased the distance between us by stiff-legged footsteps and put my hand on my side of the connecting doors. "Don't touch me again."

"Well, don't harmonize when I sing."

"Don't sing. I'm taking a shower. You'll have to use your own damn bathroom."

"I'm fine with that."

The doors slammed shut together.

It was too much. My eye fell on Lovely's pacifier, which she'd dropped as she'd fallen asleep. The steward had placed it on a lace doily next to the bed. A hysterical burst of laughter welled up in me. I was overwrought. What had the steward thought when he found a pacifier in my room?

Was it any worse than a con man in my bed?

All this, and now Priss. Things were getting out of hand. I was losing control.

I'd get it back. I straightened my shoulders, determined to pull my shattered nerve endings under some semblance of control. No more singing with Artie. No more nothing with

Artie. I would get my money and build my production company and become a director and never lose control. Mock and I would be extremely successful.

And Bax, I thought guiltily. *Bax would be there. And . . . and we would be happy.*

Right.

I took a shower and stood under the stream for far too long, hoping the warm water would soothe me.

I joined Cor and Rebel on deck for lunch, sitting under the cool lattice umbrellas. I wished for distance between me and Artie, but Cor wanted me to bond with her, and I wanted her to fall for Artie. There was no hope for it. We were going to have to spend the afternoon together after finding ourselves in a kiss that had lit an unfortunate fire in my libido.

And I simply refused to consider what might happen if he came to sleep in my bed that night.

Determined to remain calm, I waited and smiled and asked if we were waiting for Priss before ordering lunch. "Are she and Trip and Lovely still asleep?"

"Oh, let them rest up from their journey," Cor said breezily. "Like you said, it'll probably be dinnertime before we see them. Life gets so much more complicated with a toddler." Marcus appeared, his skin already an alarming pink, and pulled out a seat at the head of the table. *Sunblock is critical, Marcus. Don't you know that?* Sinjie sat by me. Even Brock appeared and wedged in between Cor and Rebel. He ate off of Cor's plate and teased her and drove everyone else up the wall.

But no Artie. Where was he?

Lunch was over, and Marcus revisited his idea of the tram up to the Sky Bridge for a lovely stroll with a million-dollar view.

"That sounds heavenly! Ellyn, will you help us figure out how to arrange that?"

I had already pulled out my phone. "How many tickets shall I buy?"

"Let's see—are we all going? Yes? Why, where's Arthur? I think he'd like to come, don't you?"

Marcus puffed up. "We don't need him, Cor. I'll take you." He meant he'd escort her, since Cor would—as usual—be paying for everything.

"Oh, let's find out. Ellyn, call his cabin, won't you?"

I found a house phone at the bar and pulled it over to Cor. I helped her to dial his cabin.

"Oh, Arthur dear! Won't you . . . Oh, I see . . . No, that's . . . are you sure? Oh. Certainly. Three o'clock? Can we be back by then?"

I nodded yes, Marcus shook his head no.

"Yes, dear. I'll meet you in the yoga studio at three. We'll perfect our rumba. Goodbye, dear—happy reading!"

She hung up and turned to us. "He's lost in that book of his about Borneo."

"Burma?" I asked.

"Burma, that's right. He's so dedicated to his craft. Well, three handsome men and three lovely women! Won't this be a delightful outing!"

I bought the tickets and arranged for the transportation. And the view from the Sky Bridge really was lovely, if slightly unnerving.

The bridge arched away from the mountain until we were walking over nothing. The sea stretched away in all directions, the verdant mountains behind us. Clear panels at the midpoint were designed to remove all sense of stability, and Cor and Rebel cooed in excited fear. Their escorts manfully walked them across the bridge.

Brock attempted to lean on me. I looked at him with a laugh.

"I'm not kidding. I really haven't got a dime, you know."

He stopped leering. "Really? Nothing? You're her niece, right?"

"Right. But she's the one with access to the family trust. Go lean on her."

"Too much competition. You're really hot. You want to bang later?"

"Thanks. A nice offer. But no."

"Not for money," he assured me. "Just for fun?"

I wasn't sure who was supposed to be paying who, but neither direction appealed to me. "No thanks. I have a boyfriend."

"It's not James Blond, is it? Because that guy's a total scam artist."

I bit off a laugh at the name, as well as the surprisingly accurate assessment. "James Blond. That's funny. No, not that guy. My boyfriend is in New York."

He shrugged and eyed Cor, ahead of us with Rebel. "Okay. Let me know if you change your mind."

"Good luck," I said with sudden sympathy for him.

"Yeah. I'm younger than all those guys. She'll figure it out." He leered at me. "Stamina." I was sorry I'd wished him luck.

"Great."

He swaggered off, and I photographed the steel girders against the forested hillside below. That was the best part of the trip.

Reading about Burma. Huh—like anyone believed that.

The walk was short. We were easily back to the ship by three, and Marcus—who hadn't benefitted from another hour in the sun—was annoyed to see Artie, beaming with approval and looking fresh, young, and glowing in a white shirt at the top of the gangway.

"Let's get ready to rummmmbbbbaaaaa!" Artie's call made us all look up, and Cor laughed delightedly.

Marcus grumbled. "I could dance with you." He was petulant and not at all swaggering.

"Oh, you sweet thing." Cor patted an absent hand against his chest and didn't notice him wince; he was more than a little sunburned. "You know you have two left feet. We've already tried. I'll see you for cocktails before dinner—and don't forget, we've got the Balinese dancers in the theater tonight before bridge. So exciting!"

Rebel and I were her attendants as she swept up the ramp to the ship, where Artie put her on his arm with warm appreciation. Sinjie and Marcus followed more slowly, and Brock had disappeared entirely. Cor was definitely having a better time than most of her suitors.

"I'd say we definitely have a leading contender," Rebel whispered to me.

"Looks like," I said. "And Cor looks like she's having a good time."

"Oh, she's having a blast."

"Then that's good."

"Agreed."

Luz met us at the yoga studio and helped Cor change into heels. Rebel and I took our accustomed place along the wall. I'd have to check the schedule again; did anyone ever use this space for yoga? I could stand some guided relaxation.

Luz sat near us in silence as the rhythms of Cuban music filled the space. She lingered instead of fading away, and I wondered idly why.

Then the answer appeared in the doorway.

"Aunt Cor!"

Priss had woken up.

Cor broke away from Artie's gentle hold. "Priss, there you are! Sweetheart—what on earth are you doing here?"

"I came back! I couldn't bear to be away from you any longer!"

She made a show of embracing Cor, kissing her cheek, and Luz looked at me significantly.

This confused me. *What? What are you telling me?*

Luz shook her head faintly and looked away. Rebel leaned in.

"So, here's niece number one, coming to horn in on the time of niece number four."

"That's not what she's doing," I protested loyally, but Luz looked at me again. Was it?

"I had such a wonderful time with you. Didn't we have a good time? I just had to join you for the last leg of the trip!"

"Well, that's heavenly, dear. And I must say—it will be nice to get to know you better without your husband and daughter around. She's precious, but she is a handful, your little girl!"

Priss froze. "They're still asleep. Downstairs."

"Oh. Well, that will be nice too!" Clever Cor. She knew Trip and Lovely had come back with Priss.

My cousin realized that bringing her toddler back might not have been the best idea and hurried to recover. "But we're still going to have a wonderful time together, just you and me!"

Luz glared at me. *What? Oh, all right.*

I stood. "And me. Don't forget about me."

They turned to look at me, Cor with relief and Priss with annoyance. "Of course! Here's Ellyn!" Cor reached out her hand, and the three of us found ourselves awkwardly holding hands in the middle of the yoga studio, "Bésame Mucho" crooning away in the background.

"Might I beg an introduction?" a deep voice said, and Artie stepped away from the wall.

"Certainly!" Cor used his intervention to release our hands. "Priss, this is Arthur Petrovitch, an author of some renown." Artie looked modest. "And this is my niece, Priss Wolcott Conner. She's here with her husband, Trip, and dear, sweet, little Lovely."

"Delighted to meet you," Artie said smoothly. Priss, confronted by Artie's size and blond beauty up close, blinked in silence at him. "And do you dance as well as your aunt?"

Artie clearly wasn't interested in a response, as he turned to Cor and took her hand, pulling her to him in a gentle tug. She laughed.

"It's our rehearsal time, Priss. We'll talk in a bit."

I dragged Priss to our bench. Luz had disappeared, apparently having witnessed what she came to see.

"That's the guy I saw in your bathroom," Priss said stupidly. Rebel looked at me with interest.

I shook my head, feigning disinterest. "Not my bathroom, remember? He's got the cabin next to mine. You saw him in his window. Not mine."

"Oh. Right." She watched Artie and Cor move through their dance. They'd gotten pretty good, and it was worth it to watch them. "This is the guy you think is after Cor's money?"

Rebel leaned in to conspire with us. "He's one of three!"

"Four," I amended. "Don't forget about Brock."

"Oh, that puppy." Rebel dismissed the young man. "She doesn't care about him at all."

Priss still watched the dancers. "I spotted Sinjie and Brock when I was here before, but they're nothing. Does she care about this one?"

"We think he's the front-runner," I said.

"I can see why. I mean—damn." Priss inhaled as she watched Artie guide our aunt into a perfect spin, catching her in a brief and graceful dip. Rebel and I sighed in agreement.

"Gigolo, though," Rebel said.

"Definitely," I agreed. No sense in implying I was on the gigolo's side.

"Well, I'll bet he's worth every penny." Priss was a convert too. I resolutely ignored the fact that I knew the thrill of this would-be gigolo's tongue against mine. That was not helpful information here. "She definitely looks like she's enjoying herself. Clearly, I got here just in time."

That furled my brow. *What are you saying?* "What does that mean?" I asked.

Priss tried to pass off her comment. "I just mean—it's good you and I are here while she's having her wonderful time. She's sure to . . . you know."

She looked at Rebel, who smiled like a cat.

I filled Priss in. "Rebel knows about the legacy. She's up to speed."

"Oh. Well, good." Priss collapsed against the bench. "I mean, we want to make sure she's having a better time with us than she did with Liv or Farrah."

"Seems to me like she was having a great time with just Ellyn," Rebel said with a smirk. "I don't see that you're needed here."

"Oh, Rebel." Priss swatted her arm playfully and changed the subject. "Now—who will be at our table for dinner tonight?"

Yep. Priss was complicating things. A lot. Like I didn't already have enough trouble with Artie perpetually going maverick on me. Some people are almost impossible to direct.

CHAPTER EIGHTEEN—ARTIE

CLEARLY, DINNER THAT NIGHT WOULD BE A MADHOUSE. FAR too many suitors; a fistfight might break out due to too much aging testosterone. Plus, there was the matter of the battling nieces, plus a toddler. I wasn't a fan of the very, very young. They didn't seem to have any respect for reason.

I offered my regrets as soon as I was invited. Fortunately, I'd run into two of the people I'd met onboard (Hannie and Chris Kettlesworth, wealthy and boring and kind) and had already arranged to meet them for dinner. After all, it wouldn't do to pursue Cor with too much eagerness. I could scare her off; she clearly thought men made a habit of ignoring women. With her history, she might respond well to my smiling rejection. That could be normal and even comforting to her.

Shame. She deserved to actually be treated with respect. Despite myself, I was coming to like Cor.

So, distance was important at this point.

I waved from across the room at the Wolcott party as they were seated in the restaurant. I enjoyed dinner without a toddler off her schedule, to say nothing of the two suitors. Sinjie was losing his British accent by the minute, and Marcus had turned an alarming shade of red and was beginning to shiver visibly.

The morose maid, Luz, had been deputized as a babysitter and was the last member of the overcrowded table for eight. I turned away with a smile, pleased to be out of the scrum and to be seen in the presence of people who were enjoying me. Let Cor see and know I wasn't always at her beck and call.

I kept an eye on the table without seeming to, and I saw when Ellyn opened her ever-present camera bag and pulled out one of the thin wool shawls she'd bought in Kuala Lumpur. She passed it to her aunt, who smiled her thanks and wrapped herself happily.

Ellyn had two shawls in the bag, which I knew because I'd already taken a complete inventory. She was reaching for the second one when she noticed Rebel shivering. With a sigh, she handed it over, and Rebel, too, wrapped up in warmth. Both of the older women thanked Ellyn, and she brushed away their gratitude.

It was a tiny moment. Nothing. And yet it was the key to Ellyn's personality.

She was capable. People followed her instinctively and did what she told them . . . and she was kind, even when her kindness left her covered in goose bumps and hunched forward to hide pert, chilled nipples from the view of others.

Well, that part was only smart. No one other than me should have been looking at those nipples anyway.

The larger point was—Ellyn was a sucker. She'd suffer so someone else wouldn't. That was something I could exploit.

And I wasn't used to feeling guilty about that.

Sheep were prey, and wolves hunted them for sport and sustenance. That's the way it had always been, the way it should be. It wasn't natural for a wolf to protect its dinner.

By the time we got to the Balinese dancers in the ship's theater, Luz had disappeared with the grumpy toddler, to everyone's relief except (I assumed) Luz, and Priss had sent her husband to get her a sweater.

They sat in a cluster on the benches, and I eyed the lineup.

There was plenty to deduce from how they'd arranged themselves. Cor and Rebel, swathed in their borrowed shawls, were in the center, of course, with Marcus and Sinjie to either side. Priss and Trip couldn't worm their way any closer, and Priss wasn't hiding her irritation very well.

Brock had reappeared from the bar, having opted to drink his dinner. He sat in front of Cor—rather, he leaned back over the low bench to lay his head on Cor's knees, and she laughed at his foolishness.

And Ellyn, to the far side of Marcus, began to turn blue from the cold.

I sat behind Cor, and she greeted me with pleasure. "Let's see if this dance troupe is as good as we are, Arthur, dear!"

Her words annoyed Marcus, Sinjie, and Brock. Priss and Trip weren't too pleased either. But Cor and Rebel were having a wonderful time, and that was all that mattered.

It was clear to me that Brock wouldn't offer Ellyn his jacket, and Sinjie feigned obliviousness to her goose bumps—likely, his jacket hid a less-than-perfect shirt underneath. It didn't look like Sinjie had had too much success as a gigolo lately.

And Marcus shivered almost as much as she did, although his was from sunburn and not from being a slim woman in a light, sleeveless dress in a theater chilled like a walk-in freezer.

She was a sheep, and I was a wolf. She was there to use, not to protect.

And yet . . . she was shivering. And helping out wouldn't cost me a thing.

So, I waited until the lights went down and dropped my jacket over her shoulders. She startled at the first brush of cloth and shot me a grateful look. She pulled it around her, and I ignored the flush of possessiveness I felt at giving her the warmth of my body, along with the lines of an excellent blue blazer.

The dancers were graceful and colorful and could move in surprising ways, holding their hands and fingers in positions I couldn't achieve without surgical intervention. They held my attention for almost three minutes. Alas, the dancing went on for more than an hour.

Instead, I reviewed the things that mattered and mentally discussed them with the ghost of Victor.

How to increase Cor's affections for me, and how to manipulate Marcus into positions of humiliation based on his age, weight, and basic lack of respect for even a minimal skin care regimen.

How to ensure I could get into and then out of Myanmar with my package, undetected and safe.

How the lights from the stage caught Ellyn's profile and made a soft nimbus of her hair.

What Priss was doing here, and how Luz was in on this mess of a journey.

Victor was silent on most of these topics, but I knew he would have frowned at me when I admired Ellyn. *Don't be an idiot, darling,* he would have said. *You can find a pretty girl anywhere. Keep your dick in your pants and your eye on your mission. Once you've got the money, you can have your pick of pussy—if you insist on that kind of thing.*

Victor had an annoying habit of so often being right. He knew more about grifting than I would ever know—plus being a remarkable carnival barker. He was the one who had lifted me from the roustabout crew when I was seventeen. He was the reason I knew I could keep conning suckers past my physical prime. Age could even be an advantage in a lot of cons; Victor proved that. And he'd begun my education when I was just a teen.

I know you're perfectly enormous, boy, he'd said, *and they need you to lug electrical cables and whatever else it is you do for this fly-by-night operation. But I've heard you speak. You've got the gift. You can dazzle with your tongue as well as with your most luscious body.*

He'd leered at me, and I'd known what he wanted. We struck a deal that very night. He'd teach me to be a barker; I'd please him physically. I became his apprentice, and my low-level scams took a huge leap in quality. I learned a great deal, he died relatively happy, and I missed him to this day.

And I know what he would have thought about Ellyn. In my mind's eye, he was shaking his elegant, shabby, gray head. *No. Not that one, dear boy. That one is your kryptonite.*

I'd never gone wrong listening to him before, but I wasn't sure I could follow his path this time. She just looked so good in my jacket.

But I was still in control.

Wasn't I?

CHAPTER NINETEEN—ARTIE

IT CAME AS NO SURPRISE TO ME WHEN MARCUS BEGGED OFF that evening's bridge game almost before the lights came up at the end of the dance troupe's performance. The man had been shivering harder than Ellyn. He tottered off to the elevators, not caring that he was leaving the field to his rivals.

He would have cared, too, for this was the night Cor announced she would teach me how to play bridge. "And Ellyn too!" She linked her arm through Ellyn's.

"Oh, not Ellyn," Priss said dismissively. "We've tried to teach her for years. She's hopeless."

The older cousin cut out the younger cousin, stepping between Ellyn and Cor and taking her aunt's arm. "Come on, Aunt Cor—Trip and I will partner against you and Rebel. Let's go!"

Interesting. Priss had conveniently forgotten she and Ellyn were a team. This merely confirmed my belief that if Priss were awarded the money, Ellyn wouldn't see a penny of it. On the other hand, if Ellyn won, Priss would have hounded her until she got her half.

Priss looked like a sheep. She clung to a sheep's image. But she had a strong streak of the wolf in her.

Good thing Ellyn was about to get an uncle on her side.

I pulled Priss's own move on her, stepping between Priss and Cor to displace the older niece as she'd displaced Ellyn. "Can you really teach me to play, Cor? I'm afraid I might be hopeless."

"Oh, not at all! It's as simple as anything. All you have to know is how to bid. Let me explain . . ."

Behind me, Priss waved to Ellyn. "Bye. We'll see you tomorrow." She and Trip followed behind Cor's entourage, and Ellyn let us go. Smart of her? Stupid? Was she glad? Sad? Confused?

I pushed her out of my head and listened to Cor review the arcane, insane bidding philosophies. Ellyn thought I was hopeless, but I'd studied this ridiculous game and was ready to give it a try.

And even though she thought I couldn't resist, Ellyn was wrong: I wouldn't cheat.

Much.

I didn't palm any cards, but I was tall enough that I could often peer into the hands of those next to me. It wasn't too much of a challenge, and as the drinks kept coming, the observational cheating got easier. They were all but begging to be scammed.

I made sure I wasn't too successful so Cor would keep teaching me. I kept her laughing and quite enjoyed our game playing against Rebel and Sinjie, who came into his own at the bridge table. He was far more natural and relaxed in the card room than out of it, and I saw why he could be trouble . . . if we did nothing but play bridge.

Priss and Trip were banished to another table and had to play against strangers. She looked pissy about it and kept leaning across the space between the tables, trying to make little jokes with her aunt. It wasn't a very successful evening for her.

By the end of the night, I was judged to be a skillful amateur. My clothes reeked of the constant cigarette smoke from Rebel and occasional cigarillos from Sinjie. And Cor was mine for the plucking.

Rebel walked with us to our cabins, so I couldn't kiss Cor good night. Instead, I merely bowed over her hand and wished her sweet dreams. Rebel watched me with a smirk and followed into Cor's suite, no doubt so the two of them could dish like high schoolers over the evening. Once Luz returned from babysitting duties, I hoped she wouldn't be kept up by the slumber party that looked to develop.

I let myself into my room and stretched. It had been a long and largely successful day, and much information had been gathered. I wanted a shower because I smelled bad, and I wanted to know how Ellyn was doing, so I got my card out to pop the lock.

But when I opened my side of the connecting door, I found hers was already open.

She was dressed in her version of pajamas, a long T-shirt and nothing else—a fact I'd confirmed by touch on both the nights we'd slept together. Over her nightshirt, of course; I don't mind pressing an advantage, but I won't go after a woman when she's asleep or unconscious. That's just not sporting.

"Show me how to pick that lock," she said. My jacket was folded neatly and laid over the sofa.

"Okay."

She knelt beside me, and I showed her the stiffened card I carry in my wallet. It looks like a credit card, but the magnetic strip is fake. "Look. These locks are easy."

"You smell like cigarettes."

"Yeah, sorry. Blame Rebel. I'm going to shower. You think you got this? Not hard, right?"

I left her to practice while I showered in her bathroom. It was impossibly luxurious. This was the lifestyle I was made to live.

When I came out, she was in bed, sitting up with the covers pooled around her waist. The curtains were drawn tight against the marine appearance of any more Peeping Tom cousins.

"Get the lights, will you?"

That gave me a buzz. Were we skipping over the "get out"

scenario? Had she accepted I'd be sleeping with her? The possibility sharpened my interest like a wolf on the scent of dinner.

I moved around the room, figuring out how to turn off all the expensive, subtle illumination. "Priss is going to be a problem," she said.

"Yeah. She is." I found the last light and stood uncertainly by the door to my cabin.

She flipped back the covers on my side—an unquestionable invitation—and kept talking, so I played it cool, too, and slid in beside her.

"What will we do about her?" Ellyn asked.

I lay back and opened my arm to her, and she came into my side as easily as if we'd slept this way a hundred times. I was glad she couldn't see my sudden smile. "Watch her. Do you trust her?"

"Hmm." She fussed around for a moment, moving pillows and rearranging me and pulling her hair out from under her, but eventually she settled, her head on my chest. I stroked her shoulder idly. "When we were kids, she was usually the one to rat us out when we did something wrong."

The idea of little Ellyn made me chuckle. "What kind of bad things would you do?"

"Oh, you know—go to the beach when we weren't supposed to. Once we stole Mr. Darby's dog and dressed her up in a tutu. She didn't mind, but he was pretty cheesed off."

The phrase was a throwback to childhood, when a kid couldn't say *pissed off*, and it made me smile to hear it. "What kind of dog?"

"Sort of beagle-y. The tutu dragged on the floor and Liv got mad. Of course, she'd made it."

"For you?"

"For Farrah, who was going to be a ballerina at the time."

The story pleased me, and her breasts were warm and soft against my ribs. The sweep of my hand got a little broader. "And what did Priss have to do with this?"

"Oh, well, Mr. Darby came looking for his dog, and Priss told her father the dog was in my room. Like she hadn't been in on the canine liberation."

I loved the innocence of the crime, but I thought Priss's character was pretty well-set. "No loyalty to her cousins, then."

"I guess not so much."

"And this is the person you've partnered with."

"Yeah." Her arm was across my chest and her fingers were rubbing over the hem of my sleeve, the soft brush of her hand sending ripples of sensation up my arm.

"Were you punished for your transgressions?"

"Oh, not so badly. No allowance for the rest of the summer, and we had to walk Robespierre every day and clean up all the dog poo in Mr. Darby's garden."

"The dog's name was Robespierre?"

"Mr. Darby was a history professor."

"Of course he was. And did Priss serve time with the three of you?"

"Not officially, but we always did everything together, so she came with us anyway. And she bought candy for the rest of the summer with her allowance and shared it with us."

"An even split?"

"Well—mostly."

"Right. I'm sure. Well, I know all I need to know about Priss, then."

"Shit. Bad, huh?"

"Safe to say she's not really on your side."

"Unf."

"But if you get the money, you'll still split it with her, won't you?"

She was silent for a while, no doubt measuring the difference between what was right and what she knew I wanted to hear. "Probably."

"You're a sucker, Ellyn," I said. I was now stroking her hair, and I tugged on it to prove my point.

"Ouch. Quit it. What do you care?"

"Well, if I get twenty percent, I'd rather have a million than half."

"Right. Of course. It's all about the money, isn't it?"

I was curled in the darkness with a warm, supple, naked body in a loose T-shirt that would slide out of the way with the slightest tug, and it was time for some reality. "Obviously, it's all about the money. That's why we're here, right?" I nudged her when she was silent. "Right?"

"Right."

I spoke with great confidence, persuading myself as I reminded her. "And no more kissing. No more harmony. You and I are going to focus on the prize. Right?"

"Right."

We lay there, and I stared at the ceiling. We'd left port during dinner, on course through the night to Phuket. We didn't have the faint lights from shore to illuminate the room through a crack in the curtains. I'd left the light on in the bathroom, though, and that cast a soft glow across the bed.

And she was still warm and soft. And naked under her T-shirt.

I still stroked her hair, and she traced patterns on my chest. I frowned as I concentrated on her fingers.

"Are you following muscle groups?"

She stilled. "What?"

"With your fingers. Are you outlining pecs? Serratus? Deltoid? Don't stop. I dig it. Why wouldn't you? I've got great definition. You should do my abs."

"Oh, God. You're so annoying." She tried to roll away, but I tightened my hold.

"I work hard for every line," I said. "Why wouldn't I be vain? My looks are my meal ticket. I keep myself in top physical shape because that makes me better at my job. And if I weren't self-confident, I'd be a crappy scam artist. So, you can mock me, but I'm this way for a reason."

She'd stilled, listening to me. "I never thought about it that way."

I shrugged. "Also, I'm extremely handsome."

She laughed and punched me in my side. I *oof*ed out a breath in response and rolled over to capture her hand.

And then she was under me.

And I was over her.

Her giggles tapered off, and her breath picked up. Not hard to measure it. After all, we were chest to chest.

Victor was a ghost in my brain. *Not this girl, dear boy. Don't forget your goal.*

Ellyn was having a mental conversation as well. She said, "Bax . . ."

"Yeah? What about him?"

"He's, uh—"

"—not here," I finished. Her fingers tightened on my biceps, and she licked her lips. I watched her do it, and my erection grew from dimly interested to *let's get a move on here.*

"This is a bad idea," she said as her hands slid up to my shoulders.

"I know. It's about as stupid as it could be." I lowered my head and nuzzled along her cheek.

She sighed, and one hand made it to my neck. "One day, you might be my uncle."

I grinned into her neck. "This would make one hell of a porno, then, huh?" She laughed, but her heart was still going like a rabbit. "I'm not going to make you do anything you don't want to do, Ellyn. But I'm not going to help you be good either. You knew I was a scoundrel when you hired me."

I lifted to look at her, and she bit her lip. "I wish I wanted to be good," she said.

Score. That was enough to work with. My dick was now fully hard. "Allow me to make the decision, then."

It was simply a matter of lowering my head, of finding her sweet, pink lips and nibbling on them. She opened to my kiss. I licked along her tongue, and she caressed mine. Her hands were fists in my hair, and the light sting spurred me on.

We kissed until we were both breathless, and then she pushed me off. "Cor," she said. "Bax. Money. How far do you think this can go?"

I yanked her T-shirt over her breasts and slipped one pink nipple into my mouth. She gasped and held my head closer.

"Wow."

Wow was right. She was responsive and hot and almost naked under me. The stroking of her hands across my shoulders and back maddened me. I needed more.

And clearly, she did too.

I spent some time on her breasts and took the time to kiss along her armpit, to the private, soft skin I'd put lotion on that day. She smiled in response to my touch, and I nibbled on her for the glory of her skin twitching against mine. "By the way," I murmured.

"Yeah?" she sighed.

"This time, I *am* copping a feel." I had one breast cupped in my hand, and I returned to lick the nipple and flick it with my tongue. She offered a half moan, half sigh that I took as a measure of progress.

"Will you take off your shirt?" she asked.

"I'll take off mine and yours." I sat up, and she gasped.

"Oh—I don't know if I'm ready for—" My shirt came off and she purred. "Fuck. Look at you. You're gorgeous, Artie."

"I know. Thanks. Let's look at you now."

I tugged and she sat up to help, and there was a moment when her arms were tangled in the sleeves and her face was covered by the shirt, and I couldn't resist. I leaned down and sucked one breast into my mouth with a strong pull.

She yipped and fought out of the shirt, laughing and cursing me. Now her hair was a mess around her in a soft cloud, and her eyes were shining. I sat up again to look my fill.

"Fuck, Ellyn. Look at *you*. God."

"Good?" She preened, her arms still overhead and her ribcage lifting her breasts up to me.

"Good." I went back to worshipping her, stopping often to drink in her kisses. The woman had the most amazing mouth—soft and hot and the perfect wetness. Glorious.

She wanted more, and God knows I did, but I couldn't stop kissing her, so I ghosted my hand down her body. She was writhing by the time I got to her crotch—her beautiful crotch. Not waxed. That was like her. I pulled back from the kiss to look at her and longed for enough light to see. Was the hair there darker? Lighter? The same flaming red that was making me crazy?

She liked being looked at. She shivered, and her hips twisted. I teased her with my fingers, but neither she nor I could endure a slow, careful seduction. We were far past that point. When I ran one long finger down the crease of her, she opened her legs to give me access.

And she was wet. Magnificently wet, and hot, and when I slid my finger boldly right inside her, she was tight. I ached to ease my cock into that tightness. But first?

The little bud of delight, her nerve endings all clustered for me to play with.

I moved down the bed until I knelt on the floor, bent over her long legs. "Oh my God," she said, one hand covering her eyes.

"All you have to say is no," I said. "And I'll stop."

She was silent, holding her breath.

I grinned and ducked to lap her with my tongue. Her breath came out in a gasp.

It was the taste of female. Warm, dark, secret. Fresh. Delicious. Possibly my favorite flavor. I licked and licked, and she just got wetter.

When her hands came down on top of my head to draw me where she wanted me, I knew it was time. I flicked lightly against her clitoris, and she jumped.

So, I held her hips with my arms and got to work, slowly at first and then with increasing pressure. She probably didn't even know she was driving, her hands on my head telling me exactly what she needed.

By the time her fingers were fisted in my hair, I ground into her, and she gasped with inarticulate yips that told me she was close.

I released one hip and slipped two fingers inside her to flick at the back of that tiny nerve bundle, and she shattered. She gave a little scream as she came, her legs going stiff on either side of me. "Oh, God," she breathed.

And then she was still, the only sound her panting breaths.

Delicious.

I wiped my face on her inner thigh and crawled up her body. I took her, boneless and limp, into my arms and held her while she recovered.

CHAPTER TWENTY—ELLYN

I THINK I BLACKED OUT. I'M NOT SURE.

Bax could give me an orgasm—if I helped. Other lovers could too. I wasn't a novice in the bedroom.

But Artie had managed to push buttons I didn't know I had. He'd taken control. Relieved me of the burden of deciding. And I came so hard that my fingers and toes were still recovering from the stretch.

What a scoundrel, I thought happily.

He was smart about the post-orgasm moment too. He was just holding me. A large erection pressed against my thigh, but he hadn't asked for a thing. He let me come down, giving me the warmth of his very large body. Breathing evenly and deeply. Not a word.

Perfection.

Out of nowhere, a wave of sensation rippled through me.

"Aftershock," he said drowsily. "Happens after every earthquake."

That made me giggle. And it made me think maybe I wasn't quite done with him yet.

"That was amazing," I said and waited for him to express preening vanity.

"You're amazing," he said instead. Another ripple fanned out from my clit. Summoning the last of my strength, I rolled lazily onto my belly beside him.

"We could use a condom right about now."

He raised an eyebrow. "Really? You don't have to."

"Fuck *have* to. I want to. Let's get to know the real you, scoundrel."

He grinned. "I happen to know you have condoms in your camera bag." He waggled an eyebrow at me.

I attempted to gather an air of tremendous dignity around me. "I use them if a microphone might get wet. I need to keep those. I happen to know you have an entire box in your luggage."

He flipped me over and landed on top of me, surprising me. "You went through my things?"

"While you were in the shower."

"Oh, God." He was kissing me again. "I'm so proud of you."

I laughed, even as excitement rose in me again. His tongue slid through my mouth as it had slid through my folds. The sensation sent a shiver through me. I was impatient. "Go get one," I said.

"Ahh—yeah," he said, but he wouldn't move for long minutes, kissing me instead and rubbing along my body with his hands. He molded and shaped me, releasing each muscle at the same time he tuned me like an instrument.

"Artie," I sighed. I yanked his head up by his hair. "Seriously. Don't you want to fuck me?"

"Fuck. Yes, I do."

He rolled off me and was through the connecting door in a moment. Then he was back. "I want to turn on the light. Okay with you?"

"Do it. I'd like to look at you more."

He chuckled. "My thoughts exactly."

He flicked on the bedside light and I blinked, briefly blinded. He stood there in nothing but tented black boxer briefs, holding a foil packet in one hand.

He liked that I was looking. Confident in his beauty, he turned in a slow circle for me. I reach out a hand and stroked his ass as it went by. That made him sigh, and he stepped away from the bed and bent forward, perfectly twerking his buttocks at me. No well-paid stripper could have done a more perfect movement.

God. He made me wet, even as I laughed. I applauded the perfection of that man's hindquarters and the ripple of muscles over his back. And before he could escape, I leaned over and ran my hands between his cheeks so I could cup his balls, tight and warm against my fingers.

This time, he was the one gasping.

I let him go, and he turned to me. I sat and moved to the edge of the bed. "Stop—I'll take them off."

He gave me a lopsided grin and laced his fingers behind his head.

"Spread your legs," I demanded. He complied.

The light was perfect. Dim and clear. Highlights fading into soft shadow. His cock strained against the cloth. It was clear Artie was proportional: a big guy with a big dick. Another ripple of sensation—an aftershock—made me clench all those muscles, and I gasped out an "ahh" that he liked hearing.

I leaned forward and sniffed him. He smelled . . . secret. Delicious. Hot in sexiness as well as temperature. I kissed the head of his cock through the fabric, where a drop of pre-cum had dampened the cloth. He sighed.

Then I peeled the shorts down, running my fingers slowly over the cheeks of his muscled ass and lifting the material away from his straining dick.

And there he was. Naked. I sighed in pleasure.

I pushed the shorts down impatiently, and he stepped out of them and kicked them away. He was right there. I opened my mouth and slipped over his head. He was velvet over steel, and I gloried in his moan.

"Yeah," he said, and his hands ran through my hair. "More."

The thrill of turning him on made my every muscle flex. Gladly, I slid my mouth up and down, running my tongue firmly along his shaft, tasting and licking and teasing and pleasing. His fingers grew more demanding, and he began to thrust into my mouth, holding my head still.

I thought I would have hated that, but somehow it turned me on even more. His excitement drove me higher and farther. I used my hands to cover the length of him that wouldn't fit in my mouth, and for a few strokes, he held my head and fucked my mouth firmly.

Then he pulled out with a gasp. "I want to be inside you."

"Yes," I said. "I want that too." And I did. I felt empty—hugely, achingly empty, and I longed to be filled, stretched, scalded by him.

He nudged me back. "You ride me," he said. He lay on the bed while he ripped open the condom and rolled it onto his cock. "Come on—get on top of me."

The thought of spearing myself on that thick truncheon set off another wave, and I shivered again. *Perhaps this wasn't an aftershock*, I thought dimly, *but a warning of things to come.*

He helped me seat myself across his hips, his hands at my waist. "Want me to do it? I can put the head inside you if you want."

"I want to do it."

He nodded. "Raise up. Lift up. Yeah—like that. You're so beautiful, Ellyn. Damn."

He held me so I could hold him. I ran the head of his cock along my seam to wet him, and then I tugged until he was barely a dome of pressure reaching up into me. He was in me.

"There," I breathed.

"Good girl. Now go slowly. Take your time. I'm pretty big, and you're tight as hell."

I whimpered as I eased myself onto him. I could only take a little at a time, but my hunger kept growing. I needed more. And more. And more. The stretch was overwhelming, and I closed my eyes to focus on nothing but the sensation.

At last, he was fully inside me, and I was seated on his hips. The stretch was agony. Delicious, tingling pressure. "I need a moment," I panted.

"As long as you need," he grunted, his hands now fists on my hips. "Take your time."

I hung my head and adapted, adjusting to the thickness of him inside me. Long before I thought I was ready, my hips betrayed me by starting to move.

At first, it was the tiniest movement, my ass going back, which forced the head of his cock against my front wall. I began to gasp.

Then I began to lift off him as I went back, pushing him into me with each return. I leaned into my hands fisted on his chest and closed my eyes, lost in the sensation now pooling deep inside me.

He'd given me control. Let me set the pace. Ripples of excitement swept along my spine. My fingers began to grow numb. And I couldn't stop moving, reaching back and up—and down and in. Hard. Harder.

Soon, I was shaking all over. The wave was about to crest, to overwhelm me. I was going to come—and come hard. I needed to let him know.

"I'm—I—you—" I gasped.

"I know. I've got you." He moaned and urged me on. "Go ahead. I'm with you."

His thumb landed hard on my clitoris and I exploded, my orgasm like a jolt of lightning shocking every nerve in my body into pure, white-hot light. I screamed and rode the waves until I couldn't bear it any longer.

I collapsed on his chest. Had he come? I hadn't even noticed. How rude—how unobservant of me. And after he'd made me come that hard too.

But he was panting, and his arms around me were like steel. He was still frozen in one last thrust into me.

And then he went limp, his breath escaping in one gasping sigh.

After I lay there for an eternity or two, I gathered my thoughts. "Fuck," I said thickly.

"Fuck," he agreed. There was silence again before he spoke. "It may have been a terrible idea, but we are really, really good at that."

"Damn straight."

"Let me get that condom out of you."

I whimpered in protest, but he rolled me off of him and retrieved the rubber. He threw it out and grabbed water from the mini fridge. "Thirsty?"

"Give me that."

I rose on one elbow to drink, feeling wrung out and wonderful. Guilt and remorse could wait until tomorrow. For now, I'd been fucked into euphoria.

The water was cold and wet—obviously. But there are times when wetness is more needed than at others, and I'd panted myself into a dry throat. I drank in huge gulps until he protested and pulled at the bottle.

"Don't be greedy. I need some."

"Fine." I collapsed on the bed, and he got in. Not content to have me curled against his side, he pulled me over him like a blanket.

"Sleep now. We can freak out tomorrow."

He'd had the same thought I had. That was reassuring.

I fell asleep with his heartbeat under my ear and his arms around me. For this moment, at least, I could ignore all the ways this relationship was guaranteed to lead to a tangled, painful disaster.

CHAPTER TWENTY-ONE—ARTIE

IN MY EXPERIENCE, ALL SEX IS GOOD SEX. MALE, FEMALE, ALL alone, with a crowd. As long as everyone involved is willing, even bad sex is good sex, and I am always in favor of it.

Sex with Ellyn turned out to be way better than just good.

I felt like my joints had all been oiled; my elbows, knees, hips, and shoulders would all slide more smoothly against each other now. Or like my chakras had been rearranged, or whatever it is the Indian mystics do. I was at peace with the world. Her weight on top of me was a gift, and she was glorious.

She was going to be so pissed at me when I disappeared.

CHAPTER TWENTY-TWO—ELLYN

I woke slowly and stretched with a groan of pleasure. I was alone in my bed, and all sorts of little-used muscles had a very pleasant ache to them, like after a hard workout.

How much could I tell about the world without opening my eyes?

The ship's engines had stopped. We were in port in Phuket.

No sound from my bathroom; Artie wasn't in the shower. Had he come and gone already? Or was he still working out and would come in later to boldly invite himself into my suite and my toiletries? I would need more shampoo soon.

The sheets where he had lain were cool. He'd been gone a while.

I stretched again and came fully awake with a smile. Sex with Artie complicated everything we were trying to accomplish, but damn. It was worth the challenges.

I lay there for a while, trying to decide how I'd handle it if he became my uncle. Just the thought made me grin at the absurdity of the idea. Would we nod and smile over the Thanksgiving table at Aunt Muffy's? Would we pretend not to see each other when we met at the floating dock off the shore of the Nantucket compound? Would I give him and Aunt Cor a silly Christmas present while he handed me enough money to start my production company?

The ideas were so ludicrous, I started to laugh. I'd have to tell him about these upcoming obstacles he and I would have to face to ensure we didn't end up sneaking off to fuck like bunnies while the rest of the family bitched about whose turn it was to hold the annual Labor Day barbecue.

Of course, I wouldn't want to hurt Aunt Cor.

That thought sobered me. A slight chill wafted through my sunny morning.

And there was Bax.

Damn it.

Sweet, lovely Bax, who wouldn't hurt a fly. This would kill him, and he really didn't deserve this kind of pain. Artie and I were clearly just a fling. Weren't we? Was this *really* a betrayal? Should I tell my boyfriend what had happened? Confess my sins and beg his forgiveness? Or hide the truth and avoid hurting him?

Artie winning Cor in marriage seemed like a long shot. But what if he did marry her? What if I not only went to family functions with a hot uncle, but Bax also had to endure that at my side? If it looked like Artie really would marry Cor, I could never tell Bax. If I didn't get a new uncle, then that would mean I would tell Bax. Or would I?

Confusion. Options and possibilities and fidelity and honesty and being the kind of person I hoped I was . . . it all flew around in my brain, and I hadn't even gotten up yet.

By the time I dragged myself out of bed, I was a lot less cheerful.

I examined myself closely in the mirror. No hickeys. No redness from Artie's scruffy chin or cheek. No evidence we'd made a pretty significant mistake the night before. I was safe; I could be seen in public. As long as no one looked at the stain on my soul.

Where was Artie? His presence would have been useful. He would have scoundrel-ed me out of this mood, mocking me for being a sucker or a wimp. A sheep—apparently the lowest of the low, in his opinion.

I checked in with Aunt Cor. She and Rebel were sitting in Cor's suite, which, after the Kuala Lumpur trip, looked even more like some crazed warehouse of dubious treasures. The feathered headdress was now on the massive flamingo's head, and necklaces were clumped together on the vanity. Not only were they already in an impossible tangle, but I could tell from looking at them they'd turn the skin green if anyone actually decided to wear them.

My two wool challis shawls were neatly folded and waiting for me. Luz was watching out for me. I scooped them up and tucked them in the proper pocket of my camera bag.

Cor and Rebel were comparing the six or seven saris they'd bought, trying to decide the best way to wrap the skirts.

"Ellyn will know! Darling, I'm so glad you're here. Could you look this up on your little phone? We can't figure out how to wear these."

I sat next to Rebel on the loveseat and checked out YouTube when I noticed Luz in the doorway to her room. She shook her head mournfully.

"Maybe Luz knows how to wear a sari," I suggested.

Cor flapped her hand. "Luz thinks she knows how to do it, but I'm sure she's wrong. Rebel and I look terrible the way she does it. I know you'll find the right way. There are plenty of plump Indian ladies who look graceful and lovely in their saris!"

Luz raised an eyebrow and shot me a look. I bit back my grin and continued my search.

We had a silly and entertaining half hour during which I wrapped them in brilliantly colored fabric and they wrapped me, according to videos.

"There," Cor said when she and Rebel were finished. "I think

I must be very good at this. Look how lovely Ellyn looks in this. It's you, Ellyn. You and Luz aren't good at this."

Rebel relaxed on the sofa. "Or it could be she's literally six feet tall and slender while you and I look more like fireplugs."

"Speak for yourself. I happen to look lovely in my sari."

Now Rebel and even Luz were both laughing outright, and finally, Cor gave in and joined us.

The silliness continued until the arrival of Priss, with Lovely and Trip in tow.

"Morning, my sweet Auntie! Are we ready for breakfast? Lovely, don't touch that." Priss picked up her daughter, who immediately squirmed for release.

"Yes, dear. Good morning, Trip. Let me get changed."

"What are you gotten up as, Auntie? That's a—a beautiful sari. How gracefully you wear it!"

Cor snorted and she and Rebel retired to the bathroom to change their clothes. Since they'd put mine on over my shorts and T-shirt, I didn't need privacy and unwound myself right there.

"What the hell are you all up to?" Priss hissed.

"What?" I looked up, surprised.

"She needs simple, classic styles. That's the only way to mask her . . . you know. Her figure flaws. Smooth lines. Single colors. Monochromatic. She looks ridiculous like that!"

I blinked, confused by the venom in Priss's voice. Lovely had succeeded in wriggling halfway down her mother's body, and Priss finally gave up and released her. The child headed immediately for the necklace nest.

"No, Lovely—you don't know where those have been. Take her, Trip, please."

Trip scooped up his daughter and took her over for an eye-level look at the garden flamingo.

"All right. What's on the agenda today?" Priss hit me with an efficient smile. "I know you've got the plan. You always know what's going on."

"We haven't talked it over yet. What would you like to do?"

Cor and Rebel reappeared. They were both wearing clothing in plain colors—walking shorts and camp shirts. Their outfits fulfilled Priss's expectations. They were classic. Simple. Monochromatic. Both women were dowdy and frumpy in those clothes, and I regretted the loss of the saris and the laughter.

"What shall we do today, Auntie dear?"

"Well, Priss, whatever we do, let's begin with breakfast! Shall we go?"

Priss plucked Lovely from Trip's arms and handed the child to Luz. "Thank God you're here, Luz! We'll be back in an hour or so. Don't let her play with that—or that." Priss eyed the evidence of wild shopping sprees with suspicion. "And don't go out on the balcony. Auntie, why do you have trees out there? We didn't have trees on our balcony—well, Ellyn's balcony now. Are those trees poisonous? How do you know?"

I gave a wave to Luz as we left. She hit me with an annoyed eyebrow and ignored Lovely tugging on her hair.

On deck, Cor's usual table was set for her. Sinjie sat in the shade, and he folded the day's activity sheet and stood as we arrived.

"My dear. Aren't you radiant this morning!"

I looked around. Artie was often wrapped in a book and seated by himself for breakfast (until he was drawn over by Cor), but we must have missed him.

Cor missed him as well. "Morning, Sinjie! Just you today? Where is Arthur? And how is Marcus? He looked awfully sunburned yesterday. I hope he's all right. Didn't we have fun last night, teaching Arthur how to play bridge?"

Sinjie looked less pleased with the memory but stood it in good grace. The six of us sat to breakfast and to plan the day.

"They say Phuket is one of the most beautiful places in the world. How shall we see it? What do you think, Ellyn?"

"I think we should go paddle boarding in all that turquoise

water," Priss interjected. "It would be nice to get some exercise, don't you think? Good for the waistline."

She looked significantly at Cor's plate, which showed the remnants of a waffle. Cor flushed and pushed her plate away.

Her crushed spirit hurt me. "Or there's a weekend market we could go to," I said. "It's not fancy. Mostly for locals. I think they're known for shoes. And it's near the handicraft shops in the Old Town area. What do you all think of that? Some trash, some treasure?"

"Perfect!" Cor clapped her hands. "And we'll bring Arthur. He was so good about carrying all the bags last time!"

"Trip will carry your bags, Auntie," Priss volunteered her husband, who was a good-natured man. He nodded agreeably.

"Nonsense, dear. I wouldn't keep you from your paddle boarding. Go and have a wonderful time. Make sure you take Lovely. I'll need Luz with me."

Cor smiled sweetly at Priss, who insisted she didn't want to miss shoe shopping. Cor allowed her to worm her way into the jaunt but insisted Priss hire someone on the ship to watch Lovely.

Priss was having a bad day. This wasn't going the way she'd expected. "Of course, Auntie. That's a great idea. Or maybe Trip should stay with Lovely. You don't want to shop for shoes, do you, dear?"

"Well, if Trip's not joining us, we definitely do need Arthur!"

Priss was now trapped between insisting Trip would be the bag-carrying Sherpa and saying Trip would stay on the ship to care for their daughter. Cor forestalled her. "Ellyn, dear, go call Arthur's room and ask if he can come with us."

But Artie didn't answer his phone. *Where was he?*

"Ah, well—we'll manage, I suppose. Look! There's that Brock! Brock, dear, why don't you come shopping with us?"

Brock was blinking his way through an early-morning hangover, but if the wealthiest woman on the ship beckoned to him, the young man could stir himself to respond.

"Perfect!" Cor said. "When should we meet to leave?"

I'd been working my phone to find a local guide with a vehicle up to Cor's expectations. "The guide can be here in an hour. Just enough time to put on comfortable shoes and plenty of sunscreen, Aunt Cor!"

She laughed at my teasing. "I think we've learned a lesson from Marcus, dear—I'll go lotion up right now! See you here in an hour, all."

That would give me time to find Artie. Marcus had been routed, and it wouldn't do for Brock to come from the back of the pack to take Artie's place as the front-runner.

I knocked on our connecting door. When he didn't answer, I proudly picked the lock. Easy!

He wasn't in his cabin, although my sunscreen was. *Scoundrel.* I took it and pulled out my phone. I texted him and almost immediately heard his phone bing. It was on his bureau. Damn. Wherever he'd gotten to, he'd left behind the only way to get in touch with him. That gave me the first vague hint of unease. I went to wander the ship.

He wasn't talking to Basilio at the poolside bar. Not in the chilly restaurant. Not at the gym, although a small cluster of women did refer to him as "King Arthur" when I asked if they'd seen him. They were annoyed he'd missed his morning workout.

Hmm.

I checked with the excursions director; had Arthur Petrovitch left the ship? He hadn't. He was here somewhere.

But I still hadn't found him by the time we gathered for our shopping spree. He'd found some out-of-the-way hiding place, then. But where? And why?

The bright spot of the markets was watching Priss's disappointment when the promised shoes turned out to be canvas over rubber soles. Cor and Rebel were enchanted with the local flavor of the market, so Priss—who preferred to live her life in Manolo Blahniks—was forced to buy a pair for herself and a cute pink pair for Lovely.

As she turned away from the stall, I caught Cor in a tiny smile and realized she was most definitely messing with Priss. I bit back my own grin and felt a burst of affection for the tough old lady who wasn't quite as needy as we'd all thought.

The handcraft shops were hit-or-miss. Some of the wares were crude and plain; some were jaw-dropping and gorgeous. Cor bought several wall hangings—scrolls of Asian gentlemen in ancient regalia—as well as a small tiara, a collection of earrings, and bells to tie around her ankles, should she decide to take up exotic dancing. Pleased with the sound they made, she bought pairs for Rebel, Priss, and me as well. We expressed our dubious delight, and she laughed outright.

That wasn't the only surprising addition to our day. When we arrived at the ship, a slim figure dressed in black from head to toe waited for us on the deck.

"Why, Olivia!" Cor called, waving.

My cousin Liv would never be so gauche as to wave, but she slunk over to us. "Where have you been? I've been here for two hours waiting for you all."

"Sweetheart! What are you even doing here?"

"I came because I had such a good time before. I wanted to finish the trip with you." Her words were wooden, but Liv often sounded like that if she wasn't whispering or giggling with her twin. "Didn't we have a wonderful time exploring each area's culture and fashions?"

Cor immediately relieved Brock of the packages—he looked grateful and took himself off to hydrate at the bar like a man who'd been in the sun too long—and showed Liv her purchases, unpacking everything right there in the main lounge.

Liv was not impressed by the scrolls or the earrings, she admired the tiara, and she was besotted by the ankle bells. Priss immediately tried to give hers away, but Cor insisted Liv take hers.

"Excellent. Thank you. Where's Farrah?"

Beside me, Priss heaved a huge sigh. Cor smiled.

"Farrah? Farrah's coming back too? How lovely! I'll have all four of you girls together!"

Liv and Priss didn't seem too excited, and I was confused as hell. All my cousins were converging on the ship? What was going on? Where was my scoundrel when I needed a strategy session?

"She's not here yet? God, that girl—she's probably in a bar. I'll find out." Liv turned away, pulling out her phone. Cor waved over a steward. "Help us get this to my cabin, will you? Girls, are you coming?"

"I'll wait for Liv," Priss said, and I nodded in agreement. If they were going to have a private confab, I would be in on it.

"All right—see you soon! What fun this will be!" She and Rebel followed the overburdened steward.

I waited until she was out of earshot before pressing Priss with questions, but before I could, Liv returned. She was annoyed. "Farrah missed her flight. Of course she did. She's going to meet us in Port Blair. Like Farrah can find her way to the middle of the Indian Ocean to South Andaman without a guide."

"Forget about Farrah—what the fuck are you doing here?" Priss let her anger show.

So, I did too. "What are either of you doing here? You had your time with Cor. This is my time, and I'm thinking you're trying to force me out of consideration. That's not fair."

"Please—fair? She's always liked you best. You were the only one who would talk to her before Uncle Carl died. This is the only way it *is* fair." Liv, usually calm, was rumpled and upset. *Jet lag*, I thought. *I know how that feels.*

Priss glared at both of us. "We don't all have to be here—I was handling it."

"Great. I'm sure we can all count on you, Priss." Liv was seething.

"What's that supposed to mean?" Liv and Priss were nose to nose.

"I happen to know you have an arrangement with Ellyn here. You're going to split if either of you win."

"Because you have that same deal with Farrah! You're twins. Of course you do!"

Voices were rising; we were beginning to make a scene.

"I'm not as worried about your deal with Ellyn as I am about your deal with me." Liv played the statement like the trump ace in a hard-fought bridge game, and my stomach fell.

"Your deal with Liv?" I asked Priss, reality beginning to dawn. "You have a deal with Liv *and* with me?"

Priss pretended she didn't know why Liv and I were now both glaring at her. "I don't know what you mean."

"So, let me understand this," I said, working through it in my mind with growing fury. "If I win, you get half the money. If Liv wins, she has to split it with her sister *and* with you?"

"Yeah," Liv said, "so I get a third and you get a third and Farrah gets a third? That's not fair."

"Hang on." I turned on Liv. "You agreed to this. Why are you mad about it now?"

"Because I didn't think she'd win!"

I shook my head. "What are you both going to do if one of you wins? Liv, would you split with both of them?"

Liv looked uncomfortable. I grilled Priss.

"Would you split with Liv and me?" She didn't answer, but that was inconsequential. I could see the answer in her eyes. Artie was right; I was a sucker. "You wouldn't. If you won, you'd keep all the money."

"Well, I have a lifestyle to maintain," Priss exploded. "You people don't really need it."

"Don't need it?" Liv was shouting now. "Ellyn and I are both trying to start businesses. We need it more than you do!"

The speed with which alliances were shifting made me dizzy. I had a thought and rounded on Priss.

"Farrah will be here tomorrow, assuming she can make it to the Andaman Islands. If I ask her, will she say she has an agreement with you too?" The look on Priss's face was enough, and Liv's eyes were bulging in insulted astonishment. "She will," I said." You've got a fifty-fifty deal with all three of us. Jesus, Priss."

"I'm done with you," Liv announced. "Our deal is off."

Priss protested, and Liv turned to me. "Ellyn, want a deal?"

"You're both crazy. Get away from me, and leave this ship. All deals are off!"

"Fine!"

"Fine!"

We all stormed out, but because we were all heading for Cor's cabin, we stormed out together, which annoyed all three of us.

We were stomping down the hallway when I wondered aloud, "How do we all even know about these partnerships?"

They turned to look at me, and I explained. "I mean, Priss—how did you know Liv and Farrah had a deal?"

"Like it was hard to figure out." Priss shook a fist at Liv.

"But how did you know? Who told you?"

Priss slowed and we slowed with her. "Um, I think . . . Luz said something."

I looked to Liv. "And what made you get on a plane?"

"I . . ." Her eyes darted from me to Priss.

"Let me guess," Priss said. "A text from Luz?"

"Well, I'm paying her enough to keep me in the loop!"

"I am too," Priss said.

We'd come to a halt in the hallway, and light was dawning. "We're being manipulated," Liv said.

"Goddamn it." Priss was redirecting her anger.

"It's worse than you think." I got their attention with that. "Rebel says Luz keeps nothing from Cor. Cor already knew about the partnerships." I ran the thought through my head and nodded. Yep. That was right. "Cor's the one who's manipulating us. This is all her idea to make us jump through hoops."

All intercousin animosity was forgotten as we turned our ire on our uncle's second wife.

"Okay," I said as they steamed. "We don't let her know. There will be no accusations. If she wants to play us, we're going to be played. Right?"

Priss shook her head in admiration. "You've always been smart, Ellyn. Okay. She gets her way, and one of us gets some money. But don't assume it's going to be you."

"I won't."

"She loves shopping with me," Liv said.

"She loves playing bridge with me," Priss countered.

"And let me guess: she loves to drink with Farrah," I said.

"Everyone loves to drink with Farrah." Liv knew her twin better than anyone.

"Okay." I scrabbled together a temporary strategy. "Take an hour. Go to your cabin, go work out, go sit on deck. Calm down. We're going to let this play out. Meet at her cabin at six for cocktails, and we're nothing but sweetness and light. We do not let on we know anything at all. Agreed?"

"You're going to go talk to her!" Priss accused me.

"Not me. I want time to think about this myself. Promise." They regarded me suspiciously. "Hey—I'm the only one who didn't make more deals than I should have. And it's my two weeks, anyway. Go chill out. Meet here at six. Right?"

"Right."

"Okay."

They went to their caves in the lower bowels of the ship, and I went to my palace. *Come on, Artie—be in your cabin.*

But he wasn't there. Nothing had been moved.

I began to get worried. I checked with the expeditions desk again. "Everyone back?"

"Yes, miss. We have a full ship and will be leaving on time in about twenty minutes."

"What if I think someone's missing?"

"No one's missing, miss, I assure you. We keep good track of our guests."

"Okay. Thanks."

I stood on my balcony, watching the docks when the ship left its berth and we headed out. If he was on the ship, I'd find him.

If he wasn't on the ship, what had happened to him?

CHAPTER TWENTY-THREE—ARTIE

I sat on a bench watching the *Empress of the Indian Ocean* move toward us through the bay, heading for her berth. Next to me, a young lady who was now no longer as hungover as she'd been when we met continued her monologue.

"I told him I wanted to go to a happening club, but he kept trying to take me to tearooms. Do I look like someone who wants tea?"

I'd already learned she didn't require much participation from her audience. She held a mango smoothie in one hand and was gesturing with the other.

"So finally, he brought me to a tearoom in kind of a groovy district, and I hopped out and paid him and he went away, and I found a nice bar where I could get a drink. And you know what happened then?"

She laughed and frowned at the same time, a relentlessly sunny personality. Way too chatty, but I liked her anyway. She was cute. Like a puppy.

"The cab driver appeared again! He wanted to know why I hadn't gone into the tearoom, because they wouldn't give him his cut of whatever I spent!"

She howled with laughter, the sound now no more than a

minor annoyance. My headache was fading. My smoothie was pomelo; the slightly bitter grapefruit taste cut through the fog in my brain, and I was more alert. Still, a long sleep would have been even better.

"So, he ended up having a drink with me, and we partied all night. I barely got here this morning. Liv would have been pissed if I'd missed the boat. Again." As if it were a common thing to do, she pulled a pen out of her bag and started drawing a cartoon on the whitewashed wall of the building behind us. Quick and graceful, a drunk and grinning cabbie holding a large drink appeared on the wall. Some dock manager was going to be furious. Or turn it into a mural.

If the red hair hadn't cued me in, her frequent mention of her cousins would have alerted me to her identity. I'd already marveled at the coincidence—"You mean, you know Cor Wolcott? That's amazing! I'm her dance partner. We're going to win a rumba contest!"—and now had no reason to worry about being identified.

Farrah, flighty and entertaining, never thought to ask why I wasn't actually on the ship now coming to the dock before us. She was singularly incurious, and after I'd gently rebuffed her flirting by telling her I hoped to be involved with an older woman, she'd accepted me as a fellow traveler.

I nudged her, breaking in on her description of the great South Andaman Island cocktails she'd discovered. "Is that one of your cousins?"

Ellyn was on her balcony, looking at the docks. The scene was a busy one; Port Blair was a busy town. It took her a moment to be sure. But I knew the moment she saw me because all the tension went out of her body. She slumped against the rail.

She'd been worried.

I liked her concern, even though I knew she was probably worried for her investment, not for any more personal reasons. Still, looking at her even from this far away reminded me of our night together, and I had to shift my position to make my growing wood less obvious.

Not that Farrah would have noticed. She'd leapt to her feet. "Hey! Hey, Ellyn! Hey, girl! Tell Liv I made it, huh?"

Ellyn was focused on her phone. Texting, no doubt. Before long, two more figures joined her on the balcony. One was Priss; one was a creature in funereal black. Liv the fashion designer, I assumed. Our cast of characters was growing.

The crew finally ran out the gangplank. Farrah grabbed her bag, I shouldered my backpack, and she and I were invited to board.

She passed through their registration easily, her modified ticket in hand, with nothing more than a gentle admonishment. "We expected you in Phuket. Your sister told us you'd meet us here, but we wish you'd called the main office."

I, on the other hand, was in for the third degree from the ship's staff.

How had I gotten off the ship without anyone noticing?

"I don't know. I left with all the others. I assumed you saw me go."

What happened?

"I met a friend. We went to a bar. I'm afraid I had a little too much to drink and missed the ship's departure."

Why didn't I let them know?

"I never thought about it. I knew you were coming here next, so I hired a captain to get me here. Nice fast boat, too—we beat you!"

Did I have any proof that I belonged onboard?

"There are multiple passengers who can vouch for me, and probably members of your staff. But here's my room key and my driver's license." Both had been taped to my instep for the last twenty-seven hours, but I'd cleaned off any signs of duct tape.

Grudgingly, they let me onboard. I showed no sign of the electrifying adrenaline that gave me an edge in this battle. This was only the next step in a long series, and everything had to go right if this was going to work.

I found Cor Wolcott and all her attendees—now a thick crowd—at her breakfast table on deck. A cool breeze and the dappled shade from the woven awning made it a very pleasant spot. I still longed for a nap, but I had the energy to make nice with my target.

"I am here to welcome you all to India!" I said grandly.

Once I had their attention, I leaned forward and kissed Cor on the cheek. "Did you miss me?"

"I missed our practice yesterday, you naughty boy. Now, where have you been?"

I pulled a chair to her side, displacing Priss, who hitched over with annoyance to give me the room. I leaned in toward Cor to confide. As expected, a dozen people tipped forward to overhear. Dupes are so consistent. Even the toddler paused in her attempts to empty the sugar bowl.

"I snuck into Myanmar."

Cor gasped. "You didn't!" She put a warning hand on my arm. "Arthur! That was too dangerous!"

"I don't care. Thailand was the closest we'd get, so I skipped Phuket, called in a few favors, and was off the boat mere moments after we docked."

I'd been avoiding looking at Ellyn, but the contrast had been so vivid—one moment curled against her sleeping softness, the next climbing down from the marine door and into the boat delivering vegetables—that I had to see how she was taking this.

She looked confused. And like she was making calculations.

She was damn smart. And of all the people here, she was the one who knew I wasn't a novelist and didn't actually need to get into Myanmar.

It was possible one of the sheep was turning into a bit of a wolf.

"How did you do it?" Rebel asked.

"I'll tell you. But it goes no further, right?"

They all nodded. The toddler gnawed on packets of sugar in the protective circle of her mother's arms.

"I told the ship's crew I got drunk in a Phuket bar and simply missed the ship's departure. In fact, I picked up a fishing boat outside the city. They took me to the border with Burma, and I transferred at sea to a Burmese fishing boat."

Ellyn was looking at her phone. That was okay. No one else would notice the distance from Phuket to the border would require one fast boat if I expected to make a round trip.

"And the Burmese fishermen took me to their coastal village. I was in. No border control, no passport check, no ID on me at all, so they couldn't identify me if I got caught."

"And what did you see?" Even Sinjie was on the edge of his seat, whispering. Nothing keeps people's attention like whispering. It's human nature; we all want to be in on the secret, whatever that secret might be.

"I saw repressions. And kind people. And fear. I saw Buddhists—yes, Buddhists, the most peaceful people on the planet—treating Rohingya villagers like vermin. I saw great beauty. I saw great sorrow."

I sold it. They drank down every word. Even Ellyn was caught up in it.

"What about the Buddhists?" Trip asked.

I'd done my research and told them about ethnic cleansing and brutality. Nothing sells a story like gory details, and after all, it wasn't such a bad thing if more people knew what was going on.

And it was a great cover for my story.

"But a patrol came by, and I missed the turning of the tide. I had to wait overnight. So, my friends brought me straight to South Andaman Island, where I picked up the ship again. And here I am!"

We all sat back, thrilled and elated by the tale. I was regarded as a hero.

"I met him on the dock," Farrah piped up. "I didn't realize you were on a secret mission, Arthur. Pretty cool!"

"Not a word to anyone, though—right?"

She nodded, her eyes bright. My secret would be a secret until she had her first prelunch cocktail, but that was all right. I was covered.

The only problem now was Ellyn. My wolfish little sucker.

"Well. If you all don't mind, I'm ragged and travel-worn. I think I'll go take a shower and wash the whiff of fish off me!" I didn't smell like fish—I hadn't been on any fishing boats—but they wouldn't notice. Once the suggestion was planted, they'd smell what I told them to smell. "And maybe take a little nap, so I'm fresh for our rehearsal. What time shall we meet, Cor? Competition's tomorrow evening, you know."

"I know! Can you bear to rehearse after all that?" She was wide-eyed and took my hand. I hid my grin of victory.

"Well, we're getting so good. Let's give it all we have and dazzle them all! What about three o'clock? Would that be good for you?"

"We can be back by three, can't we, Ellyn?"

My beautiful redheaded accomplice smiled. "We don't even know what we're doing today, but I think we can make a point of being back by three. So, yes. Make your plans!"

"Lovely!" Cor said and laughed as the little girl looked up. "I mean, perfect! You go rest, Arthur, and we'll see you at three!"

It took another half an hour before Ellyn escaped and cornered me. It wasn't hard for her to do; I was naked in her bathroom when she arrived.

She let herself into her suite, and I made sure she was alone. Then I pulled her into the bathroom and sat her on the counter and kissed her until she forgot she had questions.

The technique had its advantages for me as well.

I forgot I was trying to forestall her curiosity and began exploring her mouth. "You have too many clothes on," I murmured.

"Yeah," she breathed. But as my hand slipped under her shirt to explore naked flesh, she pushed me. "No. Stop that. I have to meet everyone in Cor's suite in half an hour."

"We can do a lot in half an hour."

"Put something on." She hopped off the counter and pushed past me. "Let's talk in your cabin. I don't want to be overheard if any of these twelve million cousins show up early."

I wrapped a towel around my waist and watched with approval as she presented her ass to me. My approval increased as I realized she was bent over to pop the lock on the connecting door. I was so proud. My girl.

She went into my room and turned to glare at me. She actually stomped her foot and pointed at the floor. "Get in here."

She was irresistible. I sauntered to her and crowded her until I pushed her to the padded bench that passed for a bed in my cabin. She lost her balance and sat abruptly.

I eyed her with appreciation. "I'm sleeping in the big bed once you all are gone. Thought you should know."

"The steward..."

"The steward has already been and gone. You didn't notice your room is immaculate?"

"No thanks to you. Did you steal my sunblock again?"

"I'll return it later." I rethought our positions. I took her elbow and tugged her to her feet again. I took her place and drew her toward me until she straddled my legs. "Have a seat."

"No." She tugged halfheartedly on the grip on her arm, and I grinned. She shrugged, surrendering for the moment, and sat. Nowhere near close enough to my dick, but the pose was still pretty good. I rested my hands on her thighs.

"Where the hell were you?"

"Me? International man of mystery? I told you: Burma. I mean, Myanmar."

"I don't care what the country is called. You're not a novelist. You didn't need to go to Burma. Where. Were. You."

"You wouldn't believe me if I told you." I pulled her forward, but she resisted. That made me grin again.

"Try me."

"Don't worry about it. I'm here, aren't I?"

Ellyn shook her head in frustration. "What am I supposed to make of this? What's going on?"

"And I'm telling you not to worry about it. It has nothing to do with you or your aunt. Everything's still good. In fact, it's better than ever because now I'm so mysterious. And charming. And really handsome. And a hell of a dancer."

"Your teeth are kind of dingy, though," she teased me and I knew I'd gotten past her most serious and obvious objections to my surprise departure.

"I fucking know it," I said to reward her for surrendering. "My teeth were so beautiful until you people interfered with perfection! I oughta sue you."

"Your teeth are still pretty good."

She watched my mouth with focused interest, so I bit my lip lightly. "Oh yeah?"

"Yeah." Then, at last, she lay forward on me, her weight firm against my swollen cock, her breasts burning against me. My arms slipped around her, and our tongues tangled.

"I missed you," she breathed.

"I missed you too."

"I was worried. I thought maybe you fell overboard."

"I'm an excellent swimmer."

"And so modest."

"Of course."

"Shut up."

"Make me."

She made me, and I was well pleased with her persuasion technique. With more time, I would have had her naked, her thighs spread and open to me. But the girl does like to be in charge, and we really didn't have the time to push her boundaries.

"Okay. That's enough. I've got to spend the day with a bunch of heartless, mercenary cousins. Can we talk about them, please? I need you to strategize with me."

I sighed and let her sit up again. The minute she left, I would be jerking off to thoughts of her. "Okay. What's going on? What are they all doing here, anyway?"

She told me about the arrival of the twins, about the discovery that everyone but her had secret partnerships with the others, and about how Luz had been the conduit of all the information and paranoia.

"But you said—" I couldn't even finish my sentence before she cut me off.

"That's right. Rebel told me Luz kept Cor informed about everything. So, I'm thinking you're romancing one clever puppet master."

I couldn't wipe the smile off my face. I was liking Cor more and more. That she was a wolf in sheep's clothing gave me a huge buzz. My kind of scam artist. "She wants attention and affection from her husband's nieces, so she arranges for all of them to show up on the last leg of the cruise, and she stirs the pot. Gets you all suspicious of each other."

"Yeah, but it's not going to work. We're on to her."

"Sure it's going to work." I picked her up and put her on the bed beside me; I needed to pace while I thought. "It doesn't matter if you know. You're all still going to be competing for her affections."

"No way. We know what she's been doing. We're not going to let her keep it up."

I stopped and looked at her, curled up like a colt. She was luminous. "You mean *you* won't let her keep it up because you're basically decent and kind. The other word for that is a sucker. But the manipulation trio? They're going to do what they can to work this. So, you need to watch them. Like a hawk."

Confusion was written across her face in a frown, a furled brow, a tilted head.

"Okay," I amended. "*I'm* going to watch them like a hawk."

"Well, not today, you're not. We're going on a glass-bottomed boat tour and then—and I know this will surprise you—we're going shopping. And *you're* going to be napping." Her contempt tickled me.

"You're taking a toddler on a glass-bottomed boat tour? I'm not sure that's a good idea."

"Lovely, I'm happy to say, will be staying with Luz across the hall, who's mad as a wet cat about it. And I hope they both howl and cry the whole time and keep you awake."

She stood and pushed past me to leave. I boldly groped her heart-shaped ass as she strutted past, and she jumped with a gasp. "We'll continue this conversation tonight," I said with a leer.

She blushed and shut the connecting door in my grinning face.

CHAPTER TWENTY-FOUR—ELLYN

THE BOAT TOUR PROBABLY WOULD HAVE BEEN MORE ENJOYABLE if I hadn't been made so damn randy by that damn scoundrel. Damn it. He got me all worked up. I stared at myself in my bathroom mirror and knew someone would ask me why I was so flushed. I wet a towel and held it to my face, but it took long minutes before I calmed enough to meet Cor and the others.

And that was the easy part. It also took about two hours to lose the urge to straddle every railing I came across and rub myself to a fast, hard orgasm. The man was dangerous.

I think I could have calmed down faster if he hadn't promised to finish our "conversation" that night. The thought of what he might do . . . and what I might do . . . and what we might do . . . kept echoing through my brain like a smutty movie played in church.

And all the while, I watched my cousins behave exactly as Artie had predicted they would. Damn him.

We knew she was manipulating us, and yet Priss cooed over that evening's upcoming bridge game.

Liv investigated local shops and designers on her phone and kept reading tidbits to Cor about where they should go when the boat docked.

And Farrah? She'd brought along a flask and poured straight whiskey down Cor's throat. She said it was a Manhattan, and the fumes coming off both of them would make it dangerous to go near an open flame.

I sat in the stern and watched them.

They knew Cor was manipulating them. And still they were playing up to her as hard as they could. Not to have a good time, and certainly not to make sure Cor had a nice trip.

Just to get the money from Cor—and keep the money away from the other three. It was depressing to watch.

Rebel moved over to sit beside me, and we watched the cousins together.

"They all have something," I said. "Some reason why Cor would like them best. And I've got nothing."

"You're the tour guide. The cruise director. The one who knows where we're going."

"Great. That's lovable."

"Oh, and you're lovable."

I scoffed. She turned to me with a smile. "You're the one who actually likes her. Who looks after her. Don't worry about it."

The one who liked her. Great. I was the pathetic one. *Sucker*, a contemptuous voice whispered in my head. *Baa-aa-aa, little sheep.*

Away from Artie, the sun shining and the breeze cool on my skin, I took a moment to figure out the strengths and weaknesses of my strategy.

The original premise was: She'd give the money to the niece who was with her when she was happiest, which was why bringing Artie was such a good idea. He could romance her and make her happy, and she'd look upon me with favor.

But now any happiness inspired by her shipboard romance would become a part of all the nieces together. I'd have no advantage. My biggest strength—Artie—had become a weakness.

Unless . . .

Unless I actually helped to ensure my aunt married the man who demonstrated that I'd been having sex all wrong.

And that made my head hurt.

Or maybe it was the sun.

I was glad when the boat tour was over and I could lead my little ducklings to the artisans Liv and Cor had agreed were "can't-miss" shopping opportunities.

Sinjie was with us, of course, and Marcus had braved the light of day. Parts of his skin were still sort of purple, but he'd gotten over his fever and was covered in several layers of clothing. Still, he huddled in the shade wherever he could find it.

Brock had known—and drunk heavily with—Farrah when she was cruising on the leg of the journey before mine. He was boozily, sleepily in love with my hard-partying cousin, and she liked having a handsome young man who could keep up with her drink for drink. So, he met us at the shops to carry bags. He also replenished Farrah's flask.

But at least Farrah and Brock drank most of the contents. Cor was essentially sober by the time we returned to the ship for her dance rehearsal.

Artie was in prime form, and the many observers (Cor's competitive family, her best friend, her suitors, a morose maid, and a small child) agreed they'd gotten pretty damn good at their rumba.

The praise pleased both the dancers, who beamed at each other and at us.

I watched them critically and decided that if they ever did marry, Artie would probably make Cor happy. And God knows he would enjoy her money. *She should marry him*, I decided. And I'd never go to another family function again. Not much of a loss —all my cousins had now annoyed or outright angered me.

Cocktails and dinner and the endless rounds of bridge . . . We'd fallen into a rut, but at least I wasn't expected to be in attendance in the card room. Both Liv and Farrah told me separately they'd be willing to room with me in my luxurious suite, abandoning the other twin. They were in another low-level cabin, like Priss and Trip. I turned them both down. This was my turn across the hall from Cor. Let the twins live together.

And let me have my sweaty, panting nights with my future uncle.

Set free as the cards were being shuffled, I went to my cabin. I changed for bed and settled in with my camera and laptop. Some of the images I'd taken on the glass-bottomed boat were pretty good, and there was a headshot of Liv I knew she'd love. She'd have it on her website as soon as I got it to her. I got lost in my work for a while.

Artie appeared near midnight. His entrance was presaged by a fumbling at the connecting door. How unlike him. He had trouble popping the lock.

Once he made it in, I saw why. King Arthur was a bit tipsy.

Oh, this could be fun.

"I have been thinking about you," he sang.

"Oh, really?"

"Oh, really. I was trying to figure it out."

"What?"

"How you got into my head."

"I'm in your head?"

"It's bad enough you're in my bed."

"Um—you mean *my* bed."

He waved away my comment as he prowled around the room. "Whatever. I like women. I like to fuck. We have a good time. But everyone knows you don't fuck someone who's part of a job. It's not even a rule of the game, because you just don't. That's a ticket to prison, baby."

"You think we're going to prison?"

"Please." He came to a halt and examined himself in the mirror. "We haven't done anything illegal. Much. No, that's not the point. I shouldn't be fucking you, and Victor would have my head."

"Who's Victor?"

"Victor." He turned to me as if I was stupid. "Victor!"

"Okay. Victor."

"So, what is it about you that makes you so special? Why am I so connected to you?"

He waved his hands around, and I was suddenly warmed by a flush of pleasure. "You're connected to me . . . how, exactly?"

"How?" He growled and threw himself on the sofa. "Physically. Emotionally. Spiritually. Musically." He threw the last one at me with contempt. "So—why you? You're hot, sure."

I sat straighter, pleased. He dashed me with his next words.

"Lots of women are hot. I've had hotter than you."

"Thanks."

"You're funny and smart and God knows you're practical. And you're a total sucker. I could con you in my sleep."

I didn't sound so good as he rattled off my attributes. "Is that a good thing or a bad thing?"

"Bad!" He shouted as he came off the sofa to prowl some more.

"Lower your voice, or we go to your cabin."

"Fine." He spoke in an exaggerated whisper. "It's bad. You're a babe in the woods and someone is going to take advantage of you. Like a cousin. Or another cousin. Or *another* cousin. You need to wise up." He rounded on me, menace in his voice, and I was suddenly uneasy.

He saw my reaction, and the fury drained out of him. He sat beside me on the bed. "Don't get so upset. No one's going to hurt you while I'm here."

I would have been more pleased with the statement if I hadn't been on such an emotional roller coaster. "No one's going to hurt me but you, of course."

"Of course," he agreed and threw himself back, his arms spread across the bed. I moved my camera and laptop to the table. "But the question I'm asking myself is—why you? You gorgeous, red-haired Bambi in the woods."

He stared at the ceiling, and I stared at him. Was he done?

"And I figured it out." Nope. He wasn't done. "It's purely sexual."

I wasn't sure this would get any more flattering to me. "Okay," I said guardedly.

"You are the key to my lock."

I raised an eyebrow. "Anatomically, wouldn't you be the key to my lock?"

"Trivialities. Let me explain." He sat up and fixed his focus on me.

"Please do."

"There is a first rule of the scam. Do you know what it is?"

"I believe we've established I'm the dupe and the patsy. I don't know the first rule of the scam."

"The rule is: figure out what they don't have."

He offered this pronouncement with complete authority, clearly believing he'd made his point.

"Who?"

"Your mark. Your pigeon. The person you're scamming. Once you know what they don't have, you know what they want. You know why?"

I was skeptical. "Because people want what they don't have?"

"That's right!" He beamed at me like a proud teacher and got up to pace again. "People want what they don't have. So, let's look at you."

He happened to be admiring himself in the mirror again as he said it, so it seemed clear his suggestion was rhetorical.

"Let's."

"Here's a woman who has no interest in leadership, but she's so damned capable that people follow her around and wait for her to decide things." He settled his fine blue blazer on his shoulders and took it off to sling over his shoulder like a fashion model. He posed in the mirror and returned to the subject. "So, what does that woman want?"

"I don't know. An aspirin?"

"Obviously, you want someone else to make the decisions."

I laughed. "I do not want that. Most people make terrible decisions. I'm better off when I do the choosing."

"Yes." He wheeled and pointed a finger-gun at me. "*Most* people. That's right. If you came across someone who was as capable as you? Maybe even a little more capable?" He prowled to me, his jacket forgotten on one hooked finger and dragging behind him on the floor. "You're telling me you wouldn't gladly turn over authority and for once do some following?"

I blinked. This abrupt turn in the conversation was unsettling. He didn't let up.

"What if someone else knew where to buy shoes in Kuala Lumpur?"

"It was Langkawi," I said faintly, but he ignored me.

"What if someone else knew the way to the café with the best—what were they called?"

"Bubur cha cha," I whispered. My brow wrinkled.

"What if someone else remembered the name of the must-try Malaysian dessert? What if someone else knew where to go and what to do and how to get there? What would you think of that?"

He stared at me fixedly. I couldn't think of what to say.

"This is where you say, 'I would like that, Artie.' Got it?"

"I would like that, Artie." The words came out of me woodenly, but the sentiment was very true. I was tired of being the one in charge.

"I know you would. That's what makes me such a magnificent scam artist. I know what people want." Triumphant, he collapsed on the sofa, watching me with his arms spread along the back.

I shook my head to clear it. "Yeah? So?"

"*So.*" He sat forward and linked his fingers, his elbows on his knees. "What do you think *I* can't have?"

His question took me by surprise. "I don't know. A big enough bed? Sunblock?"

My attempts at jokes failed. He shrugged arrogantly. "I

already have those, clearly. What else? What might I like that I can't get?"

Teachers in film school asked questions like that when they were sure the student could answer if they'd just stop being so clueless. Artie was going someplace with this, but I didn't know where. And I was definitely clueless. "I don't know. What?"

He shook his head. "You're a terrible scam artist."

"Yes, we've established that."

He rose to his feet and spread his arms wide. Even in this oversized suite, his head nearly brushed the ceiling. "I'm six-foot-five. I'm heavily muscled. And I've been this way since before I was a legal adult. I con people, including women. Do you think your Aunt Cor wants to be pushed around by some gorilla?"

"Marcus pushes her around."

He corrected me. "Marcus ignores her. It's very different. When I'm with your aunt—when I'm with any woman—I am gentle. I am kind. I am, above all things, not scary. And I have it in me to be scary. Do you believe me?"

He loomed over me, and I had to crane my neck to look at him. He blocked the light, and his face was in shadow.

"I believe you."

"You should. Because I am scary. But I don't let that out. It would be bad for the job."

He still stood over me, and he reached out one hand—big enough to crush my skull—and cradled my jaw. "So, what do you think I might secretly long for?"

"Do you want to hurt me?" I squeaked.

"Not hurt you. Never hurt you. But dominate you? Yeah. I would love that."

He didn't sound quite as drunk anymore. His voice was steady and low. My mouth went dry.

"You see?" he said, sitting beside me. One hand behind me, one hand on my knee, all sense of menace gone from his face. "I long to be in charge—to be strong and powerful. And you long to surrender authority. For someone else to be in charge. Lock and key. That's why I can't stop thinking about you."

He was scaring me. And exciting me.

"I don't think I can let go like that," I tried, but he cut me off.

"No, you're misunderstanding. Being submissive isn't about being weak. Because you're not being forced. You're surrendering. It's your choice."

"My choice?" My heart pounded in my chest, and my fingertips tingled.

"Your choice. You make good choices; that's who you are. And you can take it back at any time."

"How?" I whispered, my eyes on his mouth. "Like—a safe word?"

He smiled and smoothed my hair from my face gently. "You don't need a safe word. The regular one will do fine."

I leaned toward him, drawn by his warmth and strength. "Regular one? What's the regular one?"

"*No*, of course." He smiled. "All you have to say is *no*. And I'll stop."

I was frozen, unable to move. My head was exploding with possibility. What he described was so . . . dirty. So secret.

So exciting.

"Stop what?" I whispered.

"Using you. Like a slut. A whore. Someone designed specifically to please a man."

I shivered, and he smiled—just a little cruelly—at my reaction.

"And you won't hurt me?"

"I don't get off on pain. I won't hurt you."

"No ropes or bondage or anything?"

Now his smile was wicked. "I won't need ropes to restrain you."

"I might fight back."

It was his turn to shiver. "Really? I'd like that."

"You would? You're a brute."

"Now you've got it. What's the word? How do you stop this?"

I lowered my head and whispered it: "*No.*"

"Good girl. Now that you know that, I'm going to take over. Are you ready?"

He was poised and on high alert, but unmoving. I had to buy into this—buy into a fantasy I'd never realized I had.

I bit my lip. Surrendering to him seemed almost . . . shameful. And I wanted it so badly.

". . . yes."

He shoved me flat on the bed and had one elbow under my knee before I could do more than gasp. "Want to fight? Go on— try to stop me."

He leaned his weight on me, and I tried to push him away. I used my strength to lengthen the leg he'd bent almost to my chest and arched to throw him off.

He laughed and caught my hands, bringing more of his weight on me. His crotch was against my hip, and his erection was undeniable. He lowered his head and nuzzled my breast through the T-shirt. "That's it? That's all you've got?"

I pulled my hands free and pushed against his shoulders, wriggling to slip free.

One of his hands wrapped around my shoulder to stop me from going up the bed, and the other arm around my knee blocked me from sliding down. I was trapped under his weight and his heat and his strength, and my heart was pounding, and my core was wet and needy. "Let go," I gasped.

"No," he said with a grin. "See, I can say it. *No.* No. Again, no. I'm not letting you go. But you go ahead and keep wiggling. It feels so good when you do."

Could he really dominate me so easily? My heart raced in excitement. What was left to try? "Please let me go."

"No." He bit my nipple and I jerked. "But that was a good try. You sound scared and pathetic. Too bad you're under a total scoundrel."

"You are a scoundrel," I agreed, and he kissed me, pushing his tongue into my mouth and controlling my body. My hands were now clenching and stroking his shoulders instead of pushing him away. Had I surrendered so easily? Was that all it took?

I made a galvanic movement and managed to push my leg away from my chest. He growled and redoubled his grip. "Good one. Keep trying. Maybe twist your hips around?"

He was using my writhing to get off. "Bastard. Sicko. Freak."

"Yeah," he breathed. "You got it. Keep going. What else?"

I couldn't help it. I erupted in giggles. "Bastard," I repeated.

"Poor imagination. You said that one already. Turn over."

"Huh?"

He used his strength to flip me onto my stomach. "Cross your arms under your forehead. Like that. That's it. Now, be a good girl, and I'll make you feel good. Not that it matters in the end, because you *are* going to get fucked."

I buried my flushed face in my arms and shivered at his words.

CHAPTER TWENTY-FIVE—ARTIE

She was a dream. Responsive and hot and so excited by the idea of submitting to me that her nipples were tight buds and she unconsciously ground her crotch into me.

But on her stomach, defenseless before me, was even better. She couldn't see what I would do, she couldn't struggle or fight—she was mine to control.

I tasted metal, the flood of testosterone rocketing through me. Until I tasted it again, I never would have associated the metallic tang on my tongue with the first raw years of adolescence—when any curve, any scent, any sound of a woman laughing would make me hard.

And here I was once more, salivating like a teenager, tasting metal and all but drooling on her.

My higher intelligence reminded me this was an event to be savored. Finding a powerful, strong woman willing to submit? Not common. I should go slowly. Explore all the aspects of a hotly erotic scenario.

My instinct caused me to fist my hands in the neck of her T-shirt.

I paused for a moment.

And then I ripped the fabric apart, the sound an echo of the scream I was making inside.

Mine.

Naked.

Shred.

I'd descended into primitive behavior, and Ellyn's gasp of surprise was gasoline on the fire. "Buy a new one," I demanded in grunts.

I had to shift to get all the way to the bottom of the shirt, and the hem resisted me. But there was no way I would be defeated. My muscles bunched, and my fists were rocks. The cloth parted with a final rip.

Her spine and her luscious ass were exposed to the air—and to my gaze.

The view was gorgeous. Long, lean muscles, strong from carrying that damned camera bag everywhere. Her skin was pale and supple and gleamed like a pearl.

Her ass was curved and tempting. I had to bite it. There—on the full sweep as it rounded into the thigh. She jumped at the nip. "Hey! You bit me!"

"Be quiet," I said, all of my focus on the small pink crescents from my teeth coming up on her skin.

I'd marked her. *Mine.*

"Well, don't do it again."

I swatted her ass for her boldness and bit the other cheek. She twisted around to protest, and I put a hand between her shoulder blades and pushed her flat again. "Lie still."

"Make me," she panted. She challenged me—and she wasn't saying no.

My balls drew tight against my body, and my cock was like steel. I pushed her legs apart and shifted to lie on top of her, rubbing my dick against her ass.

I held myself on one hand while I unbuttoned my shirt with the other. She had to hold all of my weight for the moments when I unbuttoned my cuffs, but I made sure she could breathe and didn't feel suffocated.

Still, she was pretty thoroughly crushed, and I tried not to enjoy it too much.

I tugged my shirt out of my pants and fought my way out of the cloth. It hit the floor beyond the bed, and I lay on her for the sensation of her naked skin against mine.

I held her down and breathed in her ear while I kicked my shoes off and used my toes to peel off my socks. I licked her earlobe and bit her shoulder. "Don't," she breathed.

"That's not the word you need," I reminded her. "*Don't* isn't going to make me stop."

She held her breath while I licked across the bite and rubbed my cock against her ass again. "I know," she admitted. She wanted more. I was so excited I almost fucked her right then.

Instead, I got off and flipped her over. "Don't move. Lie there. I want to look at you."

Her hair was in her face and she moved to smooth it back, but I caught her hand.

"No. Don't move. I told you."

She stilled. Already so obedient.

I pushed her hands to her sides, and she held them there. With one finger, I hooked the remnants of her sleep shirt and drew it slowly down her body, until she was perfectly naked in front of me.

She was a fantasy. Slender but strong. Breasts exactly the shape of my cupping hand. A thatch of flame at her crotch. Long legs currently pressed together, her ankles demurely crossed.

That wouldn't do at all.

"Open your legs."

She was breathing hard. "What if I don't?"

I stroked the hair from her face and smiled at her so she could see I wasn't going to stop. "Then you won't get to know what comes next."

"What comes next?" Her gaze was focused, and she shivered slightly.

"Open your legs. Do as I tell you, and you'll see."

She uncrossed her ankles and I sizzled from another rush of testosterone. *Do as I tell you.* "Good. Further. Further."

I made her lie with her legs awkwardly far apart so cold air invaded the hottest part of her. I knelt beside her and took her hand in mine. "Put this one here."

I moved her until her hand cupped her breast. She bit her lip and did as she was told. "Play with the nipple." I kept my hand on hers as her fingers plucked and teased her own skin. So pretty.

She deserved a reward, so I slid my other hand over her hip bone and boldly into the fork of her legs. She gasped as my fingers found the wetness at her core and slid slickly across her folds.

Then I had her clit under my finger. She closed her eyes, and I allowed it. Her hips began to move against me, and she sighed.

"Undo my belt," I ordered. Her eyes flew open. "Let go of your tit and open my belt. Do it, or I stop rubbing you. Want me to stop rubbing you?"

She shook her head and her hand went to my belt, brushing over my cock. I jumped at the sensation. "Careful."

"Sorry," she whispered. Her fingers fumbled, but soon my belt was open.

"Now the button. And the zipper. Slowly. Go slowly."

I talked her through it and raised my hips so she could push the fabric away. "Now the shorts. Lift the band over my cock—gently. You don't want to make anything angry."

Biting her lip, she unveiled me.

My cock, my oldest friend, was hot and hard and huge against her slim hand. She was responding with perfect submission, excited to be going through the actions of revealing the weapon of her surrender, and I increased the pressure on her clit in reward.

She gasped again and closed her eyes. But I wanted her to watch what I did to her.

"Take my cock in your mouth." My demand was harsh. I would fill her soft, wet mouth, and I would fuck her tight, hot core, and she did not have the option of refusing.

She wore her surprise on her face and turned slightly so she could bend to me without dislodging the finger that teased and tormented her.

First, she simply kissed me, her full lips pouting against the head. Then her tongue came out to swipe at me. And at last, she opened her mouth and engulfed me, sliding her head over my cock. She was eager and shy at the same time, and I had to fight the urge to grab her head and fuck her mouth until I jetted down her throat.

The thought was almost too much. I pulled her off me after only a few plunges. "Stop. That's not where I'm going to come. Lie back."

She did as she was told, shivering and panting. Her hands were fists against her sides.

"Play with your nipples. Both hands. Show me how you like it."

She obeyed, sweet and eager. I clenched my jaw against the lust that threatened to overwhelm me.

I fished in my pants for the condom and shifted to kneel between her legs. "This is it. You're about to be fucked." She gasped and pulled on her nipples. "You know what word stops this?"

She nodded, her eyes never leaving me.

"You know if you don't say it, I'm going to shove my cock into your cunt and fuck you hard?"

"Yes. I know."

I grinned. "You are such a slut. You want this, don't you? You're aching for my cock."

She writhed at my words, her breath ragged. "Yes," she whispered.

The condom was in place, the pressure a faint mockery of the viselike grip I needed. "I know. Use your hand. You seat me at the entrance."

"Oh, God."

Her hand stole from her breast, and she wrapped her fingers around my thickness.

"Go on," I grunted. "Pull me down. Do it—put me where you're aching to have me."

She dragged the head of my cock down and across her clit. She moaned, and I was at the entrance to her heat and wetness.

"Go slowly—please," she begged.

"You're lucky I'm in a good mood." Nevertheless, I went faster than she might have liked—not that she said the word to stop me.

She offered small yips as I pressed inside her, and the muscles of her belly jumped against my hand. "There. I'm in you now. Feel that? Feel my cock in you?"

She shivered and gasped, her fingers clutching my forearm. "I feel it. You're too big."

"Not too big. I'll prove it." I pulled out again, my teeth clenched in concentration. "Here it comes again."

Her exhale was as drawn out as the stroke. I watched her carefully; she was just on the good side of pain. "There. Now you're being fucked. I'm fucking you, and there's not much you can do about it."

The words were exciting me as much as they were her, and I grabbed her knee again. Putting my elbow underneath, I pushed her leg against her chest so she was even more open to me.

"You're taking it now—you're taking my cock. You slut. You're getting fucked now. Take it. Take it all."

We were both panting, and her moans had become cries. Her hips pushed against me, driving me deeper. The impending explosion curled at the base of my spine, and I knew—no matter how rare, how exciting this was, I wasn't going to last long enough to draw it out and savor the experience. She was too hot, her grip too tight, her surrender too complete for me to remain calm.

Just as the top of my head was lifting off—as molten gold and fire shot through my veins—I planted my thumb on her clit and ground down mercilessly. She shrieked and then we were both coming, jittering and pulsing and out of control.

With the last of my strength, I fell to her side so I wouldn't crush her. She curled into me, and I felt the wetness of tears on my chest.

"All right?" I murmured.

"So all right," she sighed.

I slept for a few minutes. She might have too.

Then I peeled myself off her, disposed of the condom, and pulled her under the covers, spooning her against me. She fit perfectly, with legs long enough that I pressed against her all along my thighs and shins.

"You are a princess," I whispered.

She laughed lightly. "Is that how princesses are treated?"

"Not that—this." I turned her in my arms and kissed her with all the reverence and softness I could muster.

She sighed and curled under my chin. "Yes, that was nice too."

Something had shifted in my soul. I released my breath in a long sigh of pure satisfaction. I should have been more careful about being vulnerable, but by surrendering, she'd somehow gotten past all of my defenses. And I was feeling chatty.

CHAPTER TWENTY-SIX—ELLYN

It was hard to take anything too seriously after an orgasm that intense, but as I lay curled against Artie, I marveled at what I'd learned.

"I'm a submissive," I said in surprise.

"Sometimes," he agreed, stretching his long legs.

"What do you mean?"

"Well, I'm a beast, but only some of the time. I also like the way we fucked the other night."

Mmm. "Yeah. That was good too. So—I'm not always a submissive?"

He chuckled. "You can be anything you want. In a few years, when I've recovered, want to make me the submissive?"

The thought jerked me awake. "Really?"

"Sure. Why not?"

"How would I even do that? You're so much bigger and stronger than me."

"And you like that." He was smug. Fair enough. He was right; I liked how big he was. After a lifetime of always being taller than every other woman and a lot of men, being with him made me feel . . . dainty. Feminine. More than feminine—he made me feel female.

"Well, I do like that. Tonight."

"All the time." Arrogant ass. "You'd have to figure out how to dominate me. I'm pretty sure you'll come up with an idea."

The idea made me wriggle my toes. What a fun possibility.

Maybe he heard me thinking. He snorted his amusement and pulled me closer. "You're a slut. I approve."

"Thanks. You're a bastard."

"A scoundrel," he corrected. "We're a good pair."

"Seems that way." All the things that should have bothered me about sleeping with Artie had faded. Post-orgasmic stupidity, I supposed.

"Artie, who's Victor?"

"Hmm. Victor." I could hear the smile in his voice. "Victor was the master, and I was the apprentice."

"He taught you how to scam?"

He puffed out air. "I always knew how to scam. You're born with it or you're not. Victor taught me how to not get caught."

I thought about it. "What do you mean, you're born with it?"

He rolled onto his back and settled me on his chest. His other hand went behind his head and he stretched with a satisfied groan. "Well, let's see. I'll give you my backstory."

"Oh, good." Artie had a great voice; I would have listened to him read the dictionary. But this was even better.

"My father is a shithead. That's the starting point of my narrative."

"What kind of shithead? The beat-his-kids kind?"

"The unrepentant alcoholic kind. The kind who loses a union job, and those are hard to lose. So, he sits in a recliner in his living room all day and blames people and acts like someone has done him wrong. He's a shit."

The sentiment was presented with so little emotion I figured he was covering long-standing pain. He kept talking.

"My mother is still with him. Still bringing him beer and borscht and the dark pumpernickel he likes from the bakery he demands. I don't know why she stays with him. At first it was because she had four kids, but we're all grown now. She could leave."

"Maybe she loves him."

He scoffed. "Not likely."

"You're the oldest?"

"Second to youngest." He yawned through the words. He settled in for the story and relaxed. "I have an older and younger brother, and an older sister. And to hear them tell it, they had a crappy childhood."

I could hear his contempt in his voice. "Not you?"

"I had a great fucking childhood. They're wimps."

He was so casual in his dismissal that it made me chuckle. "Why was yours so much better than theirs?"

"Because, as previously noted, I was born to scam people. So here we have Hildy Petrovitch and her four children and her useless husband. How does she feed us all? She had a few jobs, but that wasn't enough. To make ends meet, she'd take one of the kids into a store to distract the manager while she tucked things under her coat."

"She stole."

"Damn right, she did. She hated it, but she did it. And my father ate every single thing she brought home too. He used to place orders—more like demands. The fucker." This time, the pain was more obvious.

"And sometimes she took you."

"At first it was sometimes, and then it was all the time. My brothers and sister were hopeless. Terrible at distracting people. Not me—I'm great at it. Soon, she stopped taking them at all. And soon she stopped going. I did all the stealing, and I was good at it."

"She was okay with that? Your mother knows what you do?"

"Maybe in the beginning she was sorry, but she got saddled with a black hole of a man instead of a decent partner. She figures we all have to do what we must to survive, and she knows I like conning people. She's good with it."

He was smug and arrogant about his history—his natural skills. "What did you like about it?"

He was silent for a moment in thought. "The thrill, of course. It's exciting. It's like—I'm more alive on the edge. You have to think fast. Read people. Make a mistake, and it's all over. That's . . . good."

"You're an adrenaline junkie."

He was far from offended. "No question. Absolutely. I love it. A great con is the most energetic buzz in the world. I'm a god when I pull off a good con. Nothing at all is more fun. Nothing."

He was so sure of himself, so satisfied. I envied him knowing his place in the world so totally, even if he was very definitely on the wrong side of the law.

"So, there you are, a little thieving child, liberating foodstuffs from across Staten Island."

"Well—I branched out. All of Manhattan was mine pretty quickly. I'm pretty independent, and I was using the ferry and the subways alone when I was eight."

"That didn't freak out your mother?"

He shook his head. "She dug it. Everybody could stay home safe, and I'd go out and get what we needed to survive."

He was proud. "You didn't resent it at all?"

"Resent it?" My question had confused him. "They were bad at it, and I was good at it. That's just the way it was."

"And they did nothing to help?"

"Oh, sure. Kaz would protect me from bullies at school, and Wendy made me clothes—anything I asked for. And as I grew, so did my innate stylishness. I looked good then too."

"And Kaz and Wendy are—?"

"Older brother and sister. And Simon, my younger brother."

"Okay, so keep going. You're a junior criminal and supporting your family of six. Then what?"

He scoffed. "Then Simon started being afraid to go to church."

I shook my head to clear it. "You're robbing stores across the city, and you're still going to church?"

"Sure. I like church. I like the hymns."

That made me smile. He and I could sing "God of Our Fathers" in two-part harmony. "Okay. So, about Simon and church?"

"Yeah. He was nine, maybe nine and a half, and I made him spill it: the new priest was after him."

"Oh, shit. The poor boy!"

"Yeah." I could hear satisfaction in his voice. "Not for long, though."

"Why? What happened?"

"Me. I happened. I made sure I got the new priest for confession. I was sitting in the confessional, and he slid open the gate, and I told him I'd hired a thug to cut his balls off. If he ever wanted to go after any other nine-year-olds, he better get the hell out of Staten Island before Monday afternoon."

"How old were you?"

"Um—eleven?"

"And he believed you."

"I was very persuasive. He was gone the next day."

"Wow. That's awesome. What about the other kids in his new parish, though?"

"That was their problem. I was eleven. I protect my own." He had no remorse, and I decided for a little kid, he'd done pretty well for himself.

"Had you really hired someone?"

"Nah. But I could have if he'd stuck around."

I nudged him in his ribs, and he grunted. "You're a hero."

"Yeah. You're just now seeing that? Anyway, word got around, and I got a reputation. Within a year, this local boy buttonholed me. Henry Dragomir. He wanted to be known as the Dragon, but everyone called him Fat Henry. Still, he was a tough bastard."

He was lost in thought for a moment and went on.

"Sometimes Kaz ran with Henry's gang, but mostly it was

older guys. And one day, Henry found me and told me from now on, I'd be stealing for him. And he had big plans for me."

"Like what?"

"Like no more lifting stuff from stores. He was branching out to breaking and entering, and my status as a juvenile made me pretty appealing to him. He said if I did, he'd let Kaz into the gang. And if I didn't, he'd let the gang into Wendy."

"The fucker!"

"No doubt."

"So, what did you do?"

"I thought about it for a while and said I'd run with him. Then I called a cop who had been bugging me for a while and told him where we were going to be on which night. Henry got pinched."

"Good for you!"

"Yeah. Trouble was, I had enough of a juvenile record by then that I got pinched too. I didn't get sent to the same place as Henry, but I was in juvenile detention with his little brother. So, I had to arrange protection pretty quickly."

He talked about a nightmarish movie-of-the-week scenario like we were sharing what we did for summer vacation. My head spun.

"So, I became lovers with two of the bigger guys there, and they took care of me."

"Lovers?" I gasped the word. "They raped you?"

"Nah. I don't do rape. It was a deal, and I was fine with it."

"And how old were you?"

"Thirteen by then."

"Oh my God. Were you a virgin?"

"Mostly. But really, it wasn't a nightmare. I'm pretty much bisexual anyway. Especially if it benefits me. But mostly, I just enjoy it. It feels good. It's not like a prison movie. I mean, it *was* like a prison movie, but a *good* prison movie."

The distinction was lost on me.

"Anyway, I got out of there with some good friends, some

terrible enemies, and a whole lot more knowledge about my chosen profession. But Henry the Fat Dragon wasn't in a forgiving mood. When I was fifteen, I told my folks they'd have to take care of themselves for a while, and I left."

"You left? What do you mean?"

He shrugged. "You know. Just went away."

"I really don't know. What do you mean? What did you do? How did you eat? Where did you sleep?"

"Wherever. It wasn't that hard. I was already tall and bulky, and I could get jobs. Dishwasher. I was a migrant farmworker for a while—that's backbreaking. It'll teach you quick that whatever you do, you don't want to work for a living. After a bit, I got a job in a shitty traveling carnival as a roustabout. That was fun. After a while, a bigger carnival hired me away. And that's where I met Victor."

He smiled again; I could hear it in his voice. He spoke of Victor with more affection than he'd shown for anyone else in his tale. "And he taught you how to be a real con man."

"Yeah. Not just a thief. Some of the jobs I pull are semilegal. That's why that guy you called? Dash at the FBI? Yeah. He knows I run cons, but none of it was bad enough to get me arrested—like conning your Aunt Cor. What are we actually doing wrong here?"

"Well . . . manipulating her? Making her believe a hot stud is interested in her?" He goosed me when I labeled him a hot stud, but that didn't distract me for long. "Maybe it's not against the law, but it's morally disgusting."

"Disgusting? That's too much. I do like her. I think she's awesome."

"And yet you're lying in bed with her niece, having fucked me into seizures or something."

"Yeah? Seizures? That's good, right?"

"Yeah. That's good. What we're doing to Cor is not good."

"Oh, please. She's a grown woman. She can make her own

decisions. And if you and I weren't here, she might fall for Marcus, who would ignore her. At least I'd talk to her."

"You would, wouldn't you?" I felt a wave of fondness for the golden brute.

"Sure. Especially if we talked about me."

I tickled him, and he growled and rolled over on me. He kissed me, and it started out sweet and sleepy. But it didn't end up that way.

Soon I was panting—again—and he was hard and nestled between my legs.

Then he climbed off me and stood, holding out a hand to me. "Come on."

"Where are we going?"

He pulled me out of bed and to the connecting door. "I only had one condom in my pocket. The rest are in here. Besides, I want you to ride me like you were earlier, on that shitty bench of a bed. It will be the best thing that ever happens in this crappy little cabin."

"Oooh. I think you're right about that."

CHAPTER TWENTY-SEVEN—ARTIE

I DROPPED A KISS ON HER NAKED SHOULDER WHEN I GOT UP. She was sprawled across the massive bed on her stomach and hidden in a tangle of hair. Edible. My mouth actually watered.

"I'm going to work out," I said softly. "I'll be a little while."

She mumbled a reply.

"What'd you say?" I asked, stepping back to the bed.

She rolled her head and one green eye looked at me. "I said why. Last night wasn't vigorous enough for you?"

I smiled at her. "Because it feels good, of course."

Her reply would have been a snort if she'd been more awake. I freed her feet from the tangle of sheets and blankets at the foot of the bed and pulled them over her. *Sleep like a princess, huh? Always tidy when you sleep, huh? Right.*

She purred at the warmth and curled onto her side, burrowing deeper and hugging a pillow to her chest. I almost got back in with her.

But serratus is an unforgiving series of muscles. If you don't work them out regularly, you don't get that pop of tiny divots over the ribs. And I like those divots.

I like how women respond to them.

I am an artist, and my body is my canvas. I make of myself

what I put into myself, and twisting crunches pay off in excellent definition.

"I'll be back."

"Unf," the redheaded pile of covers said.

I flirted idly in the gym with King Arthur's Court—that was what my regular observers had taken to calling themselves. At least two of them were ready for some form of sex in the locker room, and I could have talked two more into it. Not with each other, of course . . . although that would have been an interesting challenge.

But no. I was fucked out at the moment. Either that or I was temporarily hungrier for a very specific body type. White, creamy skin. Long limbs. Russet hair.

I was daydreaming on the rowing machine (not enough to pop a boner; just enough to know it was a possibility) when that exact body type walked into the gym.

Unfortunately, it was attached to Cousin Farrah.

She wore a short, shimmery dress that made the most of the family's leg legacy and carried a martini glass like a caricature of a New York City party girl. She growled casually at the woman on the treadmill with immediate results. The woman—a mommy with dreams of a hot fling while her husband was oblivious in sleep—fled immediately.

I amended my assessment. A mean New York City party girl.

Farrah sat on the equipment, her legs sprawled carelessly across the space between us.

"It's my dockside buddy," she said breezily. I could smell the alcohol on her breath. "Don't you look yummy."

"Thanks." I kept rowing. The toe of her high-heeled sandal was brushing my glute every time I took another stroke. I was reasonably confident she was well-aware of this, hoping her stroking my ass with her shoe would be appealing to me.

"So, Arthur. Pretty Arthur. You're very hot." She looked around the tiny gym and fanned her hand. "I mean, like, sexy. But this place is pretty hot too."

I suppressed my smile. "Only warm place on the entire ship. At least, it is once I'm finished with my workout."

"Are you nearly finished?"

"Just about. What can I do for you, Farrah?"

"Well, if you're going to be all direct about it—what's up with you and my aunt?"

"What do you mean?"

"I mean, are you her boyyyyyyfriend?" She drew out the word. I saw a different side of her. Hungover Farrah and non-drunk Farrah was a lot nicer than the gin-soaked stress queen in front of me now.

"I'm her dance partner."

"She likes you."

"I'm glad. I like her."

She pounced. "How much? Like—does she, like, do what you say?"

I had a quick flash of how much work it took to get Ellyn to do what I said for an all-too-brief half hour the night before—and how mind-blowingly worth it the effort had been.

Farrah kept talking. "Let me explain." She attempted to sip from her empty glass and pouted when there was nothing in it. "I want my aunt to like me the most. And if you help me get that, I'll be very grateful." She leered at me. "*Very* grateful, if you know what I mean."

"Wouldn't you be very grateful even if I didn't help you?" I finished my time and unhooked my feet. I stood and put my hands on my hips, looming over her.

"Jesus. Look at you."

I gave her a cocky grin. "If you want your aunt to like you, be nice to her. It's not hard. She's a sweetheart."

"Yeah." Farrah did not seem persuaded.

I grabbed a towel. "Maybe you'd like to get some sleep, Farrah. It's seven in the morning."

"Ugh. Don't remind me. This damn sunshine is *everywhere*."

She grabbed the bar over her head and dragged herself upright. "I'm going to have such a bad headache today."

"Two big glasses of water and three aspirins," I said.

"Oh, like you can teach me anything about drinking. Well, see what you can do for me, Arthur. The old lady likes you."

I found I didn't like Farrah referring to Cor as "the old lady," but as I was already treating the girl to a view of my fine, muscled ass as I walked out, I didn't bother to make the correction.

I took my usual place at Basilio's bar while he set up for the day. He made me a smoothie, and I grabbed a plate of fruit from the poolside buffet. Life was peaceful and full of restorative hydration until a streak of black appeared at my side.

Liv slipped onto the barstool next to me.

Why hadn't I foreseen this? And when would Priss make her play?

Liv opened her mouth to start. I cut her off.

"I just spent a charming few minutes with your twin sister."

"Farrah?" Liv asked, surprised.

"You have more than one twin?"

Liv favored me with a dirty look.

"She wanted to know what it would take for me to encourage Cor to feel more affectionate toward Farrah."

"Oh, Christ. She's so out of control." Liv dropped her head onto her hands. Pity (a rusty emotion in my life) reared its unwanted head. "What did she say?" Liv asked.

"Implied sexual favors for my help."

Liv winced. "Well, don't take her too seriously. I've heard from lots of would-be boyfriends that she talks a good game, but she's very selective."

I raised an eyebrow. Of course she would have followed through with me. But I let the point go.

"So, Arthur—you know about the decision Cor's going to be making soon?"

I frowned. "I know about it." I knew more than she thought.

"And can you tell me if she's leaning in one direction or another?"

I shook my head in admiration. "Why don't you ask her?"

Liv sighed. "That's not how it's done in our family. I don't know why not. It would make more sense."

"You could try."

"I could." Clearly, she wouldn't. She rallied and turned to me. "I'm not Farrah. I won't tempt you with sex." I inclined my head in acknowledgment. "But I am prepared to make it worth your while—financially—if you could tip the scales in my favor."

"You'd cheat against your own twin?"

Liv closed her eyes and offered a shudder. "Farrah would literally party away all the money. She could very well drink herself to death. It would be the worst thing in the world for her if she won. If the money comes to me, at least I could take care of her."

She almost sounded like a martyr. It was nicely played. "Very noble of you."

"I've watched over her all our lives."

"Well, out of curiosity, what kind of money are you talking about paying me here?"

She leaned in. Basilio leaned in, too, and Liv glared at him. He moved away. "Five. Thousand. Dollars."

I played it close and did not laugh out loud. "It's worth that much to you," I said with a whistle.

She nodded gravely and laid one slim hand on my forearm. "Please help me, Arthur. For Farrah's sake. She's not well."

I finished my smoothie and stood. "Thanks, Liv. It's been . . . interesting talking to you."

"Does that mean you'll help me?"

"No." I smiled. "It means it's been interesting. See you later."

I left her fuming, frustrated, and glaring in the brilliant morning light. The twins were not sun-worshipers.

Priss was actually lurking in the hallway outside my cabin. She looked up with a jerk when I arrived.

"Oh, Arthur—there you are!"

"Priss. Christ."

"Keep your voice down. I want to talk to you."

"Let me guess. You want me to influence your Aunt Cor to like you best."

Priss blinked. "Oh. Are you already working with Ellyn on this? She and I are partners. Anything she knows, I can know too!"

Bold as brass, this one. "I'm not working with Ellyn. I just had conversations with Farrah and then with Liv. And now you. I've been approached by everyone *but* Ellyn."

"Typical." Priss deflated. "Miss Do-the-Right-Thing all our lives, like a boat dragging an anchor. Please. So, who are you working with? Will you work with me?" She placed a hand on my chest and blinked up at me soulfully. "Will you help me protect a legacy for my child?"

I stepped away from her hand and chuckled. "You Wolcotts. Damn."

I opened my door, but before I went in, I turned to her. "What are you offering in exchange? Just so I'm clear."

She gave me a sharp look. "Why? What did the twins offer?"

"The promise of sex and five thousand dollars."

She huffed. "No question of who offered which." She eyed me. "None of those was to your liking, huh? Well, what do you want?"

I shook my head. "Nothing, Priss. I want a shower and a peaceful morning. I'll see you later."

I closed the door on her objections.

I'd finished showering and applying the day's sunscreen and was back in my cabin getting dressed when the muffled knock came at the door. Who now? Was there a Wolcott I'd missed?

I opened the door and cursed myself as a fool for missing it.

It was Luz, the sad-faced maid.

"Hi, Luz," I said, not at all sure how to play this one.

She raised her chin and stared at me. The silence drew out

painfully, and she said, "I take care of my lady."

"I know you do," I began to bluster.

She raised an imperious hand. "I take care of her. I watch over her. And I watch *for* her." She gestured with her head, and I turned to look behind me.

Damn it. The door between my cabin and Ellyn's was open.

"Oh—uh—"

"I see you go into this room from the gym. I hear the shower going on in her cabin. And now here you are, clean and fresh. You think I don't know what's going on?"

"No—it's not what you think. I'm too big for the bathroom in—"

She held up her hand. "Stop. Come with me now. Bring your phone."

My phone? What the hell was going on here?

She refused to say another word. She stalked through the ship until we came upon a crowd of Lycra-clad women leaving the Sunrise Stretch class in the yoga studio.

Luz waited. Once the room cleared, she went inside and pointed to the sound system.

"Bésame Mucho."

"I'm sorry?"

"Put on the music. Do it now!" She stomped her foot and all of a sudden, she looked imperious. Queenly. Despite my alarm, I grinned at her powerful attitude—so different from her silent, morose subservience.

I did as I was told and returned to her at the center of the room.

"Now," she said, holding her arms up, "now I will show you the rumba."

Jesus.

She began to dance and I followed, purely in self-defense. She'd been to all of the rehearsals with Cor, sitting on the bench a little away from Ellyn and Rebel, and she knew our routine. And suddenly everything flowed together like water.

She was breathtaking. She danced away from me and beckoned, and I came willingly like a magnet. She pushed me away, and my feet found the rhythm and pulled me along. We came together with sinuous, snaky hips, we parted, I spun her, and she held the dip as graceful as a reed.

Despite my every cynical instinct, I slipped into enchantment. Luz was enchanting me.

The dance finished with a flourish, with her draped over my arm in a sensuous fall. I shouted with delight.

She came out of the pose like a jack-in-the-box, startling me. "Now. We do it again until you get it right. You can lead my lady better. You can be better. I know. I *am* Cuban."

For the next astonishing forty-five minutes, Luz taught me how to lead—how to place Cor to best effect. She did what she'd said: she showed me the rumba. By the end, I was sweaty and panting. And I was better.

"All right," she said. "That's as much as I can do before tonight. Now you are not completely hopeless. Do not tell her I worked with you. Do. Not. And I will not tell her. This, she does not need to know. You make sure she wins that contest. That's what she wants."

"Thank you, Luz."

She nodded and stalked from the yoga studio. By the time we'd returned to our stretch of hallway, she'd lost her regal posture and was back to being sad. But she stopped me before we parted.

She hiked a thumb at Ellyn's door. "That one? She's the only one worth anything. Stick with her. And don't hurt my lady."

I briefly thought about protesting, about insisting I wasn't with Ellyn. Instead, I raised my eyebrows in acknowledgment. "Thank you, Luz."

She nodded. Then she went into her cabin.

So much had happened, and I burned to tell Ellyn about it. I needed her take on things, her improvements on my plans. She and I needed to do some strategizing.

CHAPTER TWENTY-EIGHT—ELLYN

THE BEDCOVERS WERE RUDELY RIPPED FROM ME, EXPOSING ME
to the frigid air. I groaned in protest.

Artie landed next to me, one large, warm hand coming onto
my stomach. He began to pet me.

"Damn. Still gorgeous. Look at you."

I hid my grin and fished around for the sheets. He relented
and covered me again, rolling off the bed. "I've got to grab a
shower."

"You were just in the shower," I complained.

"That was an hour ago. Wake up. I've got a lot to tell you."
He swatted my ass on the way past and I jumped. Parts of me
were very tender.

"You worked me hard last night," I grumped and sat. The
sheet fell away from my breasts, and he turned to ogle me.
That gave me a zip of excitement in tender places, and I
arched my spine. I liked him looking at me. I liked him
wanting me.

He leered. "I've got a few aches and pains myself. Worth it,
though?"

"Oh, fuck yeah."

"Maybe I'll skip the shower."

I held up my hand. "Go on. I'm still waking up. And when you're done, I really don't want to hear about your abs workout."

"Abs are critical," he teased. "But I've got more news than that for you. Give me a minute."

Good thing I had access to a second—if tiny—bathroom in his closet of a cabin, since I had to pee. I'd thrown the remnants of my sleep shirt in the trash and pulled on jeans and my hoodie by the time he came back, which he did while he was in the middle of applying my sunblock generously to a very large expanse of skin. I would have been more annoyed if it had been less fun to watch.

"You have way too many clothes on," he complained.

"You have too few." Just a towel. Low on the hips. Mmm. He saw me looking and flexed.

"Still think an abdominal workout isn't worth discussing?"

I groaned. "*So* vain. What story do you have?"

He prowled back and forth between our cabins, getting dressed and telling me about his discussions with my cousins.

"Farrah offered sex? Unlikely. She has a bit of a fierce cock-tease reputation."

"That's what Liv said. And Liv offered me . . ." he paused to build dramatic tension. Then he whispered, "Five. Thousand. Dollars."

"Wait—what?"

He burst out laughing, and I had to join him.

"Christ," I gasped. "She's so cheap! At least I offered you 10 percent."

"You offered 10," he agreed, falling to the couch beside me. "And I talked you up to 20."

"Oh. Right."

"Plus half of anything you get over the total. So, if your partnership with Priss is over, and you get the full five mil . . ." He added many zeros. "Five hundred thousand is 20 percent, plus you were only expecting two and a half mil, so I get half of the increase . . ."

"Hold on." We began arguing about percentages and totals and agreements, and he pulled my feet into his lap and began to massage them. His strong thumbs pressed into the arch of my foot and I groaned out loud, like a fool. The words dried up in my mouth. "Stop that."

He grinned. "We'll argue about money after you win. I saved the best for last—or rather, for Luz."

I sat up again and stopped drooling. "For Luz? What the hell?"

He told me about his dancing lessons with the maid and his promise to hide Luz's instruction from Cor.

"And Luz knows about . . . this?" I gestured between us. I wasn't sure what our relationship was, except for very dirty and very delicious.

"Apparently. You get her vote for Miss Congeniality, and I'm supposed to stick with you and not hurt Cor."

"Agh," I said incoherently. So much to unpack there, including my relationship with a scoundrel, Luz's surprising support, and whether my secret partnership with a con man would become common knowledge.

Artie watched me as I ran through these mental scenarios. He probably knew exactly what I was thinking.

I regarded him. "You *have* had a very busy morning."

"I have," he agreed. "Lots to add into our calculations. And we've run out of time for me to demonstrate again that my attraction to you is entirely sexual. What's my next move?"

We discussed his options and decided together to make no overt moves yet.

"All right," he said. "Then I've got to get on deck to be a lone wolf during breakfast, and you need to get sunblock on all those lickable parts."

I swatted him away with a grin and he departed, pulling the connecting doors closed behind him. *Should have made that a habit before he opened the door to Luz and her quick eye.*

But hindsight wouldn't fix that issue, and there was nothing to be done about it. Luz would spill my secret relationship with Artie, or she wouldn't. There was more for me to consider. I sat for a moment, thinking about what we'd learned about my cousins. The longer I thought about it, the sadder I got.

By the time I met my family for breakfast under the woven awning on the sun deck, I was in a blue study.

I sat and looked from cousin to cousin. What had happened to us? We used to spend our summer vacations together, as well as all the holidays. When we were growing up together, we were inseparable. I knew each one as well as I knew anyone. And yet here we were, trapped in some kind of war over stupid, corrosive money. Battling over someone no one really considered part of the family—someone I actually liked.

I was chewing my thumb and staring uselessly at a half-finished glass of papaya juice when Cor nudged me.

"Earth to Ellyn. Hello, darling. What are you thinking about so hard?"

I looked up surprised and found them all looking at me. I made a quick decision.

"I was thinking about what we could do today."

"What *is* there to do today?" Priss tossed her napkin onto the table. "We've got three days at sea on the way to India. No shopping to do."

"No culture to explore," Liv added.

"There's always the bar," Farrah said from behind a large pair of dark glasses.

"Bridge?" Rebel looked hopeful.

"Just wait," Cor said. "Let's hear what Ellyn is thinking. She's such a good organizer!"

She smiled at me warmly and I thought of Artie, understanding somehow that I didn't always want to be the one to make the decisions. Muscles deep inside me flexed in memory, and I ignored the sensation. He sat several tables away, ignoring us in favor of his book on Myanmar. Or was it Burma?

"Well, I thought . . . Aunt Cor, why don't you host a dress-up party in your suite for lunch?"

There was silence for a moment, and Liv said, "We're not girls anymore, Ellyn."

"And I'm not much in the mood for a lunch party," Farrah chimed in. "I thought I might get a nap before the rumba contest tonight."

Priss shook her head at me—but she did it while watching Cor. Hedging her bets, as always.

Rebel was my unexpected ally. "You're thinking of the saris we tried on."

"I am. That was fun. What if you had the ship's staff deliver a delicious lunch to your suite, Aunt Cor, and we had a girls-only dress-up session? Liv could make those saris gorgeous, and we could try on your new jewelry."

"I *would* like to wear that tiara," Priss admitted.

"It would look great on you," I said encouragingly.

"Or the yellow feathers," Farrah laughed. "It would be so you."

"I want the yellow feathers," Liv said, a hint of laughter in her voice.

Cor smiled. She bounced in her chair. "This will be so much fun! No men—and something to do this afternoon to keep my mind off the rumba contest!" She waggled her fingers across the deck to Artie, who nodded at her with a smile and went back to his book. "Just us! Ellyn, will you get the cook to meet with me about the menu?"

"I'll find the purser. Shall we say one o'clock? That will give Farrah time to sleep. Sound good?"

"I'm leaving Lovely with Trip!" Priss sounded triumphant; the rest of us tried to mask our relief. "Unless you think Luz would . . . ?"

"We'll need Luz to assist us," Cor said firmly. "All right. This might be the most fun afternoon of the whole trip! Good idea, Ellyn!"

The purser was delighted to assist. He and I worked with Cor and Rebel to put together what started out as light finger food and soon morphed into all of Cor's favorites. She lost him on the subject of egg creams, but he kept up most of the time, delighted to provide a pricey meal to the wealthiest woman on board.

I slipped out and updated Artie. He called me a sucker for trying to bring my family back together but agreed it was a good way to keep Cor calm before the rumba contest.

"What will you do while we're playing dress-up?"

He rolled his eyes. "I've got some grooming to do. You think this look happens by accident? I'm going to look good tonight. You wait and see."

I rolled my eyes back at him. "I suppose this manscaping is going to happen in my bathroom?"

"*Our* bathroom," he corrected, "so don't let any of your cousins into your suite."

"I'll keep them across the hall."

When the luncheon party began, both Liv and Priss were uptight and awkward, and Farrah was hungover. But I handed all three glasses of champagne, and they began to perk up.

Cor had persuaded Luz to untangle the nest of necklaces, and all of her new jewelry was spread out on the coffee table and desk. The various saris were draped on the bed along with a rainbow of scarves and shawls, and shoes were tucked into every available space.

There was a moment of silence. Cor looked anxiously at the faces in front of her.

And then Liv reached for one of the rolls of batik fabric. "Will you let me cut a length of the stuff we got in Papua New Guinea, Aunt Cor?"

Farrah sat at the desk and began pawing through rings. And Priss whipped a pashmina shawl the color of a flaming-orange sunset around her and preened. "I love this," she said.

And all the tension went out of the room.

Liv really was skilled at fashion; she managed to make both Cor and Rebel look beautiful in their saris, and she draped a batik sundress on me that I wanted immediately. She pulled out a sewing kit and sat cross-legged on the bed to piece it together. Priss forgot she was a society matron and plopped onto the floor to try on shoes.

And Farrah forgot her headache long enough to show us a modified Dance of the Seven Veils that had us all howling.

"Remember when Priss made the cookies with salt instead of sugar?"

"You ate them, Farrah—how bad could they have been?"

"Ooh, they were awful. Liv dared me to eat one. Gross! And you served them at dinner!"

"And remember Ellyn under the table when the Secretary of State came to dinner?"

"It wasn't State—it was Treasury."

"Whatever. And she fell asleep, and they didn't find her until she had a nightmare and hit her head on the underside of the table?"

"God, you were so cute, Ellie."

"Still am, thanks."

"Not like then. We used to send you in to ask if we could go to the Creamery because none of the parents could resist you."

"Well, I'm irresistible."

"Especially in that headdress. The yellow is so perfect with that blue-and-orange sari."

"I'm going to add emerald-green shoes," I said. "Cor, why are your feet so small?"

"Don't stretch them, darling—try these instead."

I put on the gray rubber-and-canvas shoes she'd bought at the market in Langkawi and struck a pose. We all howled with laughter. "Ask me now if we can go to the Creamery! I am magnificent!"

"You need a necklace."

"She needs twenty necklaces!"

Even Luz, standing by and ready to assist with hairstylings or safety pins, managed to crack a smile. It was the warmest, happiest afternoon I'd had since Uncle Carl died and all the lawsuits had broken out like measels across the face of the Wolcott family. I felt like I'd gotten my sisters back.

And they were going through the same warm fuzzies. Liv and Priss shared the sofa, leaning together to decide who'd put together the best collection of bangles, and Farrah gave Aunt Cor the quick sketch she'd made of Cor and Rebel in their saris. Rebel nudged me and gestured with her chin to Cor, whose eyes were shining.

"This is very good for her," she whispered.

"Good for all of us." I nodded.

"This evening—the competition. You know she's scared about it, don't you?"

I turned to Rebel, surprised, and drew Priss's attention. I smiled and reached for one of the apricot pastries. "These are great. Have you tried them, Rebel?"

Rebel patted her generous stomach. "Too many! Have you tried the chocolate with cardamom?"

We admired the food, and Priss lost interest.

"She's scared?" I whispered.

"She thinks she's going to make a fool of herself. She thinks she's a short, fat, old fool dancing with a boy half her age—less than half her age. Help her if you can. She could use a win."

We turned to the room and watched the feminine finery, listening to the laughter.

"This is pretty good, though," Rebel added with a smile. She nudged me again. "Good job."

"Give me the feathers, Ellyn," Farrah called out. "I need them."

I plucked the ornate headpiece off my hair, brushing the fall of canary-yellow feathers away. "You want it *with* the tiara?"

"And the necklaces. I'm going for 'island goddess.'"

"Then you'll need this collar too," Cor said, fishing out linked plates of bronze that draped over Farrah's collarbones. "There. You're like a Pilgrim on a spree."

"An impure Puritan," Liv chimed in. "Ellyn, take off that sari —try this sundress on. It's ready for a fitting."

I stored up the happiness. Competition and greed were waiting for us right outside the door, but at the moment we were together. For now.

CHAPTER TWENTY-NINE—ARTIE

I SAW IT RIGHT AWAY. BY THE TIME I SLIPPED INTO MY CHAIR next to Cor, her nervous energy had turned into blind panic.

"Arthur! Where did you go?" she hissed. Her grip on my arm was more talon than finger. Her fear was visible in the darkness of the ship's nightclub. The bright lights following the current dancers picked out the tension of her face, the slight tremble in her lip.

"I'm sorry. I was just gone a minute."

"Half an hour! You've missed the last three dancers. And they were good, Arthur. *Good*. I think . . ."

Her voice trailed off and she looked nervously to the couple now on the floor. They were both tall and slim, and the woman wore a tight, revealing dress. They weren't particularly skillful, but they had a lot of flash going for them. If we'd drawn a low number, she wouldn't have had to watch all the other competitors, but we were number nine of eleven entrants, and the wait was doing her no favors.

"Cor. I went to the men's room."

"I thought you'd left. Like when you went to Myanmar."

"Sweetheart—we're in the middle of the Bay of Bengal. Where would I have gone?"

My attempt at humor didn't penetrate. "And for a moment I thought I wouldn't have to dance, and that would be . . . so wonderful!" Her hands fluttered in the air. "Oh, I'm sorry, Arthur. You deserve someone so much better than me. Younger. Prettier. A much better dancer."

I knew exactly what was happening. She'd lost the personality she'd built after Carl divorced his first wife and married her. She'd forgotten she was easily the wealthiest woman on the ship. All of that had been stripped away by her fears, and she was back to being plump, little, inconsequential Corinne from Queens, saving her pennies so she could go to secretarial school. Every insecurity was laid bare and raw.

This was the moment every scam artist strives for. Her emotions were laid before me like a tangle of yarn; I could tug gently on one strand and unravel her completely. This was the moment I could own her, heart and soul.

And I found I couldn't do it.

She was so afraid.

I looked around the table, where Cor's family was grouped and nervously watching her terror. "We're all right here for you, Cor," I said and gestured to Rebel.

Her best friend took her hand, and Cor gripped it tightly. Ellyn rose and moved behind Cor, putting her hands lightly on her aunt's shoulders. Liv and Farrah both reached across the table, unable to touch her but still trying. Priss leaned past me to put her hand on Cor's arm. "We're here, Aunt Cor. It's okay. You're going to be wonderful."

Cor gulped. She hadn't expected a show of support, and I saw her eyes fill with tears. I tugged on her chair and pulled her into me.

"It's my fault, Cor," I whispered.

She startled and turned to look at me. "No, Arthur—you're perfect! No, it's me. I'm the problem. I'm short and dumpy and . . ."

I cut her off. "I've been a bad lead. But I'm going to fix that. You'll see. This will be our finest dance yet, I promise."

She blinked at me. "Our finest? But we haven't practiced any changes."

"No, I'm not talking about making changes," I soothed. "You're just going to have a better partner. But if you want to practice, let's do it up there in about five minutes. Just you and me, and your family to watch us—like we were in the yoga studio before cocktails. Forget about everyone else. Okay?"

She gulped. "You think I can do it?"

"I think *we* can do it. Who's better than us?" I gave her my cockiest grin, and she gave me a watery smile in return.

"Who indeed?"

"All right then!"

We both turned to watch the couple finish their routine. "Not bad," I whispered to her. "Her arm could be stretched out more."

"I thought the same thing! It would be a much better line."

"So, they're not as perfect as you thought, huh? Maybe not even a little perfect?"

Cor sat straighter. Bravery was making a comeback. Priss nudged me with her shoulder and smiled. Across the table, Luz held the sleeping toddler, but she nodded to me in approval. And Ellyn's hand ghosted down my head.

Cor noticed the movement and turned to see what it was. Ellyn recovered and plucked a small yellow feather from the shoulder of my white dinner jacket. "Making sure you're both perfect," she smiled.

"Am I okay?" Cor asked.

Ellyn nodded. "You look wonderful."

"And you'll take a picture?"

Ellyn held up her camera. "I'll catch the whole thing so you can remember your triumph forevermore!"

"A triumph," Cor breathed. "Yes. Let's have a triumph."

It was our turn. The emcee announced us and I rose, taking Cor's hand in mine. "Let's just rehearse once before we show them how to do it."

"Just a rehearsal," she gulped. "Just us. All right."

We took our place under the blazing lights. A titter of amusement went through the audience as they saw an overly tall man partnered with an overly small woman, and Cor looked around nervously, trying to see who was laughing.

I pulled her into our starting position and whispered to her before the music began, "Let's show them what a girl from Queens and a boy from Staten Island can do."

And as I said it—as I worked to soothe her nerves and bolster her spirit—I realized I meant what I'd said. Neither Cor nor I had been born first-class passengers, but that didn't mean we didn't belong. "Let them *try* to keep *us* down."

She blinked at me and inhaled. She straightened in my arms, and her head came to an arrogant angle. "Fuck them," she said. "Let's do it for us."

I grinned at her and winked. She raised an imperious eyebrow at me, and the music started. I pushed her hip away to spin her out, and we were off.

From the very first pass, her confidence grew. My lesson with Luz had made all the difference, and I was leading my partner instead of focusing only on the steps.

As we danced, as we progressed through our routine, I realized Ellyn was part of this as well. Because it was Ellyn who taught me that in a powerful partnership, one person led—and one person allowed themselves to be led. There was nothing passive in either position, if only both partners trusted each other.

It's traditional for rumba dancers to look stern and arrogant, but I couldn't help the grin that would not be suppressed. *It takes the right partner to learn how to lead.* This was a somewhat earthshaking revelation for me to be having, especially while so much of my brain was taken up with the performance.

Cor had relaxed into the dance as she never had during our rehearsals. She was trusting me. In fact, she trusted me enough when we did our dip that for the first time, she threw her head and her arm back in a graceful line, sure I would catch her.

Which I did, as tenderly as if she were Ellyn herself.

The *ooh* of approval that swept through the audience made it through our concentration and got to Cor. She looked at me for a split second and returned the wink I'd given her at the start of the dance.

I laughed and pulled her up. We finished our rumba with the clever series of spins that made the most of her height and mine.

And when we finished with a dramatic sweep, the applause was genuine and delighted.

Our rehearsals had been focused exclusively on the dance itself; we hadn't worked out how to respond to applause at the end. But we were in such sync that she turned to me and swept into a curtsy as I bowed to her. Then, as if we'd planned it, we turned to the audience and did the same.

It was too professional an ending for the two of us, and I was filled with too much affection for her. So, when we stood, I swept her into my arms. I cradled her against my chest, one arm below her knees, and twirled her until she shrieked with excited laughter. She threw an arm high and I carried her from the stage to stomps and whistles.

Our entire table was on their feet, applauding and laughing.

I set Cor gently on her toes and kissed her upturned cheek. "You were magnificent!"

"I was, wasn't I?" She was breathless and laughing. "*We* were magnificent!"

"Yes, we were!"

Rebel pulled Cor into a breathless hug and had to surrender her when all of the nieces wanted a turn.

I looked to Luz, sitting stoically with the sleeping Lovely in a graceless sprawl across her lap, and she inclined her head to me just once with terrifying grandeur. I nodded to her, my hand on my heart.

"You're going to win," Ellyn said as we sat. "Wait until you see the shots I got. You were so good!"

"I don't care if we win or not," Cor said breezily. "That dance was prize enough."

She patted my knee, and I knew at that exact moment Cor was never going to see me as either lover or husband. I was a son to her. A partner on the dance floor, and nothing more.

I was her trusted friend.

That's what did me in. We sat in the darkness while two other couples performed, and I had a knockdown, drag-out mental battle with the ghost of Victor.

Fine—you've lost your heart to the niece, but you don't have to give up your mark. In my imagination, he sat on soft gray cushions, the color of cigarette smoke. His legs were crossed elegantly, and he brushed a hand through his thick silver hair.

"I have not lost my heart to the niece," I protested.

Darling boy. Fool yourself if you like, but don't think for a minute you can fool me.

"Victor . . ."

No. I told you to never get emotionally involved. You know better. Ghostly fingers batted at my wrist, soft as a current of air. *This is a job, not a romance. Keep your eye on the prize, darling. So what if the old lady trusts you? That was the point all along, wasn't it?*

"She doesn't want a lover. She wants a friend. She wants her nieces. She wants a family."

Don't be maudlin. Every family needs a daddy. You can be that daddy—that very, very wealthy daddy. Don't be silly. This is the opportunity of a lifetime. Believe me, I know. He turned, offering me his profile and raising a dismissive eyebrow. *Fuck the girl on one of your many yachts while the old lady is at the salon. But don't lose your chance now.*

"I don't want to do that. I don't want Ellyn to be a secret. And I don't want to hurt Cor."

Better you than someone else. With that much money, you know someone else is going to come after her.

"Then I'll stop them."

Sweet child, think of what you're saying. At least three hundred and fifty million, and it's no less than you deserve. Didn't I teach you better than this? Do it for all of us who were dismissed and ignored. You were given talents for a reason. This is that reason. Pay attention to what you're saying.

He implored me. Or maybe—just maybe—it was the larcenous voice inside myself begging me to stay the same. To resist change and growth. To hide from the terror of not being sure.

I didn't have to look at Cor beside me to know she still sat there. I could feel her energy. Her excitement. Her happiness. I knew what I could do and what I couldn't, and I told the ghost of my mentor so.

"I know what I'm saying. Talk to you later, Victor."

My decision made, I sat in the darkness of the club next to a fortune. Next to the future I always thought I wanted.

I caught Cor's hand and kissed it. She laughed, not knowing I was kissing my luxurious future goodbye.

Still, I had backup plans, and all was not lost.

I looked across the table to Ellyn, who was examining the photos she'd taken of my dance with Cor. Her head was bent forward, and her hand shielded the light from her camera screen so she wouldn't interrupt anyone's view of the final couple on the dance floor. Always thinking of the others around her. *Sucker*, I thought, and found I was smiling instead of sneering.

And that instinct, the admiration I felt for her *because* she was kind—that was startling enough to shake me. Where was my contempt? Where was my belief that sheep were pathetic and only a lone wolf could control his own destiny? When had she become the person I wanted to strategize with?

What the hell was going on with me?

She must have seen a photo that pleased her because she looked at me with a smile.

I smiled back at her, and she held up her camera. In the light from the dance floor, I saw her mobile, soft lips mouth the word, "Good."

I nodded. Now that I'd abandoned the idea of being her uncle, I needed to figure out how I could keep her in my life.

She wouldn't like how this would play out, though. Unless I was very, very lucky.

CHAPTER THIRTY—ELLYN

WHEN COR AND ARTIE WON THE RUMBA CONTEST, NO ONE was surprised. There were at least two other couples who'd had more technical expertise and had danced a more complicated rumba.

But Cor, dancing in and out of the arms of handsome, large Artie, had captured the spirit of the dance and delighted the audience. When the votes were tabulated, it was a total rout.

Cor and Artie went to the dance floor to receive their silly plastic trophy, and Cor got a bouquet of flowers. Apparently, roses grow even in the most exotic locales. I captured their jubilation with a classic stage photo. The overbright stage lights screwed up the white balance and left everything overexposed and harsh, yet her laughter and his broad grin were as visible and defined as any studio portrait.

Those of us at the table were clapping our hands off and screaming our approval, and we weren't the only ones. Cor was walking on air, and Artie was gorgeous in his dinner jacket. *James Blond*, I thought with a proud smile.

There was only one thing wrong with the entire picture, and it lay all but forgotten on the table by my wine.

A little yellow feather, plucked from his jacket.

I'd found it on his shoulder after he'd been gone for a good half hour. In the men's room, he'd insisted.

For half an hour?

I wished I hadn't recognized the feather. I wished there had been Las Vegas showgirls in feathered headdresses between here and the nearest men's room—showgirls who had perhaps pulled him into a broom closet and had their slutty way with him.

That would have been better than the truth.

Because I recognized that feather. I'd pulled several of the same out of my hair that afternoon—and out of the hair of my cousins.

Artie had been in Aunt Cor's suite.

And he'd chosen a time when she, Luz, and Rebel were in the nightclub, watching the competition. He'd chosen a moment when it was guaranteed no one would walk in on him.

I knew he could pop open any of the locks on the cabin doors. He was so proficient that he'd taught me how to do it. So, he could undoubtedly get into Cor's suite.

The question was—why?

What was he doing there?

The competition over, the emcee invited everyone to the dance floor, and the sound system filled the cavernous room with "Everybody Likes to Cha Cha Cha." Artie, who hadn't known the dance before we got onto the ship, laughed and pulled his partner into his embrace. They led the room, and the tables emptied as people rushed to join them.

Almost instantly, Cor was lost to sight, but Artie remained half a head taller than everyone else, his blond hair catching the spotlights. Somehow, he'd learned the dance, and he and Cor were laughing as they adjusted to match the length of his steps to hers. I watched him until Sinjie surprised me by asking me to dance.

Farrah already giggled through the steps with Brock, and Luz took Lovely to their cabin. Priss and Trip were already on the dance floor, and Marcus (sporting a golf cap that thankfully hid the peeling skin on his bald spot) bowed to necessity by asking Liv. I remembered that according to Cor, Marcus had two left feet. *Good luck, Liv.*

Sinjie held out his hand to me. Up I got, smiling and happy.

We all danced, changing partners and laughing and having a wonderful time. And by the time I got back to our table, the feather was gone, along with the dregs of our drinks. *Good. Out of sight, out of mind.*

More cocktails were ordered, more toasts and salutes given to our dance champions, and the spirit of affection that had begun that afternoon lasted into the evening. Everyone was happy. Everything was fine.

Except—just because the feather was gone didn't mean it hadn't been there.

Artie made sure to dance with all of my cousins before dancing with me. He held me loosely as we moved robotically through the box step. The original lesson—forward, side-together back, side-together forward—was just three weeks in the past.

It was a lifetime ago.

He watched me. "What?"

I shook my head and smiled. "What what?"

"What's on your mind? Everything's going beautifully. Why are you only pretending to be happy?"

Was I that easy to read? "I'm not pretending."

With one eyebrow, he telegraphed his skepticism. We were turning in a gentle circle, and I realized I followed him without question. I flushed to realize it, and he read me once more.

"You're not subservient to me," he said. "It's not like last night." I smothered a gasp and looked around. Someone could hear. "No one's listening, and everyone else is a lot drunker than you and I are. It's not subservience. It's like when you were dancing with that guy."

"What guy?"

"Our dancing lesson. In the bombed-out church rec room."

The church wasn't bombed-out; it just needed repair. I knew what he was talking about. "When Eddie taught you the beginning of the rumba. He's going to be so proud of you." The plastic trophy sat proudly on our table, next to more drinks and Aunt Cor's unnaturally green feather boa, discarded as the heat in the club rose.

"It wasn't Eddie who taught me how to lead."

He looked at me fixedly and it made me shiver. "I know. It was Luz."

He shook his head. He spun me out and pulled me in. "It was you. I figured it out. If there isn't trust, there's no partnership."

He was talking about him dominating me—and he was talking about more than that. "Trust is important," I agreed, wishing I didn't know what I knew.

"So, what's the problem?"

I worried my lip, thinking. "Is everyone drunk enough for us to leave yet?"

He tightened his grip slightly in reaction. "Why? You want to go to your cabin?" He leered at me. "Or you want to *talk* in your cabin?"

I laughed shakily. "Talk first?"

He sighed. "If we must. You go tell your family good night. I'll stay here and dance for another half an hour. Okay?"

"Okay. Thanks."

We danced in silence again, his body too close to mine and nowhere near close enough. As the song ended, he leaned down. "It's going to be okay," he said.

But even he didn't sound like he believed it.

I made my apologies to my family. Rather, I said good night to Liv and Cor, in heated and tipsy debate about some Pacific Island tribe's face painting practices, and to Rebel (giggling and happy and holding yet another cocktail). Artie swept Farrah into a dance, and Priss and Trip were waltzing like they couldn't wait to make Lovely's baby brother or sister.

"Oh, Ellyn, darling," Cor enthused, breathing rum happily into my face. "Hasn't this been the most wonderful day?"

I smiled. Her joy was contagious. "The most wonderful day. I'm going to pack it in. Want to come with me?"

"Nonsense! I'm going to dance all night, aren't I, Sinjie?"

Sinjie and Marcus were both ready to lead the champion to the floor, and I left them all lining up the next hour or so of rumbas and fox-trots and cha-chas and I don't know what all.

I let myself into my cabin, glad to take off my heels and put on my hoodie. I was downloading my photos when Artie arrived. He boldly came through the hallway entrance instead of the connecting door, and that chilled me.

"What if someone saw you?" I said, unnerved by how easily he could pop any lock. To my cabin—or to Cor's.

"No one saw. They're all dancing and drinking; there was talk of a bridge game. They'll be up there all night."

He moved to pull me against him, but I resisted. He stopped and stepped back to look at me. Then he sat on the sofa and spread his long arms along the top. I wanted to crawl inside the wings of his coat and curl against him. But I couldn't. Not yet.

"Go ahead. Tell me what the problem is," he said.

I set aside my camera and laptop and paced uneasily. *If there isn't trust*, he'd said, *there's no partnership*. I swallowed my apprehension and turned to him.

"What were you doing in Aunt Cor's room tonight?"

He was immobile, watching me and betraying nothing. The moment drew out painfully.

He sighed and leaned forward, resting his elbows on his knees. "How did you know?"

I wish I hadn't known. "I pulled a feather off your jacket. From the yellow headdress in Aunt Cor's room."

He shook his head. "The damned feathers." He sat back and patted the seat beside him. "Sit. I'll tell you a story."

"I don't want a story. I want to know what really happened."

He nodded, suddenly tired. "That's what I'm going to tell you."

I sat in the corner of the sofa, facing him, scared of what he was going to say. "Artie, did you steal something from Aunt Cor?"

He laughed. "No. Now, hush and I'll tell you. Remember I told you about my brothers and sister?"

I remembered. "Kaz and Wendy and . . . what's your younger brother's name?"

"Simon. This is about Kaz."

"He used to protect you from bullies on the playground."

He smiled. "Good memory. That's right. Kaz did his best to take care of us, but he was more muscle and less brain, you know?"

"And you were more brain."

"And less muscle—at least, back then. So, I got pinched and spent a while in juvenile detention, and after that it was smart for me to get out of New York."

"Dishwasher. Migrant farm worker. Carny."

"Yeah. But that left my family without . . . a breadwinner." He stumbled to describe himself that way, but I realized it was accurate. His family had relied on their young son to steal for them. As illegal as his activities were, he *was* the breadwinner. "It took a long time until I made enough to send money home again. And meanwhile, Kaz tried hard to pick up the slack."

Suddenly, he scrubbed his face with his hands, and I realized I was seeing guilt. "It's not your fault they had to fend for themselves, Artie."

"Sure it was. Things were fine until I let myself be caught by the cops. I mean, I saved Wendy from Fat Henry the dragon, but I left my family in a jam. I bolted out of there."

"*Did* you ever send money back to them?"

"Whenever I could. But not enough, at first. And that's not the same."

"So Kaz decided it was up to him."

"Yeah."

"But Kaz is more muscle than brain."

He acknowledged my assessment with raised eyebrows and a nod. "He joined Fat Henry's gang. He's a big, strong guy, and they used him for that. You know—muscle. Pretty soon he'd taken one punch too many to the head, and after that, he didn't . . . you know. Make good choices."

His brother had been beaten or fought his way into mild brain damage. I winced. If you thought your brother had to do that because you left, then yeah, maybe you'd feel a freight of guilt. Artie went on.

"He decided he could make more money as a dealer. Heroin, meth, coke, weed—whatever. The problem with that was he also discovered using."

The admission was apparently bitter in his mouth, as he got up and jerked a bottle of water from the mini fridge. He drank deeply and went on.

"All the money I sent them wasn't enough. There was always a need for more, more, more. I got home three weeks ago and was immediately pulled into the offices of Terence the Accountant."

"That doesn't sound so bad."

"Yeah." He laughed. "That's why he's such a success in the drug world. Legitimate offices in Manhattan, client base, all on the up-and-up. Meanwhile, he's running a thriving little empire. And my brother is heavily in debt to him."

"How heavily?"

"The total was nearly ninety thousand."

I whistled. "Shit."

"Yeah. And Kaz is a fucking mess. So, Terence calls me into his office and says I have three choices: either I pay him the money, or he kills Kaz, or I go to work for him. He's got some scams he wants to run on his competitors, and I'm the guy for the job."

Artie rubbed his neck like his shoulders ached. He sat next to me again.

"And to make sure I got the point, Terence had me chained to some pipes in his back room and had his guys use me as a punching bag. One blow to the belly, one rib-cracker, and a monstrous right cross to the face, after which he nudges me out the door and I stumble into the nearest Starbucks and collapse on a bench to think it over. He took my wallet and my phone. I had enough change in my pocket to buy one small coffee. And all of a sudden, this chick with crazy striped hair is all in my face. *Hey, mister—can I photograph your eye?*"

His voice had gone high at the end in imitation of me, and I smiled as I lay a soothing hand on his arm.

He looked at me. "And she says she can pay me a quarter of a million dollars."

Wow, I thought. *Damn.*

"You were like . . . I don't know. Like an angel in a coffee shop. Like a miracle. Evidence that there was a God and he wasn't too pissed at me. Because of you, I would be able to save my family. Get my brother into treatment. And maybe . . ." He smiled, lost in thought. "Maybe marry a rich old lady and give up this life of crime. That sounded pretty good to me about then."

"I'll bet." My heart went out to him. I couldn't blame him for anything he'd done. It all made sense.

But hang on . . .

"Well, what were you doing in Cor's room tonight?"

He sighed. "You like me, right? I mean, we get along, don't we?"

I got nervous. "What's going on?"

"Just remember that you like me."

"What's. Going. On."

He shrugged. "I left Mock's apartment that first day and went back to see Terence. He's practically across the street. I told him I could get him the money. Probably."

He looked at me, and I saw apology in his eyes. "After all, I would only get paid if you got the money. So, I gave him an additional option."

"Which was?"

He rolled his eyes, uneasy. "Drug mule."

I was confused. "Drug mule?" It was as though he suddenly stopped speaking English. And then I understood. "You didn't just pretend to go to Burma. You really went to Burma."

"Myanmar. Terence arranged the contacts. High-speed powerboats across the border. I picked up a brick of heroin, shoved it in my backpack, and was waiting for the ship in South Andaman, where I met your drunk cousin Farrah."

"With a brick of heroin."

"Yeah."

We sat in silence. "How big is a brick?"

He held out his hands. "Bigger than a book. Smaller than a shoebox."

"What's it worth?"

"Depends. Maybe a hundred grams, and each gram would be cut with something else and then sell for about a hundred and fifty. So—figure about thirty thousand."

"You'd risk your life for thirty thousand?"

"I'd risk my life to show Terence he could set up a pipeline through high-ticket cruise lines."

"Damn." I was silent again, thinking. "So how are you going to get the heroin through customs?"

He rolled his head on the sofa and looked at me, and my stomach rumbled uneasily. He said nothing, and I saw the plan all too clearly.

"You're not going to get it through customs," I said. "Someone else is."

He looked at me.

My skin flashed with heat, and my spine was icy. My innards, my emotions, my life tangled into atonal disharmony.

"You hid it in Cor's suite. You hid it in her stuff." The full truth hit me with an almost physical impact. "You're letting her bring your drugs in under her diplomatic contacts. Your fucking heroin is buried in the dirt of her two damned palm trees."

His forehead was wrinkled and his hands were clenched, and still he said nothing, just looking at me.

"If she gets caught, you'll be dooming her to prison. To prison, Artie," I hissed.

He closed his eyes on the truth. "She won't get caught. The State Department will get those trees through customs."

"The fuck they will!"

I was on my feet, fury and pain boiling through me. I grabbed my room key and was out the door, Artie on my heels.

"Don't, Ellyn. Please?"

I popped the lock on Cor's suite like I was the expert and flicked the lights on inside. I ran across the room and yanked open the sliding doors.

"It's my brother's *life*, Ellyn—please! It's my life. Please don't do it!"

He never touched me, and he could have restrained me easily. I was crying and he was curled in on himself, his big shoulders hunched forward to protect himself from an attack that never came.

The two palm trees were visible in the moonlight. I didn't wait to see which one held its deadly burden; I simply heaved them both, one after the other, over the balcony railing and heard them splash into the water far below.

I waited, panting and crying, but no one called out. No one set up a "man overboard" shout or anything. The evening was as peaceful after my life had been shattered, as it had been before.

I turned to Artie, knowing he was there only from his bulk. My tears were falling too fast to make out any details.

"Get away from me. And stay away from my family."

I left him and went to my cabin. No sense in insisting he leave too. He could get into Cor's room whenever he wanted.

I, however, made sure to wedge both my front and my connecting door firmly closed.

Wrecked, I crawled into bed and quite literally pulled the covers over my head. But I couldn't hide. His ghost was on my pillows, tangled in my sheets, sliding along the loneliness of my skin.

I slept alone that night. Or would have, if I'd been able to sleep.

CHAPTER THIRTY-ONE—ARTIE

Ellyn was a sucker.

She was made to be a dupe. In this world, there are people who are predators and people who are prey. She was prey, and I was better off to be rid of her.

I am a predator.

I am a loner. I work best alone. I work best when I trust no one. That's what Victor taught me. That's what *life* taught me.

Her anger and pain and disappointment washed off me like spring rain. What did I care if she was hurt? She knew I was a scoundrel when she hired me. What did she think would change? Life isn't like a sappy movie. I didn't look into her big green eyes and suddenly reform my evil ways. *Sorry, sweetheart. You're the sucker—not me.*

I left Cor's room filled with resolve. I was right; my attraction to her was purely sexual. She meant nothing to me.

I changed out of my slick dinner jacket and put on gym clothes. There was no way I was sleeping after that high-drama scene. She was pathetic, a hysterical woman. I'd put in a few miles on the treadmill, burn off some nervous energy, plan my next moves.

It was almost midnight; the lights were off in the gym. That suited me fine. I set a punishing pace and started my run, grateful as hell I had trusted no one.

Obviously. Cor wasn't going to marry me. That was the long shot and the glossiest prize, but not getting there was no surprise. I wasn't going to pay off Terence that way.

And it seemed clear I'd been fired by my employer. After my "heartless betrayal" (I rolled my eyes), Ellyn was unlikely to pay me, even if she won the five million.

Plus, it was obvious—at least to me—that Cor was going to divide the money between all four nieces. Duh. She wanted to be loved; she wanted a family. She wouldn't piss off three of them only to win the affection of one. Ellyn would walk away with $1.25 million. Not as much as she'd hoped for, but hardly chump change.

By rights, I got 20 percent of that, or $250,000—the original quarter million she'd offered. Would she pay it after I'd tried to turn her aunt into a drug mule?

Actually, I probably had a fifty-fifty shot. If she were like me or the rest of the world, she'd shoot me the middle finger and tell me to sue her for violating the contract we never signed. If she continued to be a sucker, she'd make a halfhearted effort at paying me, assuming she could bring herself to look at me after what I'd done.

And I'd done the only thing a non-sucker could have done. Damn it.

Fortunately, I wasn't relying on her for my lifeline.

Ellyn had thrown the wrong hiding place overboard.

The paper-mache flamingo was easy to cut open. I'd used handy-dandy duct tape to cement the brick of heroin in the garden statue's body. It would be a piece of cake to retrieve it after Cor's luggage was passed through customs under the protection of the State Department.

And while the value of one brick of heroin wasn't enough to pay Kaz's debts to Terence the Accountant, it was enough to buy me time to set up a nice pipeline via my new friends: the staff on this and other cruise ships.

I probably wouldn't be able to do my traveling on a ship as nice as the *Empress of the Indian Ocean*, but we'd been surrounded by lesser cruise lines at every stop, and I could make it work.

It wasn't the future I wanted, but it was the future Kaz and I could live with.

I pounded along the rubber treadmill that spooled out endlessly before me, going and going and going and never getting anywhere. I cleared my mind of Ellyn's tears, of the horror on her face before she ran for her aunt's suite.

Of my unreasoning burst of pride when she popped the lock without a moment's hesitation. *Atta girl*, I thought—and wiped the image clean.

I'd run for almost an hour and hadn't overbalanced my energy with muscle fatigue. I was tired of staring at my own stupid reflection in the night-dark window.

No—I was bored. That was all.

Bored by how mundane everything was. How stupid Ellyn had been, and how smart I'd been.

I toweled off and wandered through the ship. Most of the rooms were empty, although the nightclub was still crowded and noisy, partiers spilling out into the hallways. I didn't see Cor—I didn't want to see Cor—but I was sure she was still kicking up her heels.

The thought of our dance, our triumph, surprised a grin out of me, but I wiped that away too. Cor was a dupe. Someone would relieve her of all her money, and it would be her own fault.

She was a fool.

The icy air on my sweaty body was refreshing at first, but soon I was chilled. I prowled out to the sun deck and sat at the poolside bar. Basilio wasn't there, of course. He was the daytime bartender.

But the night guy poured me a reasonably good bourbon, and

then another one. If I couldn't burn off my energy, maybe I could drink myself to sleep.

But every time I thought of going to my cabin—to that pathetic excuse of a bed, cramped and short and boxed in like prison—I got angry all over again.

Why did I have to sleep there? When Ellyn rolled around in a bed big enough for an army?

No, I wasn't going back.

I fell asleep on one of the sofas, the ocean breeze blowing wisps of hair across my face and irritating me until I finally dropped off.

Basilio woke me at seven when he came on duty. He told me I couldn't sleep all night on the deck; it would look like I'd passed out.

I pointed out he and I were—as usual—completely alone. All the suckers were sleeping off their hangovers in their large, comfortable beds. He shrugged and offered to make me a smoothie. I growled at him and stalked to my ridiculous closet of a cabin.

The shower I took was enraging. I couldn't stand straight under the nozzle and bumped into all four walls at various points. Damn her. *Damn her.*

By the time I got out, there were new noises coming from Ellyn's cabin. They caught at my ear like a fishhook.

I wouldn't be caught dead asking her what was going on. She was nothing to me. But only an idiot would refuse information when it was so stupidly offered. So, I eased open my side of the connecting door and pressed a drinking glass to her side. Primitive amplifier.

I heard Priss. And Trip. And then—no need to listen through the glass—I heard the evil toddler crying.

By that time, I knew this happy little family was settling in. Ellyn had swapped rooms with Priss, and Priss was thrilled about it.

I didn't slam my side of the connecting door because I was

not an idiot, but I wanted to. No more big bed for me. No more large shower and enormous bathroom. No more top-shelf sunblock. She was escaping me, huh?

Like I cared. Like it mattered to me *in the slightest*. She was no more valuable to me than a hotel room would be.

We had two more at-sea days. No shore excursions, no shopping, no glass-bottomed boats. The ship's crew did what it could to keep the passengers entertained, but the most successful events always included a heavy pour on rum and gin.

I spent an afternoon tipsy, but it went against my nature. Drunkenness leads to unguarded speech, and that's not smart for a scam artist. So, I mostly wandered around, looking for distraction and finding very little.

Ellyn never once appeared. Cor told me Ellyn had picked up a bug and wanted to be left to sleep; she'd swapped with Priss and was holed up in a small cabin deep in the cheap section of the ship. I assured her I didn't care at all, and she chatted happily about our rumba victory. Should we enter the cha-cha competition?

I begged off. I told her I thought Marcus or Sinjie would like a chance to show off with her. (Marcus elbowed Sinjie out of the way and stepped hard on Brock's foot. Two left feet, and both of them on the younger man. He won the hand of the fair lady—for the competition, anyway.)

I assessed her as Victor would have had me do it, and I realized she wasn't ever going to marry Marcus (or loan his company money), she thought Sinjie was an utter delight and nothing more, and she simply liked to look at Brock because he was pretty. I probably fell into that category too.

Not so easy a pigeon after all.

The thought should have annoyed me, but it was one of the few bright spots in my day.

On our last at-sea afternoon, Cor found me at Basilio's bar. Unusually, she was alone: no Rebel, no Luz, no fawning nieces. No would-be gigolos surrounding her.

Just Cor.

She stood at my side and gave me a searching look.

"What?" I finally said, and perhaps my tone was a touch grumpy.

She shook her head. "Come over here. Sit with me." She picked facing sofas tucked next to a windbreak and shielded from the sun. "Sit, please. Let's have a chat."

This would be a waste of time, but what else did I have to do?

"What is it?"

She drew herself up. "Don't be petulant with me, young man. I have done you no harm."

The same could not be said of me about you, I thought, and slammed the door shut on that thought. I acknowledged her words. "I apologize."

"Now, was that so hard?" She smiled. "Can't you do the same with Ellyn?"

I frowned. "Ellyn? What about Ellyn?"

"Oh, please." She rolled her eyes, and I smiled despite myself. "I'm an old lady, not an idiot. You and she are dying for each other."

I shifted uncomfortably. "Cor, I—"

"Don't interrupt me. You've smelled like her sunscreen since practically the first day. Not being fully blind, it has been clear to me from the beginning that you and she were very careful to not even look at each other." Exactly the tell I'd mocked Ellyn for. Was I doing it too? "In fact . . ." she looked at me archly. "I wouldn't be surprised if the two of you knew each other before you boarded this ship."

My heart pounded, and I fought to keep my face still. "Well—"

"I thought so. Don't worry about it. My darling husband's attempt to make my nieces like me was bound to create a stupid level of competition."

I goggled at her in amazement.

She went on. "While he tried to do right by me, he actually set those girls against each other. Bringing in a ringer to romance the old lady was practically a given. There were times when I wondered if Brock wasn't Farrah's plant."

She saw me blink through the idea and waved her hand dismissively.

"Oh, he's not. He's simply too dim for anyone to think he could be an asset. Still, he and Farrah are having a wonderful time doing lasting damage to their livers, so at least she's having a lovely romance."

"Cor, I'm sorry."

"Don't be sorry. I've loved our time together. You're a wonderful boy, and dancing with you was a highlight of my trip."

"Thank you. I enjoyed it, too, more than I thought I would."

"I know." She smiled smugly. "I'm pretty wonderful once you get to know me. But not as wonderful as Ellyn, hmm?"

She watched me closely, and I looked away from her investigation.

"Ellyn is . . ." I sighed. She wouldn't speak, forcing me to finish the sentence. "Ellyn is a sucker." It came out with more venom than I expected, and I bit my lip against the sudden flush of emotion.

"Not a sucker," Cor corrected. "She's a sweetheart. Life hasn't beaten her down yet. Do you know, even before Carl died, she was the only one who would talk to me at family events? She's kind, Arthur. She's not like you and me."

I couldn't help it. I did love Cor, after all was said and done. I smiled at her ruefully. "A Queens girl and a Staten Island boy."

"We know what it is to make our own way in life. We take care of ourselves."

"We do."

"But Arthur, all four of those nieces had the same advantages: money, family, a guaranteed safety net if something went wrong. You and I never had that, but they did. And only Ellyn is still instinctively kind. It wasn't privilege that made her the way she is. It's her character. Her spirit."

I caught my lip between my teeth, wishing I wasn't hearing this. Cor was flooding me with a lethal combination of honesty and kindness, and she was drowning me. And she didn't relent.

"And I want to protect that kindness in her. I don't think she should have to become cynical and tough like you and I had to. What she has is rare. What she *is* is rare. I'd like her to stay kind. And I think you want that too."

My shoulders were tense. My hands clenched in my lap.

"She's rare, Arthur. She's precious."

Despite myself, I nodded.

"And she's hurting. What happened between you?"

I looked up, startled. What had happened was I tried to turn a sweet old lady into a criminal for my own benefit. I opened my mouth but found there was nothing I could say.

"You had a fight, huh? A lover's quarrel?"

Guys like me, we don't cry. It was the wind stinging my eyes. I blinked to keep all that moisture in.

"Can you fix it, Arthur? Could you just apologize?"

"She won't talk to me."

"Have you tried?" Her voice was gentle. I shook my head.

"She's in cabin 226. The rest of us are going to play bingo. I know it's stupid, but Lovely likes the stampers. I'm going to have to give Luz a really big bonus."

"Luz is awesome," I said as Cor rose.

"She is."

She moved to stand next to me on her way out and laid her hand on my head in a gentle benediction. "Don't feel bad, Arthur. You and I were never going to end up together, you know."

"We would have had fun. I promise."

"Lots of fun." She smiled and slid her hand until she cupped my neck. "But haven't you guessed? I already have a lover."

Astonished, I jerked away so I could look at her. "Not Marcus?!"

She laughed. "Don't be silly. What would I want with another old man? I've already been through the death of one man I loved. I don't want to do that again." She forestalled my protests. "And I don't have the energy for a young man."

"So . . . ?"

She smiled at me, and I tried to puzzle it out. It came to me. "Not . . . Rebel?"

She nodded, happy with my deductions. "Since secretarial school."

"You're a lesbian?"

"I'm bi. Rebel is a lesbian. So don't fuss too much—you were never going to win the old lady. But there's still a chance you could get the girl."

She leaned down and kissed my cheek, closing my gaping mouth with her hand.

I caught her fingers. "I'm happy for you, Cor. I'm glad you have someone."

"You deserve someone, too, Arthur. Staten Island and Queens—who's better than us?"

"No one."

"Who deserves love more than we do?"

"No—no one."

"You don't sound very sure."

"Well—"

"Go talk to her. See what happens. Say you're sorry for whatever it was you did wrong. Trust an old lady."

I nodded and blinked again. Damn wind.

She smiled. "Well, I'm off to let Marcus, Sinjie, and Brock down easy. *So lovely to have met you,* I'll tell them. *We must exchange Christmas cards. Goodbye.*"

I laughed, and she turned back to me.

"You, I want to see more of. Give me your phone. I'll put my number in it." I was obedient to her every whim, and she typed her information in efficiently, like a one-time executive assistant. "No matter what happens with Ellyn, you let me know you're okay. Right?"

She handed back my phone, and I nodded.

"But make sure you apologize to my niece."

Cor left. I sat for a moment. Cabin 226.

There was just one thing I had to do first.

CHAPTER THIRTY-TWO--ELLYN

OF COURSE HE DIDN'T BOTHER KNOCKING. HE KNEW I WOULD have refused to let him in.

He popped the lock on the cabin door. I'd stopped wedging it the day before, tired of pretending to the room stewards and my cousins that I wasn't blocking myself into a little cave of insecurity.

I closed out the email window—there were several people I needed to talk to when I got home to New York, and I was determined to set them up before I lost my nerve at telling the bad news—and shut my laptop.

"Get out."

The words were wooden and emotionless. I'd done enough crying already.

"I will," Artie said, taking up what little empty space the room had. "I need to say a few things first."

I shook my head. I was dead inside. How could he hurt me more? The worst was that I had only myself to blame. I'd hired a scoundrel. Why was I surprised when it turned out he had neither honor nor integrity? "Say what you need to say, and leave me alone."

"Okay." He bent to sit on the matching twin bed, but I glared at him and he straightened. "Okay."

He lost his place in whatever mental script he was running through, and I scrubbed my face with my hands. I pushed back on my bed to lean against the wall, hugging my pillow to my chest. *Get it over with.*

"Have you ever ridden a unicycle?" he asked.

This was why he had to break into my cabin? Frustration filled me with coils of tension. "Oh, sure. All the time. What the fuck are you talking about?"

This time, my glare didn't stop him. He sat on the bed and leaned forward, pulling words together.

"I learned when I was with the carnival. There was a guy who could ride them, like, ten feet tall. I was never that good. But after a while, I got so I could really move. And there's something really . . . freeing about a unicycle. You can turn on a dime. I mean, literally—he'd put a dime on the ground, roll up to it, turn a circle on it, and roll off."

"Great. Is there a point to this?"

"Yes. Hang on." He inhaled and examined the hands clasped between his knees. "I'm . . . a unicycle guy. Fast. Flexible. Too quick to catch. A loner. One guy only. One guy, one wheel."

"I get the picture." I rolled my hand in every director's *hurry up* gesture.

"Right. Well, I'd forgotten how nice it is to ride a bicycle."

I wrinkled my forehead. "What?"

"A bicycle. You ride a unicycle; you have to watch you don't fall to the side or forward or back. But when you're on a bike . . . well, you can still fall forward or back, but it's a shit-ton harder. A bike is . . . well, it's a lot more stable. And I forgot how good that felt."

"Artie."

"I'm talking about partnerships," he burst out. "A partnership with you."

I thought about it. "Like when we were fucking."

"No. Well, yes—when we were fucking. But also when we weren't fucking. We worked on this plan together."

"You rewrote the plan."

"And you made it better. We worked together. I had an ally. I had a partner. And you showed me that a partnership is about . . . Oh, God, it sounds so corny."

He was breaking my heart. "What does?"

"It's about trust. It's about being a better lead because someone is willing to be led. It's about shifting that trust back and forth. I was stronger because I was with you. Not just with someone, or anyone. It was you. I was stronger with you."

My nose was running because the tears I blinked back were rolling down inside my body, inside my soul.

"F-fuck you," I choked out. "You trusted me until you decided to plant heroin in my aunt's luggage."

"Yeah." He looked at his feet. "Yeah, I did. Because it was my brother's life or do that. And I made the choice."

"Clearly." I clutched the pillow to me, and it wasn't protection enough. "Get out."

He nodded and rose. "I'm sorry," he said. "Honestly, I am."

"Mm-hmm." Staring at the wall wasn't helping; tears were rolling out of me. At least I could be silent about it. He had no honor. No integrity.

He pulled the door open again and faced the hallway. "But you should know—you threw the wrong things overboard. I hid it in the flamingo."

He looked over his shoulder and saw my startled face. "Don't bother," he cut me off when I opened my mouth. "I just pitched it over the side."

"Artie. You threw away . . ." I stood and shoved the door shut again. "You threw away the heroin? What about your brother?"

He inhaled sharply. "It won't come to that. I'll go to work for Terence. You taught me how to be a part of a team. Maybe I can be good in his team."

"No—Artie—"

"Yes. Goodbye, Ellyn. Thank you for letting me . . . love you. If only for a while."

I put out a hand to stop him, but he was gone.

Oh, God. Things were getting complicated.

IN A BURST OF GENEROSITY, COR ATTEMPTED TO UPGRADE ALL of our flights to first class on the way home ("Not that Arthur, though—if he couldn't apologize to you properly, let him sweat it out in economy"), but when we made it to the airport, there was only one additional seat available for the upgrade. I offered to swap with someone, but Cor refused to let me.

"Each of my nieces flew first class on the way out and on the way back. You get your first-class ticket home. Now, for the last available seat, I'm going to upgrade . . ."

She eyed the family before her. Priss hoisted her daughter higher on her hip and tried to look pathetic, and Liv and Farrah both feigned indifference. Trip knew he wasn't even in the running.

Cor teased them all and made her pronouncement.

"Luz. Luz will be riding with us at the front of the plane."

For a moment, Luz looked startled—even very, very faintly pleased. Then she offloaded the diaper bag and backpacks full of toys onto Trip's shoulder and came to stand next to Cor, her face like an Easter Island monolith.

She rode up the escalator with Cor, Rebel, and me while the others stood mournfully below, watching us enter the luxurious Serendib Lounge for first-class passengers.

Somewhere below, Artie sat waiting for the flight to be called. I'd seen and ignored him on the cruise line's bus to Bandaranaike Airport, and unlike the flight out, I wouldn't be getting up to check on him in his economy-class seat. Instead, I sat and brooded for the entire flight on the conversations I needed to have once I was on US soil.

My fellow travelers waited for me after customs, except for Artie. I scanned the group nervously, but he either hadn't gotten through customs yet or he'd already gone. Not that I cared.

"Ellyn, what took you so long?" Priss asked. She was querulous, and who could blame her? Lovely was sharing her discontent with all the passengers hurrying past them as she hung from the push bar of a luggage cart piled with bags, screaming tiredly.

"Someone gets pulled for a closer search every flight. This time, it was my turn. Look—there's Mock!"

My wonderful friend and creative director bustled up to meet me, carrying a sign like the drivers who met business travelers. His read ELLYNMOCK PRODUCTION COMPANY, and I wanted to burst into tears when I saw him.

"Cute sign." Farrah had a Bloody Mary buzz going and she grinned at Mock, who kissed her. He turned his back on Liv, who sniffed and ignored him.

"Ellyn, let Farrah and me give you a ride into the city," Liv said.

"Not at all!" Mock protested. "Her chariot awaits! I can't delay another moment before hearing everything!"

Seeing him was a relief—the end of a too-full journey—and it broke my heart. I kissed Cor and Rebel, and then, to her astonishment, I kissed Luz. I hugged Priss and Liv and resurrected a complicated childhood handshake with Farrah. And with one eye on the arriving passengers, I grabbed Mock and my suitcase and fled.

"Thanks for coming to get me," I said to Mock. "What kind of chariot awaits us?"

"Oh, that," he said. "I just hate that Liv."

"So we're . . . ?"

"Bus, sweetheart. What else? Where's the hunk? Shouldn't he be here?"

"I don't want to see him."

"Uh-oh. That doesn't sound good."

We climbed onto the M60 bus and grabbed two seats toward

the back. And I unfolded the entire drama—including my brief, horrific love affair with Artie.

"Oh my God!" Mock squealed. "Tell me everything! How was he? Was he huge? I mean, *huge?*"

He held his hands apart with such a gleam of delight that I laughed, even as I started to cry.

"Oh, sweetie." Mock stopped asking questions and let me cry on his jacket. We made it all the way to 125th Street before I could draw a deep breath, and he wisely took me for pho.

He plopped the large bowl of noodle soup in front of me and made me eat every drop.

"Okay. Now start again at the beginning."

It took hours. By the end, we were in my apartment, and my laundry thumped in my tiny washing machine. I'd scrubbed Sri Lanka and Artie out of my system and had my wet hair in a towel. Mock had gone for ice cream while I was in the shower, and we were spoon-deep in the good stuff.

"So, anyway, Aunt Cor is dividing the money between us. No one gets five mil, and you and I don't get 2.5 to start our company."

"Ellyn, if you think we can't do damage with a million and a quarter—" he started, but I shook my head.

"We owe Artie 20 percent."

"The fuck we do! After he packed heroin in Cor's fucking flamingo?" Mock's voice climbed octaves until only dogs could hear him.

"I don't care. He didn't make her do it—in the end, he dumped it himself. I promised he'd get 20 percent of what I got."

"Shit. Give him ten. At least don't give him the full twenty."

"No, I've been thinking about it. A quarter million, and we'll be done with him forever. Think you and I can get something going with a million?"

He looked at me, my best friend, and shrugged. "Absolutely.

At the very least, it will reassure a bank that we're not totally without funding."

"Right." I brightened. "And I thought about the story for our first production. Handsome scoundrel imports drugs from Myanmar."

"Burma," Mock corrected automatically. "That could be good."

"I've got ideas for the plot. We'd need a screenplay."

"And a handsome scoundrel. But then, everyone needs a handsome scoundrel."

"Don't remind me." We plotted and brainstormed and eventually laughed. Maybe not everything in my life had turned to shit.

BAXTER MET ME EARLY THE NEXT MORNING, BEFORE HIS current temp job as a substitute teacher. We met at a falafel cart near his house, and he tried to kiss me hello.

I put out a hand and stopped him. "No, Bax. We need to talk."

This conversation wasn't as much fun as the one with Mock.

"But you're not seeing him now," Bax said when I finished, his voice thick. We walked slowly along, our breakfast forgotten in our hands.

"Definitely not. It ended badly."

"Are you okay?" Bax was so sweet. I was breaking up with him, and he was worried about my safety and my emotional health.

"I will be. But I think you and I need to step back from our relationship."

He walked in silence, his brow furrowed. "Why?" he said at last.

I looked at him in surprise. "Bax, I told you—"

"Yeah, but you're not seeing him now. We don't have to break up. Ellyn, I love you."

I stopped walking. We'd said it to each other so easily in the past, and now I realized I hadn't understood at all what those words meant.

"I love you, too, Bax—but I'm not in love with you."

"We can get it back. I don't care if you had a vacation fling. That's okay."

"It's not okay. If my relationship with you had been stronger, the fling wouldn't have happened."

"So—it's my fault you slept with that beefcake? He can't even dance, Ellyn."

I didn't correct him. Bax was wounded, and that blow was already deep enough.

"I'm sorry. I wish it didn't hurt you. Or me. But I need to be honest with you. I'm not in love with you."

"And it doesn't count that I'm in love with you?"

"I'm not so sure you are," I said gently. "And you deserve someone who's head over heels for you, Bax."

"That's right. I really do. Well, here we are at my school. Go on. Get going, Ellyn. I've got to go to work."

He blinked back tears and balanced on rage. My presence wasn't going to help anything. "Bye, Bax."

"Yeah."

———

I HAD ONE LAST STOP TO MAKE—THE HARDEST OF THE morning. I sat in the coffee shop and waited until I saw Artie head into the office building across the street.

I switched on the GoPro, double-checked its position, and followed him.

The woman in the reception area tried to stop me, but I was bigger than she was and easily pushed past her. The right office was just a few steps down the hall.

Artie was shirtless and stepping into his jeans. It was a nice view.

He turned in astonishment when I walked in, as did the three tough-looking guys around him and the nerdy man behind the desk.

"Ellyn?" Artie said in surprise.

I ignored him and pulled open my camera bag.

Stepping forward, I put the brick of heroin on the desk.

"I think this is what you're looking for."

CHAPTER THIRTY-THREE—ARTIE

IF A BOMB WENT OFF, IT COULDN'T HAVE TERRIFIED ME LIKE seeing Ellyn in Terence's office.

"What the fuck—"

"Who are you—"

"Jesus Christ—"

Reactions were rapid and alarmed. Ellyn, on the verge of tears, drew herself upright.

"Are you Terence?"

He watched her in astonishment.

"Are you?"

"Who are you?"

Hambone and Iggy both had their hands ready to reach inside their coats. My heart stopped. I was paralyzed.

"I'm the woman with a block of heroin."

Her tough-chick bravado went poorly with the wrong word. Terence laughed at her.

"That's a brick, sweetheart."

"What?" She was trembling faintly.

"A brick of heroin. Not a block. You need to learn the lingo if you want to play with the big boys."

"A brick, then. It's my brick."

I shook my head. "Ellyn, honey—don't."

"You shut the hell up." She shot lightning bolts at me from her eyes and swiveled to the man behind the desk. "I'm looking for someone named Terence. Is that you or not?"

He assessed her with a glittering grin. "I'm Terence. And you are?"

Automatically, she reached out to shake his hand. "Ellyn," she mumbled.

"Just Ellyn? No last name?" He held her hand for too long, and she pulled back. He laughed and let her go. Hambone and Iggy were on either side of me. My focus was on Terence, but I registered their presence just the same.

"Ellyn will do." She attempted to regain her bluster.

Terence's smile was more natural—and crueler. "That's okay. I think we can figure it out, Miss Wolcott."

She looked daggers at me, turned suddenly, and thrust a hand out to Iggy. "I'm Ellyn. How do you do."

I fought the urge to scream at her for her insistence on always shaking hands. *Not now, Red.* But the thugs around us all went through the formal introductions, like their mamas taught them. George's last name turned out to be Town; who would name their son George Town? She nodded nervously and turned to Terence.

"Okay. I have this brick of heroin."

"Seems to me *I* have a brick of heroin." He held the package in his hand, and he smiled at her easily.

She lifted her chin. "I'm selling it. It costs thirty thousand. That's what you said it was worth, right?" It was the first time she'd included me in the conversation, and I nodded cautiously.

"It's not yours to sell. This is mine. Artie was bringing it to me."

"Too bad. He lost it. Now it's mine, and you can have it for thirty thousand." Terence raised an eyebrow, but she kept talking. "And I want that to go on Artie's tab."

If she'd balled up her little fist and hit me with it, the impact wouldn't have been as shocking as her words. "Ellyn."

"Shut up. So, do you want it or not?"

Terence shook his head in wonder. "Why would you do that for him? It's clear you don't like him."

She clenched her jaw and blinked. "He tried to save my aunt. I mean, first he set her up, but then he tried to save her. And that's enough, I figure."

"That's sweet." My stomach was queasy. Terence would eat her for a snack. "Very sweet. Why should I deduct money from his tab when I have the heroin, and you don't?"

Adrenaline had me on a hair trigger. I saw her shoulders square as she faced up to him. "Because I've got something else to sell you too."

That stopped him. "What's that, little girl?"

"I'll tell you how I got *that* through customs." She gestured with her chin at the brick.

Terence grinned. "Too late, angel. He already told us the plan. Your rich auntie bought herself some diplomatic immunity."

A sense of doom crushed me. Ellyn didn't seem to know it. She tossed her head in irritation and shot me another glare. "She canceled the diplomatic immunity after he threw two palm trees overboard."

This wrinkled my forehead. I hadn't thrown the palms over. She had.

"After that," Ellyn said, "my aunt called her lawyers and canceled the State Department's intervention. I had to figure out a different way to smuggle this in. Which I did. Right past a drug-sniffing dog in LaGuardia yesterday. And I'll sell you the information on how I did that. It'll cost you the rest of his debt."

The room was silent. My muscles were going to crack if I couldn't hit someone soon.

"That's interesting," Terence said mildly.

"I thought you might think so." Ellyn was upright, and her

eyes were dry again. "So, how much of his debt would that be worth, do you think?"

Terence shook his head. "Nothing."

"Nothing?" She was startled. She looked to me. "But Artie knows your contacts in Burma now."

"Myanmar," Terence corrected automatically.

"Whatever." She dismissed him and maintained her focus on me. "You know the contacts, Artie. We could skip him entirely. You and me, a partnership—based on trust, right? What do you say?"

Terence came from behind his desk, and I stepped forward. Hambone and Iggy crowded me. Terence stopped in front of Ellyn.

"He doesn't know the guy. He'll never find him again. He doesn't know the officials I bribe. He knows nothing. And"—he wheeled to glare at me—"do you have a distribution network, Artie? Dealers? Runners? A lab? Quality control? Men on the payroll in the government *and* local banks? No. You don't. But I do."

He went back behind his desk and sat, lacing his hands behind his head and putting his feet on the desk. "So, dollface, let's forget that idea, shall we?"

She was trembling again. And then she stomped her foot—a movement so childish that Terence chuckled. "I don't want to know anything about this!" she cried. "I don't care *what* happens. This is between you and him." She thrust an elbow toward me. "So, let me tell you how it's going to go now."

"By all means, tell us how it's going to go."

"I'm leaving here, and he's escorting me out. Just him." She nodded at me. "And when I know I'm safe, I'll tell him how I got through customs. And he can come back and make whatever deal you want. Then we're through. Got that?" She hit me with the emerald blaze of her eyes, and I nodded.

"I don't think so." Terence dropped his feet to the floor. "I think we're going to take you in the back room and see if we can't persuade you to tell us right now."

Fury coursed through me, and every muscle was rigid. "No," I said.

That was all, but Terence looked at me in surprise. George backed up a foot, and Iggy reached for his gun. I kept my eyes on Terence and sent the message with every atom of my being. *No.*

After a moment, he shrugged. "All right. Tell Artie how you did it. If I don't like the answer, I think I know where to find you, Miz Wolcott. Go with her," he said to Hambone, who nodded.

"No," she said. "No Hambone, no Iggy, no George. Me and him, and that's all. And I don't tell him until I know I'm safe." She turned to me and noticed for the first time I was barefoot after my most recent strip search. "Put your damn boots on!"

I shrugged and sat to tug them on. Everyone watched me do it, and no one moved. I stood and gestured her out of the room before me.

She moved to walk out, and they let her do it. I turned to Terence as we left. "I'll be right back."

"That's fine," Terence said, his voice hard. "I know where your brother lives. And your mother."

I shook my head but got the hell out of there.

She stood beside me as we waited for the elevator and wouldn't let me touch her. She was still trembling.

"Ellyn," I said.

"Shut up. Not a single word. Hear me?"

I nodded. We rode the elevator and walked across the lobby, and I could almost feel bullets lacerating my spine. As long as they didn't hit her.

She led me across the street and astonished me when she turned into the Starbucks where we'd first met. She walked me directly to our table. "You sit with your back to the window," she demanded.

I did as I was told.

She sat in my place, pulled her camera bag onto her lap, and unzipped it. She detached a camera and then, confusingly, handed it to the man sitting at the table next to her.

He took it as smoothly as a relay racer takes the baton. "Wait here," he said.

And then he was gone.

I blinked.

And Ellyn smiled at me.

She *smiled* at me.

"You're going to want to sit here next to me." She patted the bench at her side, and I decided I'd better wait a minute before moving, since the world was reeling under me.

"What just happened?"

"Come here, Artie. Sit with me. Don't you want to watch?"

Her smile was glorious. A work of art. And it was directed at me. Hypnotized, I shifted to sit by her side.

"Don't look at me, stupid. Watch Terence's building."

I couldn't look away. Fuck Terence's building. She wasn't glaring at me.

"Are you angry? Do you hate me?"

I watched as her eyes filled with tears. "No, Artie. I don't hate you."

It was English. I knew it was English. I recognized all the words, but I couldn't make sense of what she was saying.

She smiled at my confusion. "I couldn't tell you. I didn't think you'd play it right if you knew."

"If I knew? Knew what?"

She raised an eyebrow at me. "Who's the sucker now?" She gestured, and I looked up in time to see Terence being led out of his building in handcuffs. Following after him in a little parade was Gorgeous George, Hambone, and Iggy. And Maggie the receptionist, having a bad day at work.

"By the way," Ellyn said, "Agent Ashwood sends his regards."

"What? What?" She'd made me dizzy, and that made her laugh.

"I figured it out, you know. I'm not entirely stupid. The yellow feather headpiece was on the flamingo. It wasn't anywhere near the palm trees. So, I went back to Cor's room and checked it out. I found your . . . brick." She looked around to make sure we weren't overheard. "I took it. It was already gone by the time you pitched the flamingo over the side."

"I—I didn't—"

"Didn't throw away the evidence? No. I had it."

I was speechless, and finally summoned a syllable. "Why?"

She smiled sadly. "For you. For Kaz. For anyone who that bastard sold to. As soon as I had it, I called your Agent Dashwood. Remember? You wrote his number in my notebook."

I nodded. That, at least, I understood.

"I asked him if he knew anyone interested in a drug dealer named Terence the Accountant, and he hooked me up with this task force trying to get evidence on the guy. They were really excited to hear from me. You know how you get a brick of heroin through customs at LaGuardia Airport?"

I shook my head.

"You tell the FBI about it, and they escort you. Good idea, huh?"

"But . . . " I had to make sense of the tangle of thoughts in my head. "How did you know where to find me?"

"That very first day, after we met in Mock's apartment. Remember?" I nodded. "When you left, I followed you. I didn't know if I could trust you, and I wanted to see what you'd do. That building is where you went, into an office suite listed as belonging to Terence Dalloway, CPA. And you told me about Terence the Accountant, and I put it all together."

"And the FBI needed evidence."

"Right. So, I filmed our whole meeting. See?" She showed me that she could unzip the entire end of her massive camera bag, leaving a dark mesh that a camera could film through. "I got him to confess to everything and admit the heroin was his. Got him to threaten me and promise violence to you and your family. It's all on that GoPro the FBI now has. So, he's been arrested. With the heroin. And he's going to jail for a long time. And you're not."

She smiled at me, satisfied.

"I'm not?"

"Nope. And neither am I. We just have to sit here until the FBI comes back. They want our statements, and I imagine someone's going to want to talk to you about your trip to Myanmar, but the deal is no prosecution for you, so feel free to tell them the truth."

"Ellyn . . ."

Heartless, she still wasn't done with me. She fished again in her camera bag and pulled out a check. "This is for you."

"What—"

"That's what I owe you. Cor split the money evenly. That's your 20 percent."

"It's a quarter of a million dollars."

"I know. And your big debt just got hauled off to prison, so I think that expense can be considered canceled. That's all yours."

Gravity felt wrong. My arms and legs were moments away from detaching and flying off into space. "How much does that leave for you and Mock?"

She laughed. "Suddenly your ability to do math has deserted you? We've still got a million. It's enough to inspire some backers. We'll be okay."

An absolute bedrock truth occurred to me, and I grabbed on to it in gratitude. I thrust the check into her hands. "I want to invest."

"What?" At last, she was the one looking surprised.

"I'm going to be your first investor. I'm investing my quarter million. I want to be your partner."

I said it and realized the word meant so much more.

I turned and grabbed her hands, crushing the check between us. "Ellyn. Don't say no. Don't stop me. Let me be with you. Let me lead you and be led by you. Please—please be with me."

"Oh," she said. "Oh, Artie."

"No one but you. Keep the money; I don't care. I've never wanted to be a pair before, but I am so much stronger with you. I think it's love. It's bigger than love. You're oxygen to me, Ellyn. Don't say no."

She was crying. "What's the question?"

Everything in me poured into her. "Can I love you? Will you love me? Don't say no. You'll kill me if you say no."

She laughed through the tears on her face. "Yes," she said, and my heart exploded. "You're a hopeless scoundrel, and I love you back."

"Oh, thank God." I fell into her in the most inept, clumsy kiss of my life. I was such a sucker. This was paradise, and we were together.

The End

WANT JUST A LITTLE MORE?

"But then what happened?!"

For a look at Artie and Ellyn together on dry land, just sign up for my newsletter, Bliss & Giggles, which you'll find at https://pruwarren.com

In your very first email from me (automatic; it's not that I don't love you, but don't you want the epilogue fast??), you'll be able to download the epilogue to all three of my books; take your pick!

You can unsubscribe to the newsletter after you download the epilogue if you want; I won't be offended. But if you stick around you can watch me make myself giggle through newsletters about whatever has caught my eye and whapped my funny bone on that particular day!

BUT WAIT! THERE'S MORE!

I realized that I was writing in alphabetical order. CYN, DASH, and ELLYN. Nice! (How about prequels, featuring Azariah and Madcap Maddy, and then some romance for Maddy's daughter, Belinda?)

At that point, I already knew I was drawn to Ellyn's party girl cousin. Her name was Cara at the time, but I switched her to Farrah so I could uphold the alphabet in the ampersand series.

Want to read her story? Her book, FARRAH & THE COURT-APPOINTED BOSS, is available now. Turn the page for the first chapter, presented here for your amusement!

SNEAK PEEK: FARRAH & THE COURT-APPOINTED BOSS

Chapter One—Farrah

"What about a martini? Don't you think our arraignment would be more pleasant for everyone if we all could have martinis? I don't see why courts can't have bartenders."

I spoke to Willow, my absolute best friend since last night when we'd first met each other in a dive bar. One look at her this morning and even on such short acquaintance I could tell she regretted our evening of glorious excess. Another reason why every courthouse should serve drinks. Who wants to go through the legal system sober?

"Farrah, please. Don't mention alcohol," she said, swallowing. Poor darling. She was a lightweight, booze-wise.

"All right," I said. "My bad." She needed a large glass of water and two aspirins. I patted her knee, once again admiring the dress she wore. Polka dot. Very retro. Gorgeous on her medium-brown skin. She looked far too good to be sitting on a courtroom bench waiting for the judge. "Tell me again. Why are we in divorce court?"

"Not divorce court. Diversion court. That lawyer guy explained it."

Wills gestured across the room to where a suit sat at a table. He was losing control of a stack of manilla folders.

"Right. That guy. Dermott Something. Special court to..."

"I don't know," Wills said wearily. "The city got some grant. To keep people out of prison. The lawyer acted like we got lucky."

Huh. I was in favor of getting lucky. At least theoretically. Life was fuzzy and fluffy, and I asked Wills another question. She was so good at answering. "What city are we in, again?"

She stared at me through her smeared glasses. For the first time I realized she was young. Much younger than my twenty-eight years. "Baltimore?" she said, not questioning the location. Instead she wondered why I didn't know.

"Baltimore. Right." I had no idea why I was in Baltimore. I live in Manhattan and had been in Florida. Hadn't I? Boozy Lucy would know. Where was she?

Damn it. Now I was sobering up.

"This is the end for me," Wills said. "The absolute end. My parents are going to string me up. If I actually get to go home. I might have to go to jai..." Her voice gave out. She couldn't say the word. Really, a quick drink would have helped her stiffen her resolve.

"Don't worry. Divorce court will keep us out of prison."

"Diversion court. With some retired judge everyone loves."

She absently fingered a fold of my dress as we sat side by side on the bench. This much I remembered from the night before. Wills liked fabric. She learned about people by touching their sleeve or their shoulder, but she was reading the cloth, not the person. She'd caressed Lucy's arm, but not as a come-on. She'd done it because Lou wore a silk shirtdress in a particularly gaudy Hawaiian print.

Wouldn't have mattered if Wills had been coming on to Lou. My drinking buddy since grade school when we snuck glasses of wine from our parents' cocktail parties, "Boozy Lucy" had no interest in sex. She was all about the party, and parties always

SNEAK PEEK: FARRAH & THE COURT-APPOINTED BOSS

involved just one more drink. Lou was kept on an allowance by her family, so she loved to drink with me. Who wouldn't? I had a generous trust fund. I picked up all the tabs. And where was she in this court mess, anyway?

"Burnout velvet," Wills murmured. "Sometimes called devoré. So supple and soft. Hard to work with. Expensive to match the pattern." She wasn't talking to anyone. It was more like a calming mantra, inspired by my emerald dress.

This special divorce judge was taking his sweet time. I might be going to "jai..." too, but did he have to keep me waiting?

As my buzz faded, I became, regretfully, more aware of my surroundings. Dermott Something was seated with a bunch of other suits. He was our court-appointed lawyer for the arraignment. He'd impressed me mostly for how poorly he handled his paperwork.

I'd never seen the inside of a prison. A holding cell, sure. Couple dozen of them over the years. But a prison? No. This would be a new experience. Unless divorce court held new opportunities.

People came and went. They were all so busy. Not from our bench, where maybe fifteen other hapless idiots waited vacantly with us, watched by the two policemen who'd shepherded us over from the holding cells.

No, the comings and goings were from the free side of the court. Whee—freedom. Lawyers bustled importantly. Court employees came and went with boredom or urgency. A few spectators.

And then a new type.

Tall guy. Young-ish. Tidy. Thick, brown hair. Impeccably groomed beard and mustache. Nothing unusual except all that "usual" added up to something handsome. I nudged Wills. "Cute. Look over there."

She straightened and inhaled. "That's my One Phone Call."

"No shit. That's yours?"

"Sort of. That's Mr. Gee. He's the guidance counselor at my high school."

Oh, God. High school? I stared at her. "Wills. How old *are* you?"

"Turned eighteen this June."

She was a fucking baby, and I'd partied with her in a bar until we wandered out in search of more excitement. "Damn. I must have been potted last night."

"You were pretty drunk," she agreed. "How are you not feeling sick now?"

"Oh, well." I drink a lot. I'm good at it. I leaned back to look at her One Phone Call. "Mr. Gee is hot," I commented. "But he is one thoroughly tucked-in man. Check out the precision on that beard. He looks like he irons his underwear."

Wills snorted and then held a hand to her forehead. Bad headache; hangover. Nasty way to confront a calm morning, much less the end of freedom in a courtroom with, I must say, extremely unflattering lighting. She was handling it well. I liked her all the more.

"You don't know the half of it," she said. "See that medallion he's wearing?"

He'd found a seat and was waving at Wills. She nodded at him carefully, the way I move when my head is throbbing. I could see a chain around his muscular neck, with a medallion on it. Worn over the buttoned shirt and tie. "Yeah? What about it?"

"That's his purity medallion. He's a virgin, and tells everyone about it."

"Shut up. That guy's a virgin?" He was more interesting to me now. Like a rare animal in the zoo. I took a long look. A cute, bearded, tucked-in virgin. I'll be damned.

"Yeah. He says virginity is nothing to be ashamed of and all the kids at school need to know it's a good thing to be a virgin."

She rolled her eyes and I joined her. "Really."

"Really. But he's a pretty good guy anyway. I mean, he's here.

Maybe he can help me get out of this." She didn't sound very hopeful.

The clerk appeared and made everyone stand for the Honorable Ferbus T. Cracklepot. Not his real name. He was actually Judge Tim Dooley, but if ever anyone looked like a Ferbus T. Cracklepot, it was this guy. Black guy, white hair, imposing bulk, frowning presence. He could have had a walrus as a stand-in.

At last. Let's get this show on the road.

We were going through the opening of court rigamarole (a dance, I'm sorry to say, I've personally witnessed in several states, although this one had some new stuff about diversions and a grant from the MacKenzie Foundation. Whatever) when all the oxygen left the room. The doors in the back opened and a king and his entourage swept in.

I sighed. "Here comes *my* One Phone Call."

In fact, my phone call had been to my beloved twin sister, but I should have known she'd try to protect me by dragging the family into this. Dermott What'shisname, my court-appointed lawyer with the file folder problem, was about to be seriously upstaged by a master showman with an ego the size of the planet.

Like everyone else in the courtroom, Wills stared at the late arrivals.

The first (and, in his opinion, most important) was a five-thousand dollar charcoal gray suit draped lovingly around the body of my father's law partner. Søren Andersen himself had gotten on a private jet to rescue The Wayward Daughter. The charges must have been pretty serious, then.

Behind him came a matched set of law clerks—one in the male form, one in the female. They carried briefcases and efficient laptop totes and made sure to stay slightly behind Søren.

And bringing up the rear was—hallelujah! My twin, Olivia. Hi, honey!

She uttered a peep of excitement when she found me in my line-up of reprobates, and waved with far too much glee. Even for Liv, who always took care of me, this was a surprisingly joyous greeting if I was heading for prison this time, and I forgave her for bringing a huge corporate lawyer into this.

I looked my question at her and she mouthed something incomprehensible but obviously exciting. Huh?

The walrus on the judge's stand blustered at the interruption until he got a good look at who'd come in. "I'll be damned!" he barked. He even sounded like a walrus. "Søren Andersen! My God! I haven't seen you in years!"

"Tim—good to see you back on the bench! We won't interrupt. Talk later."

Feigning humility, Søren made to sit, glaring at the two men on the bench he'd chosen. They scuttled away like crabs in the shadow of an eagle.

No—a pterodactyl. A crab-eating pterodactyl. *Awrrrk.*

The walrus restored order and got on with his judge-ish pontificating. Utterly ignorable. I watched Liv instead. She still mouthed something and gestured to me. If I'd had a simple martini...

...and then I got it.

No, *she'd* gotten it.

Unthinking, I stood, filled with a rush of excitement. "You got the job?!"

My shriek cut across the walrus, drawing every eye. He was furious and the policewoman at my end of the bench stepped forward threateningly, giving me the I'm Not Kidding hairy eyeball.

I sat—but that was okay. Liv nodded at me.

She'd gotten it. Head designer at the Bellini House of Fashion. Oh my God.

It was her dream. She'd be working on her own show for Fashion Week. Actual New York Fashion Week, along with Donna Karan. Calvin Klein. Giorgio god-damned Armani.

And Liv Ridley for Bellini.

I started laughing. I couldn't help it. I was probably looking

SNEAK PEEK: FARRAH & THE COURT-APPOINTED BOSS

at several years of incarceration, but Liv would show the world her gift. I was lighter than air. She was crying and I was crying and we were both laughing and the walrus wasn't having it.

BANG BANG BANG

My spirit thumped down from its flight. The gavel pulled everyone's attention back to the judge, where he clearly liked it.

"All right," he said. "Let's get rid of the trouble-maker first. Start with her."

He pointed at me. Dermott Something the Overworked immediately lost control of his manilla folders which cascaded impressively onto the floor. "Hold on," he said with his head below the table, fishing for dropped files. "That's one of mine. Hold on."

The clerk checked with the policewoman and called out our names. "Farrah Elizabeth Ridley and Willow Starmer Vernon. Please stand."

Just one martini. Was that so much to ask? I stood.

WANT MORE? Here is the link for Farrah & the Court-Appointed Boss, available now:

Farrah & the Court-Appointed Boss

HOW TO THRILL AN AUTHOR

Cookie, lean in here and lemme whisper in your shell-like ear:

I would PLOTZ if you clicked a star or posted a review on Amazon or on BookBub or GoodReads. Nothing pleases the massive smile-based book-selling overlords more than to see a novel that is greeted with enthusiasm.

And nothing pleases me more, either!

So if you've got it in you, gimme a review. Short and sweet is enough! Or click on the number of stars you think I should have. Somewhere in the vast digital world, I'll be doing the happy dance.

Thank you!

ABOUT THE AUTHOR

Pru Warren (who is writing this in the third person as if simply too modest to toot her own horn) bores easily and thus has been a daydreamer since roughly the Bronze Age.

She is addicted to writing because in a novel, you can make things come out the RIGHT way. Life and karma really ought to take note; there are BETTER SOLUTIONS to these pesky daily annoyances!

Beside her in-the-laptop God Complex, Pru laughs often and easily, loathes cooking, and plays way too much solitaire. She's plotting world domination even as you read this, as long as she doesn't have to wake up too early to accomplish it.

ALSO BY PRU WARREN

Cupid's Quest:

Cupid's Quest Season One

Cupid's Quest Season Two

Cupid's Question Season Three

The Muse Books (contemporary, not romcoms)

City Muse

History's Muse

Untamed Muse

The Ampersand Series:

Cyn & the Peanut Butter Cup

Dash & the Moonglow Mystic

Ellyn & the Would-Be Gigolo

Farrah & the Court-Appointed Boss

The Surprise Heiress Series:

Breath of Fresh Heiress

Full of Hot Heiress

Vanished Into Thin Heiress

You Decide Books:

Emma's Mission

A Spirit Guide for Anna Maria

Joan's Journal (Love Gone Viral) (out of print, alas, but available free in
ebook form to newsletter subscribers) (hint, hint)

Printed in Great Britain
by Amazon

27912178R00176